In Different Times
A Fictional Memoir

by
David Gregor

Alki Press
Seattle, Washington

Thanks to:

The Kinks,
The Mamas and the Papas,
The Animals, Bob Dylan, Dave Clark Five,
The Righteous Brothers, Merseybeats, The Birds,
Long John Baldry, Lovin' Spoonful, Spencer Davis Group,
Four Tops, Dave Dee Dozy Beaky Mick & Mitch, Donovan,
The Hollies, Freddie & the Dreamers, Sam & Dave, Gerry &
the Pacemakers, Zombies, Beach Boys, Herman's Hermits,
Jan & Dean, Manfred Mann, Searchers, Scott McKenzie,
Yardbirds, Monkees, Billy J. Kramer and the Dakotas,
Them, Los Bravos, Cilla Black, Pretty Things, The Who,
The Sonics, The Wailers (with Rockin' Robin),
Don and the Goodtimes,
The Beatles

for the music.

Typeset by Hermetic Press.

Printed and bound in the United States of America.
ISBN 0-9631094-0-5

First Trade Edition.
6 5 4 3 2 1

In Different Times

For my father who cared,
my mother who taught me to laugh,
and especially to Victoria
for believing.

1

That summer we unearthed the skeleton of the Indian woman from the hillside that flanks the Manette Bridge and rises steeply above the east bank of the narrows which separates the two sides of town. It was a shallow tomb, little more than a foot below the ground, and it looked more like a bed than a grave. The skeleton, intact, was resting on a thin layer of oyster shells and mussel backs. The skull was propped up and tilted forward by a pillow of dirt. The eye sockets, filled with dirt, looked eerily alive. The skull was pointed west across the narrows toward a hillside now dotted with cabins. The Indian woman was short and small-boned. There was evidence of two broken ribs, and the small ridge of calcium around the breaks indicated they had not mended before her death. Bone fragments were later dated and found to be over three hundred years old.

The discovery of the Indian woman's remains was the first such find in the county; it made the front page of the *Bremerton Sun* and resulted in several follow-up stories. In one article the *Sun* interviewed Indian historian Albert Dravis, who recounted a legend he believed might explain the lone discovery. Two young lovers had set out by canoe in the dead of winter in search of the Heart of the World. They believed that a water route, like the blood running through their veins, would eventually lead to the Heart of the World. For weeks they paddled the sound following the shoreline until one morning a dense fog obscured the spurs and headlands by which they navigated. Without visibility or bearing, the two Indians were drawn by the tides into a narrow channel where they moved with the tide flow. Far into the narrows the canoe capsized, and the two young people were thrown into the divergent tides which pulled them to opposite shores.

In the days that followed, both tried to swim the channel but were defeated by the tides. They built signal fires, but in the heavy fog no light crossed the narrows, and neither knew of the other's fate.

Alone and buried in the blinding mist of winter, the Indian lovers came to believe they had reached the Heart of the World. They built no more fires and no longer tried to swim the narrows. They accepted their place, apart, on Earth and believed they would rise together from different shores to meet in a higher place. And so they did, according to Dravis. That place is called Legend.

The Indians named that narrow channel of water Enetai, the "crossing place" where strong tides meet. Early settlers learned the Indian name as did the U.S. Navy when it built the shipyard at the mouth of the narrows. The area was named after its German founder, William Bremer, but the shipyard eventually became Bremerton, and little of the area's past was ever remembered or passed on.

After the Dravis article appeared in the *Sun*, many people wrote letters to the editor saying they believed the Indian skeleton was proof of the legend. One reader felt a search should be made for the remains of the young Indian man. Reverend Tillis of the Union Gospel Church, however, wrote emphatically in his letter that "any claim of Bremerton being like Heaven is sacrilege." Public comment on the issue ended abruptly two days later, on June 21, 1966, when the front page of the *Sun* was bannered with more startling news:

"Teddy Tarbox, 18, from East Bremerton, died of wounds suffered during a rocket attack outside Saigon, South Vietnam."

As a student, Teddy had been one of the most distinguished young men Bremerton had ever produced. In 1965, he had been named the "State Student of the Year" after lettering in three sports while maintaining a four-point grade average his senior year. He had joined the army after graduating early, and within six months he was dead—Bremerton's first combat casualty since 1953. It was the first time most people in Bremerton had ever heard of Vietnam—the first time any of my friends had lost someone. Teddy's death relegated local Indian lore to forgotten history, and it would be six months before anything more was written about Indian bones.

Meanwhile, the remains of the Indian woman were carefully boxed and labeled at the site, and then moved to an empty room at Olympic Community College. Miss Ashburn, our anthropology instructor who had overseen the excavation, asked for volunteers to clean and catalogue the remains, but there was little interest. The war and the draft and the news of Teddy Tarbox turned most students away from cleaning bones. Discussions in the student lounge now centered on talk of deferments or where people might go to avoid being drafted. At the time, I was not concerned with either. I was fascinated with a legend.

I volunteered to clean the Indian bones two days after I had decided I wanted out of all my unwanted obligations. I had left home for the third time and had moved into a cabin down on Washington Beach with Jack Hill. Jack and I knew each other from the P.X. snack bar in the shipyard where Jack worked as a busboy and where I took my lunch breaks from bagging groceries across the street at the commissary. We talked about music, and he liked my sideburns, but it was a fight over the length of Jack's hair that eventually brought us together. I was on my lunch hour, and Jack was cleaning up the two broken beer bottles around a table of sailors. Suddenly one of the sailors grabbed Jack and held him from behind while another cut off a chunk of his hair with a small knife. Without even thinking, I was across the room and throwing punches. The short-lived brawl left one sailor with a split lip, me with a black eye, and Jack and me without jobs. The following week I found a job as a relief clerk at the Enetai Hotel, and with the assurance that Jack's closest friend Flex would quickly join us, Jack and I immediately moved onto Washington Beach.

Washington Beach is just three blocks from downtown Bremerton, yet in the summer of 1966 it was still a forgotten part of town. The small white cabins, perched on pilings, were separated from town by an embankment that rose straight up from the stony beach. A narrow strip of grass, protected from the saltwater by a wooden bulkhead, stretched behind the cabins.

The smell of the water and the kelp drying on the beach was always strong, and only when the breeze off the water died down did you smell the peat that covered the hillside. The heather and laurel, dampened by the moist air, were so green that the hill looked black in any light. Wind-seared pines and twisted cedars canopied the beach, and in the deep green shadows below, a walkway wound through the blackberry vines down to the sound. Swift currents hissed during flood tide and then seethed shoreward where the rock bottom smoothed to a pebbly floor and rose sharply up to the beach.

When Jack and I moved to the beach, there were only two other people living there: Joe the Squid and Danny Peezor. Joe lived in the cabin closest to ours, about fifty feet down the beach. Joe had six months left in the navy, and he spent the better part of each day listening to Bob Dylan and Zoot Sims. He was also working diligently on his list of women yet-to-bed who came to the Enlisted Men's Club. He said it was his way of ensuring he would never return to Bremerton after his discharge. I liked Joe right off. His beer was always cold.

Where Joe was a guy's guy, Danny Peezor was strictly a lady's man. When we first met Danny, he was dating more women at one time than either Jack or I had in our entire lives. It was easy to see why too. He wasn't tall, but he was strikingly dark and handsome. He wore Ivy League clothes—pin-striped shirts, chinos, polo shirts—and was always meticulously groomed and appropriately scented. Danny was blessed with the gift of patter. He knew just enough about a lot of subjects to get his foot in the door, and from there he could turn on the charm with flowers, soft lights and music, and just enough flattery to not seem forced. After knowing him only two weeks, I was certain if anyone could have swayed a nun, it would have been Danny.

While the population of Washington Beach was growing slowly, the rest of town was booming. The Puget Sound Naval Shipyard employed its highest number of workers since the end of World War II, and both the Bangor Naval Ammunition Depot and the Keyport Torpedo Station were adding civilian laborers at a steady rate.

Young people from all over the Puget Sound area were flooding into Bremerton to enroll in the college, which spurred plans for the construction of a new campus dormitory and a music and art building.

In town, musicians, their friends and girlfriends filled the booths of Olberg's Drug Store, the aisles of Sherman Clay Music and the major street corners. Jack Hill grew obsessed with fishing Oyster Bay and the sound, and it wasn't uncommon for days to pass without me seeing him. He grew so forgetful about everything except fishing—and music—that after a month on the beach, he forgot about paying rent. Two days before we were to be evicted, Jack pawned his radio, a nice pair of waders, and ten of my albums. We made the rent, and Jack promised to pay back the records, but I knew it was a lost cause. Hard as I tried, I couldn't stay mad at him. Jack wasn't malicious. He just didn't always think beyond himself.

Our first two months on the beach were like heaven. There were parties, and there were girls. Jack and I knew a lot of musicians, and between his piano playing and my drumming, we were able to sit in with some talented people upstairs at Sherman Clay. But even when there wasn't a party or female visitors or somebody playing music, life that summer was good. Jack fished religiously, Danny used his summer school classrooms at Olympic as laboratories for the refinement of his suaveness, and I routinely cut classes to spend more time working on the Indian bones. There was a playful, carefree ease to our life on the water that took a turn about the time the beach went blue.

Bungalow "C" was a small white house perched halfway up the hill above us. It was surrounded by blackberry vines and had been vacant for over six months until, in August, it was rented by a woman named Motherbright. Though she kept to herself at first, I did see her a few times from our porch, if only in fleeting glimpses. She was tall with long legs and straight, brown hair that hung past her waist. She wore her clothes in layers of shirts and vests, along with scarves and beads. She also wore bright yellow head wraps, and one evening I saw her wearing an orange and green and red cape that seemed to dance in the dark with what appeared to be a hundred tiny lights. It was hard to tell exactly how old Motherbright was, but she was definitely older than us.

The first time Motherbright actually spoke to me, I was going down the stairs late one night as she was coming up from the beach. She wore only a towel, and her long hair was shiny and wet. The first and only thing she said to me was, "It's good to see you up close, Eddie Carr. Life's paths are far too littered with unrealized opportunities." I nodded without knowing why. Before I could say anything, she smiled and walked up to her house. Two days later, Motherbright physically changed the beach.

She began in the morning with hammering and sawing. Around noon she started painting the outside of her house a vibrant, royal blue. Our landlord, Mr. Froege, watched the transformation from his porch, across the stairway, with utter disbelief. "Frog", as we called him, was short and squat with a scrunched-up face that made him look like a bulldog. He was eight years retired from the shipyard, and his disposition was a notch below that of a cat dropped in water. Frog was never without a cigar stub wedged between his teeth, and as I watched him watching the transformation of Motherbright's cabin, I could see his growing anger in the rapid puffs of smoke he blew. I kept tabs on the project until it got dark, and then I called it a night. At six the next morning, Frog was banging on our door.

"I see you boys with paint," Frog screamed, "and I'll run you out! Understand?"

I reassured him that we had no intention of painting anything.

"That!" Frog said, pointing up the hill, "is a threat to decency."

I stepped onto the porch and looked up the hill. Motherbright was adding red to an already yellow trim around the windows and the door.

"If that was my rental," Frog said, "I'd burn the place down."

Motherbright and her blue house overshadowed us from that day on. Her bathroom window faced the sound, and at night when she showered, she was silhouetted against the misted window. Every night, like clockwork, the bathroom light caught the color of her house and veiled the hillside in a blue haze.

Danny Peezor wasted no time learning that Motherbright was from Florida by way of Denver and San Francisco. She had also just started singing at Dook's Tavern, and while none of us had ever doubted Danny's abilities with women, it was with Motherbright that our faith was first tested.

2

The inversion hit the sound the morning after our party for Scooter Hayes. He had been drafted five months earlier and was home on leave before shipping out for Vietnam.

I woke up at first light with a dry mouth and a headache. Scooter was asleep on the second couch, and Mooch was passed out on the floor, stark naked. I tried to rub away the rumbling sound in my head, but it wouldn't go away. I stepped over clothes and empty beer bottles. I caught my foot on a pink slip and stumbled into the kitchen. I peeked into the bedroom. Jack was gone. I had a drink of water and lay down again on the couch. I had just closed my eyes when the rumbling returned.

Leaping over Mooch, I ran to the windows. The glass rattled lightly, and the floorboards vibrated. The rumbling got louder. Suddenly, I saw it. I shouted at Mooch and Scooter and shook them.

"Get up! Come on, wake up! It's coming!"

Scooter rolled over, and Mooch pushed me away. I kicked Mooch and shook Scooter again.

"Listen!" I said. "Can't you hear the ferry?"

"Go away," Mooch said. "The ferry doesn't come in here!"

A loud, deafening blast of the air-horn brought Scooter off the couch and Mooch to his knees. I pulled Scooter to the windows. The fog horn blasted again, and the window next to us cracked.

"Under the tables!" Mooch yelled. "Go for cover!"

"Grab something," I said. "Make some noise."

Scooter and I grabbed two pans from the kitchen and ran to the front porch. We banged our pans on the railing and yelled into the fog.

"Beach! Beach! Turn back! Stop!"

We stopped banging. The sound of the engines grew louder.

"Beach!" we hollered. "Turn back! Beach!"

The engine vibrations rumbled deeper. We banged our pans harder. The bottom of mine collapsed. I tossed it into the fog.

"It's right out there," I shouted.

"Let's get out," Scooter yelled.

Mooch came onto the porch. The goggles of his leather aviator's cap were down, and he was carrying our record player.

"What the hell's with that?" Scooter said.

"I'm ready to evacuate," Mooch said.

The sound of the engines changed, and through the fog I saw the outline of the ferry. Scooter scrambled up the porch railing to the cabin roof as the engines rumbled deeper and then suddenly became high-pitched. A foamy prop wash surged over the porch. Mooch screamed. I grabbed his arm and pulled him onto the window sill.

"This is it!" Mooch cried. "It's the end!"

The wood pilings under the cabin creaked loudly as heavy waves hit with such force that the outside deck floor buckled. But the pilings held. The waves fell slack to a heavy wash. The ferry receded into the fog, and its engines grew more distant. When I felt sure that the ferry was moving away, I climbed off the sill. Scooter was breathing hard. Mooch was shivering. I stood stiff, staring out into the fog; my arm muscles ached, until I slowly loosened my grip on the railing.

"Just like the films in school." Mooch spoke quietly. His voice was a soft, hushed whisper. "But no flash."

Scooter, lowering himself to the porch, said, "You're sick, Mooch."

Mooch stared out into the fog. "I saw us going up in a fireball. Sucking down radio dust."

"Your head's already filled with radio dust," Scooter said. "You're infected with that doom shit, and it shows in your ratty face."

"What's wrong with my face?" Mooch said.

I turned and stared at Mooch. The way his wet, stringy hair hung down his face, he did look like a rat. I laughed.

"And what's so funny?" Mooch said, turning to me.

"I thought it was a hangover," I said.

Scooter laughed. "I saw that baby saving me a flight to Saigon."

"One of these days, the big one's going to hit," Mooch said.

"You're an endangered species," I said.

"Oh yeah!" Mooch said. "So what of it?"

I pointed at the record player. It sat in a pool of water on the porch. Mooch pouted. "Sorry, Eddie."

"Jack's gonna peel your head like a grape," Scooter said.

"He wouldn't do that, would he, Eddie?"

"Jack's mental," I said.

Mooch's eyes and mouth drew tight.

"Jack ate those slugs, didn't he?" Scooter said.

"I'll fix it," Mooch said. "I'll clean it up, Eddie, and make it right." Mooch picked up the player, and water ran out the bottom.

"It only looks bad," he said. "It'll be okay, Eddie. You'll see."

Mooch took the player inside. Later when Scooter and I walked into the kitchen, Mooch was sitting at the table wiping up water, grinning at us. Delicately, he raised the tone arm and dabbed his shirt over the wet metal.

"See Eddie," he said. "It's almost dry."

"How about inside?"

Mooch looked strained again. "What about it, Eddie?"

"It's the inside that's important."

"Jack won't see inside."

"You're right," I said. I picked up the player and threw it in the corner with the trash.

"Take him with you," I said to Scooter. "Mooch is ready for far off places."

"The army won't take him."

"I'll throw in the record player."

"I'll have it fixed," Mooch said.

"Come on Mooch," Scooter said. "Grab your head. I'll drop you off in town."

Scooter put on his knit cap, and we waited on the porch while Mooch looked for his clothes. It was hard not to rib Scooter about his shaved head, but we had all promised not to rub it in. Being in the army was bad enough.

The beach was still thick with fog. We leaned over the railing, and neither of us spoke for a long time. Finally, Scooter cleared the air.

"Between Motherbright and that ferry," he said, "I'm ready for anything."

"Hell of a farewell."

Scooter turned to me. "You won't say anything to Danny about last night."

"What's to tell?"

"The whole town must've heard her. She's not like other girls."

"She's a woman, Scooter."

"More like a banshee. Screams in the night and gone in the morning."

"I wouldn't worry," I said. "What Danny doesn't know won't hurt him. That's the way he plays it."

"Just promise me, Eddie."

"Nothing to promise."

"Promise!"

I smiled. "I promise."

Mooch finally found his clothes and came outside.

"I couldn't fix it, Eddie. It just started smoking, so I unplugged it."

"I'll tell Jack you tried."

"You're a pal, Eddie. I'll get Jack a new one. I know right where to go."

"Chain him up Scooter."

"Come on, rodent, up the hill."

I sat for awhile on the railing and listened to the waves wash on the beach. The incident with the ferry had felt like a bad dream where you have no control over what happens. I thought about how helpless we had been. Then I began thinking about what I was going to say to Dean Scoggins about my withdrawal. I needed his okay for the college to refund my tuition. I had started inside when I heard splashing. For a moment, I thought someone had fallen from the ferry. Then I saw a figure walk out of the water. The fog partially obscured the figure, but it passed close enough for me to see it was a woman, and she was naked. It was Motherbright.

As she slowly walked toward the bulkhead, she pulled back her long hair. Her heavy breasts moved as she walked, and the tuft of hair between her legs was dark against her pale skin. I couldn't believe she had not the slightest care of being seen. She lifted her dress from the grass and toweled off the inside of her thighs. I was a believer. I must have sighed louder than I thought when she cupped her breasts inside her dress, because she looked right at me.

"Hard to see in all this fog," she said.

I cleared my throat. "Didn't mean to stare."

"I'm flattered." She finished wringing her hair. "I enjoyed your party. Your friend Scooter seems too nice for war."

"He'll get around it," I said. I could still picture Motherbright without her clothes. "Isn't the water a little cold for swimming like that?"

"It's quite stimulating. You should try it."

"Did you see the ferry almost run aground?"

"Thought it might be providence."

"Looked like the Willapa. Right off the porch here."

"I didn't know they came in this far."

"They don't," I said. "Unless they're off course."

Motherbright climbed the bulkhead stairs up to the grass. I tried to think of something clever to say to keep her from leaving, but my mind was a blank.

"Care to join me—for breakfast?" Motherbright said.

I looked at my watch.

"I have an appointment."

She gave me a long look. "There will be another time, Eddie." Motherbright climbed up the stairs and disappeared in the fog.

3

On campus classes were in session, and it felt quieter than usual because the fog had not yet lifted. There were two students behind a small table at the foot of the stairs to the administration building. Above the table was a banner:

DRAFT BEER NOT STUDENTS

"Sign our petition to stop the draft?" the shorter one said.

"No thanks," I said. Politics bored me. I walked on. "I'm a Red!"

"Hey!" the taller one yelled after me. "We're communists too!"

When I was in high school, Dean Scoggins had been my counselor. He had worked out of a white-tiled office—the size of a closet—right next to the showers. The walls of the small room had been covered with pictures of him as a defensive lineman in high school and college. His desk had been littered with trophies used as paperweights. Now he was Dean of Admissions at Olympic College. That was the worst thing about living in Bremerton. No one you hated ever left town. They just kept turning up in higher positions.

His secretary said, "Dean Scoggins will see you now."

Scoggins was standing behind his desk. "Good to see you, Eddie. It's been a long time."

We shook hands. "About two years," I said.

"My God. Two more seasons in the can." He gestured to the chair in front of his desk. "Make yourself comfortable, Eddie."

Bookcases lined the walls and were filled with trophies.

"This is a lot different from your shower-room office."

"Not a bare butt in sight," Scoggins said.

"Hard to adjust?" I said.

"Well, there are times when I miss the smell of sweat." He swung an imaginary golf club. "It's the smell of competition, and competition breeds success. There's no smell quite like it."

"I know what you mean."

"How's the family?"

"They're fine," I said.

"And your mother is adjusting?" he asked.

I hated it when people who hardly knew you brought up family and talked about them like they were old friends. My mother had been in a car accident when I was ten, and a broken neck had left her paralyzed. Scoggins had played off my mother's condition before to appear friendly, and I hated him for it.

"She's stronger than most of us," I said.

"Must be hard," Scoggins said. "A close friend of mine in college broke his neck tumbling. Saddest thing I ever saw. He was one hell of an athlete. That's really sad, Eddie."

"Life goes on," I said.

"That it does." Scoggins paused, looking directly at my head. "I see by the length of your hair that you're testing some new ground."

"Hear we're due for a cold winter."

He grinned. "So what can I do for you, Eddie. Hope there's no problem."

"Not so much a problem." I reached inside my coat pocket.

"Good. I much prefer hearing about things going well."

I handed him my withdrawal form.

"I want out," I said.

The smile on Scoggins' face disappeared. He stood up, glanced at the form, and sat down on the corner of his desk.

"What's this nonsense all about?"

"I just need your signature to get my tuition back."

Scoggins re-examined the form. "You've got two quarters left to graduate, Eddie, and you want to throw what you've accomplished out the window? Stupidity, Eddie. Pure stupidity."

"I'm just tired of school."

"You'll have to do better than that."

"I don't belong here," I said. "I have no idea why I'm here. I just want out and my money back."

Scoggins paced in front of his windows. He removed a golf club from his umbrella basket and leaned on it like it was a shovel.

"If there's one thing you know about me, Eddie, it's that I don't like quitters. Nothing cools my blood faster than one of my boys throwing in the towel," he said, pointing his club at me.

"I'm not here to cause trouble," I said. "I really need my money back. It's nothing personal."

Scoggins went back to his desk. "My job, Eddie, is to insure that you go into the world prepared. A good education is the best foundation. What kind of counselor would I be if I sanctioned *this* with my signature? I have to answer for every refund, and I will not authorize the excuse of a quitter."

"I'm not a quitter."

"Precisely, Eddie, because I won't permit it. How old are you?"

He caught me by surprise. "Nineteen."

"Right now you have a deferment. Are you aware what your decision will do to your draft status?"

"I just want out, Mr. Scoggins."

"The draft board will be notified, and your name reactivated. If you've been following the news, Eddie, you know that shouldn't be taken lightly."

There was no way of explaining to Scoggins exactly what was happening with me and most of my friends. The problem was time. Time felt very important. There was an unspoken, but strongly felt, concern not to waste it doing things that other people felt were important. We wanted to live in our time, in our own way, so what we did would mean something to us. There was a feeling that a part of our time was running out. Scoggins would have never understood.

Scoggins stepped around his desk, tapping the handle of his club into his open hand. "Is this decision of yours in any way based on your—affinity for the bohemian?"

"No sir! I'm American."

Suddenly, with an overhand swing, Scoggins cracked the club over his desk.

"Don't get flippant with me, Eddie. I won't have any gypsy with hair to his ass making a fool of me."

Scoggins went to the windows. "Come here, Eddie. I want you to see what you're up against."

I went but kept my distance.

"Just look out there!" he said. "See all those kids? Six thousand students are enrolled here, and you're the only one who says things aren't right. Doesn't that strike you as a little curious, Eddie?"

"I don't belong here, Dean, and I'd like my money back. Sixty-five dollars won't break Olympic. I need my money back, and I'll get it one way or another."

Scoggins whirled around. "Don't threaten me. You're free to leave Olympic College, but you'll do so without my approval. I believe this discussion is over." Scoggins faced the windows. "You *do* remember the way out?" he said, without turning around.

I walked toward the door, but in the next instant his shelves of trophies loomed up before me. Without another thought, I took one of the small trophies and threw it against the far wall.

"What the hell!" Scoggins yelled, whirling around.

I grabbed the largest trophy and cocked my arm.

"No Eddie! Not that one! It's from the League of Coaches."

"You have something of mine that needs your signature."

"Put the trophy down and we'll talk."

"Just sign the form!" I said.

"You'll never get away with this, Eddie. My signature under duress won't work. One call and the paper is worthless."

"One throw and your athletic career is a memory. Just sign the paper."

I enjoyed seeing Scoggins squirm, rekindling his sense of fair play. Justice was truly a matter of position. "You better hurry," I said. "This baby's getting heavy."

I shifted the trophy from my right hand to holding it over my head with both hands. Scoggins went to his desk and signed my withdrawal slip without a word.

"Think of this as building character," I said.

I walked over and grabbed the paper and quickly backed my way to his office door.

"Where you going with that?" Scoggins said. "We had an agreement."

"We still do. But I believe you *would* call the cashier, so I'll just keep this as insurance. As soon as I get my money, you can retrieve this."

"Don't ever set foot on this campus again, Eddie."

"It's been a pleasure learning from you. You should be very proud."

I went out the door and closed it behind me. His secretary smiled pleasantly as I walked by her desk. I clutched the trophy in my arm.

"Dean Scoggins is letting me show this around," I said.

"That one is *so* beautiful," she said.

"Oh yes, inspirational."

The cashier passed me my money, and I signed for it. I set Scoggins' trophy on the counter and asked her to call Scoggins. Then I left the building feeling totally cleansed of higher education.

Fog still covered the campus, and the smell of the air reminded me of the summer mornings I had spent picking berries as a kid. I had the same anxious feeling of getting on that yellow school bus, going off to new places with new faces, without ever knowing for sure where I was going. For just a moment, on my way to the car, I felt like I was stepping off the morning bus again ready to harvest another ripe field.

4

Walking past Frog's apartment on my way home, I heard quick slaps of leather, like a razor being stropped. The sound came from behind me and quickly grew louder. I looked up the street and saw Danny Peezor running toward me. He was shirtless, and there was a huge red-bearded man chasing him. Danny jumped the stairs, clawed through the hedge, and fell against the bulkhead below me. I leaned over the railing and watched Danny press himself into the corner of the cement wall.

"You haven't seen me, okay?" he said, breathlessly.

A moment later, the big man was standing in front of me. He bent over and coughed, sending sweat flying from his red hair and beard. He cleared his throat.

"You see a guy run past here?"

"I saw a guy," I said.

He spit. "Well, which way'd the sonofabitch go?"

I looked down the stairs and pointed around behind the manager's apartment. "Back up the way you came."

"Damn it!" he said. "I catch that bastard—if you see him, you tell him, his ass is mine. Got that?"

"Got it. His ass is yours."

"That skinny little shit."

He started down the stairs but changed his mind and headed back up the street. I watched him prowl between the buildings. When it was clear he wasn't coming back, I gave Danny the okay.

"Had me worried there," Danny said. "You oughta see the bugs down here." He brushed himself off and slashed through the laurel, knocking over a garbage can. Frog's screen door flew open, and he popped out, chewing on the butt of his cigar.

"Holy Christ on a stick," he bellowed. "What in the Sam Hell's going on out here?"

"It's me—Danny, Mr. Froege. I missed the stairs, but I'm fine."

"I don't like that kind of stuff." Frog looked up at me and rolled his soggy cigar stub around in his mouth. "Won't put up with no weirdos or hell-raisin'."

"Won't happen again," I said.

"See that it don't," Frog said, and the door slammed behind him.

"Let's move," Danny said, "before somebody big reappears."

We walked around to his apartment. I kept an eye on the street while Danny fumbled with his keys. "Hope you don't mind warm beer," he said.

"Do I have a choice?"

"Nope. My fridge died, and Frog's in no mood to hear about it."

"That reminds me," I said, and ran back up the stairs. I listened outside Frog's door for a moment. Then I snatched his newspaper and slipped back to Danny's. "I didn't tell you about the ferry this morning."

His apartment was small and dark, with a low ceiling, and the place smelled of dead air. Tennis shoes and rackets, clothes, and album jackets were strewn over the living room. A bunch of red carnations, their heads drooped lifelessly over a vase, were on the coffee table surrounded by four empty Rainier bottles and a half empty wine glass. As I finished my account of the ferry incident, Danny grabbed two beers, and we settled into the kitchen nook which caught most of the morning sun.

"Who was that gorilla?" I asked

"Just another humorless jerk. Hell, if it isn't a love-struck blonde trying to rope you, it's a heartless goon who wants to tear your lungs out. What's this world coming to, Eddie?"

"A string of bad luck maybe."

"Bad luck! That goon's wife never told me she was still married. How's that for courtesy?"

"When did that make a difference?"

"I would've at least kept my shoes on."

Danny could be cold when it came to breaking off women, though he always seemed to do it with a finesse that made it look sacrificial on his part. Danny was a master of mood and atmosphere. He knew which Montovani records would give him the most mileage, and why every guy's first investment should be a set of satin sheets and a mauve lamp shade.

Danny leaned back, hands clasped behind his head, and a grin slowly spread across his face.

"You know," he said, staring at the ceiling, "married women have something special."

"I wouldn't know."

"Something you just don't find in single women."

"Husbands," I said.

"They're relaxed, and they know what they want and why. Maybe they know what they want, because they know what they're missing. Ya know, Eddie, life's too short to get all bogged down in one little pasture."

I shrugged my shoulders.

"Husband or not," Danny said, "she was pretty damn lonely. She told me herself that her old man only got romantic when somebody else showed interest."

"I thought she never told you about him?"

"She never used the word 'husband'."

"Better you didn't know then."

"Better! Hell, that creep beat a hole through the bedroom door." Danny stared off. "But married women have just got . . ."

"Husbands," I said.

"You can be real depressing, Eddie."

We finally got around to toasting my leaving school, but Danny's enthusiasm seemed forced. I sensed he wished it was him who was dropping out, but his aunt paid for his apartment, living expenses, and tuition as long as he stayed in school. It was good that he didn't have to worry about money, but he hated everything about college except the women. Danny had successfully talked his aunt out of cutting him off for getting straight D's spring quarter, but now he was sweating his grades for summer. Danny wasn't stupid. He had a quick, but one-track, mind. All thoughts led to women. So did mine, right then. There was nothing worse than being on your own without a steady girl.

I said no to a second can of warm beer and opened the damp newspaper. I heard Danny talking as I read the comics. Suddenly, the tip of a can opener popped through the paper, and Danny's face was quickly where the funnies had been.

"Am I talking to myself?" he said.

"I heard you."

"What did I say?"

"Motherbright's beautiful, and her boyfriend was crazy to leave her. How's that?"

"So what makes a guy leave a woman like her?"

"Maybe she swam in the nude in Florida, and he didn't like it."

"I should've been with you this morning. I bet she was something to see."

She was something, I thought, remembering the way she pressed her breasts dry with her dress and wiped the inside of her thighs so slowly that it made me wish I was a fingernail.

"The fog was pretty thick," I said, folding up the paper. "Say, what the hell's a banshee?"

"A banshee? I've heard of screaming like a banshee. Maybe it's a wild bird. Why?"

"Just something I heard." I belched the sour taste of warm beer. "Fix your fridge, Danny. Drinking here is no fun."

At the door Danny reminded me of the party Friday night across the stairs at Toshi's. I didn't really know Toshi, but I told Danny I'd be there after my night shift at the hotel. I knew if Danny was going, a lot of women would be there.

I opened the door, and in the light I noticed that the wall by the door looked wrong. At one time there had been a dozen photographs on the wall of Danny and a blonde girl named Sara. "What happened to the pictures?" I asked.

Danny picked up several torn pieces of photographs off the rug. "Sara and I had a little disagreement the other night."

I looked at the one picture still intact on the floor. "She never looked like the violent type."

"Surprised me too," Danny said, "but we're still friends. I'm starting fresh now, Eddie. Too many women complicate your life."

"Never had that problem."

Danny pointed to Motherbright's blue house. "She'd be enough for any guy."

I thanked Danny for the beer and started down the walkway. "I almost forgot," I said. "That big gorilla told me to tell you— your ass is his."

Danny laughed. "Seems only fair," he said. "I've had his."

5

My need to celebrate had not been totally quenched at Danny's, so I walked to Joe the Squid's to beg a cold beer. I knocked several times. Just as I was about to step off the porch, Joe stuck his head out the door. His eyes were little more than slits.

"Is that you, Eddie?"

"Sorry," I said. "Didn't mean to wake you."

"What day is it?"

"Wednesday," I said.

"Thank God. Thought I'd slept through today and this was tomorrow."

"It's today all right."

"Well hell," Joe said, "come on in. I've got another day."

"Who is it, Joe?" a girl said, from inside the cabin. Her voice was familiar.

"I'll come back later," I said. "I thought you were alone."

"No problem," Joe said. "I've got a whole 'nother day."

Margy Vasina stepped out next to Joe. She was short and still baby doll cute, with wide eyes and pigtailed hair. She had the firmest looking breasts I had ever seen. Margy had her arm wrapped around Joe's bare chest, and that caused her short, Japanese robe to ride up her thighs.

"Hello, Eddie," she said, coyly. "That was a good party."

"Hell of a send-off for—what's-his-name?" Joe asked.

"Scooter Hayes," I said, remembering that Margy had come with Scooter.

"He looks so different with no hair," Margy said. "I liked him better when it was longer. He's just not the same anymore. He should've moved down here with you, instead of joining the army."

"He was drafted," I said.

Joe stepped forward. "I didn't know you two knew each other?" Joe said.

Margy smiled, and when Joe turned to me, she winked. "Eddie and I have been *together* before," she said.

"I just came over to borrow some beer." I spoke quickly before Margy could say anything else. "We're cleaned out."

"Well come on in," Joe said. "Let's drink a few."

"I'll just take one to go."

Joe shrugged and went inside. Margy stepped outside and leaned against the side of the cabin. She touched my shirt sleeve and ran her finger down my arm.

"Were you ignoring me last night, Eddie Carr?"

"Just busy," I said.

"We should get together sometime soon," she said, with a smile. "It's been a long time."

"A long time gone, Margy." Joe came out and handed me two beers. "Sure you won't stick around?"

"Maybe later," I said. "But thanks for the beer."

I walked off the porch.

"'Bye Eddie," Margy said. "See you again real soon."

I waved over my head without turning and walked on. The radio was on when I got back to the cabin, but Jack and his fishing gear were gone. I headed further up the beach.

The Hole, as Jack called it, was a drop-off north of the Manette Bridge. It was thirty feet deep and a great place for bottom fish. When the tide was out and he couldn't fish off the front porch, Jack would usually go to the Hole.

"Thought I'd find you here," I said. "How's the fishing?"

"Rotten!" he said. "Dogsharks keep stealing my bait and gear. I had to start bringing them in just to get my hooks back."

Jack was a fanatic about fishing and in addition, he was obsessed with one particular fish. He had caught a salmon the winter before off Point Herron. It had snapped his forty-pound test line, and Jack swore the salmon weighed a hundred pounds. Jack believed the salmon was still near the narrows because the water was cold and deep with a good food supply, and the currents were swift. Everything an old salmon could want, according to Jack.

I handed him one of Joe's beers. "Maybe this will change your luck."

"Thought we were out?"

"Joe the Squid. Margy's with him."

"She gets around," Jack said. "She was with Scooter when I left the party."

"Margy's like a bad dream that won't go away."

"She can't be *that* bad," Jack said. "She looks great."

"Looking is one thing, and being around her is another. The last time she came on to me, she started talking marriage." I took a drink. "Why is it all the good-looking ones want to get married?"

Jack reeled his line in slowly, and I could tell he was thinking. I threw some rocks into the water. I liked the plopping sound they made when they hit.

"It's hormones," Jack said.

"What?"

"Hormones," he repeated.

"What's that got to do with anything?"

"That's Margy's problem. Bad hormones. Simple as that."

"Stick to fishing, Jack."

"I'm serious, Eddie. Hormones are the answer. You're just afraid I might know something you don't. Well, I'm telling you, I know what I know."

"And what's that?"

"I know it's hormones. We had a neighbor lady who just went weird all of sudden like Margy."

"Probably living next to you."

"She started crying one night, in the middle of a dinner party. Crying like a baby, in front of all kinds of army brass for no reason at all."

"So what happened?"

"Well, eventually she ran off with her husband's driver. A colonel's wife taking up with a corporal is really strange."

"Maybe she liked him."

"My mother said it was hormones."

"And you figure that's Margy's problem."

"Bad hormones, Eddie. Either bad or maybe too big."

I lay back on the gravelly beach, my hands behind my head. High clouds peeked through the clearing fog, and I closed my eyes. I felt removed from everything—the bridge traffic above, the people in town, and all the plans I had tried for months to assemble. I felt like I had been tossed high into the air in slow motion and was suspended, floating above all that lay before me.

"Jesus!" Jack yelled.

I sat up and saw him yanking back on his pole, bending it nearly in half. "What is it?"

"Maybe dinner."

Jack walked his line a few feet down the beach. I watched him work his fish in closer, rhythmically pulling on the pole and reeling in line.

"What's the time, Jack?"

"Give me a minute," he said. "I'm a little busy."

"What did you find out about that job?"

"Bastard said to come back when I got a haircut." Jack pulled hard on the taut line. "You want to grab the line so I don't lose him in close?" I took the line and tried to see the face of Jack's watch.

"Well," I said, "washing dishes is a shitty job anyway. I could check with Hawkins and see if there's any work down at the hotel."

Jack backed up as he brought the fish in closer, but when its high dorsal fin broke the surface, Jack flew apart and threw down his rod.

"Shit! I had a feeling that's what it was."

"Dogshark?"

"Can't get away from the bastards."

Jack stormed out into the water, running his hand along the line, pulling in his catch as he waded out to his knees.

"This sonofabitch is going to pay," Jack said.

I started winding in the slack line until I saw that Jack had the harmless shark in tow. He was careful, however, to keep his hand clear of the poisonous tail barb. Once Jack dragged the shark out of the water, he tried pulling it up the beach. It moved about six inches before the line snapped, sending Jack onto his backside. I held my laughter. It was clear Jack was mad enough.

"That cracks it," Jack said. He stood up and kicked the shark. He wedged a piece of wood between its jaws. Then holding it up off the beach, Jack repeatedly slashed at its throat with his knife. Finally the heavy body fell to the rocks, and Jack held its head.

I stared at the jerking head and the body flopping below.

"Jesus, Jack," was all I could say.

Jack dropped the head to the ground, slit open the mouth, and after some tearing, he removed his hook. The bait was still attached. Jack dropped the hook into his tackle box, and standing on the shark's tail, he opened its gut with one hard pull on his knife.

I shook my head. "What'd you do that for?"

"Sending a little message," he said.

"Just leave it," I said. "It's dead."

"I want his friends out there to *know* that."

Jack grabbed the dogshark by the tail and threw it out into the water. The current swept the body quickly downstream where it dropped below the surface momentarily. Then one of the whirlpools brought it right back up, swirled it around, and finally sucked it down again. We watched the surface to see if it would rise again, but it never did. I kept my eyes fixed on the water until Jack took the pole from me.

"What time did you say it was?" I said.

"I didn't," Jack said, lifting the shark head, "but it's ten till three."

"Hell!" I started up the beach. "Hawkins will kill me if I'm late again."

"Leave me a note. If he fires you," Jack said. "I'll go right down there."

"Forget it. He's bigger than that dogshark."

"Not for that," Jack said. "I'll pick up your job."

"Well, in the meantime, clean up your message to the fish world. You're fouling up the neighborhood."

I saw Jack cock his arm, and I ran faster. The shark head flew past me, skidding over the wet rocks ahead of me. I just kept running.

6

The once grand Enetai Hotel now served a group of poor residents who stayed by the month. The faded, musty smelling lobby was spacious with large sculptured pillars, yellowed from smoke, and an ornate front desk near the foot of the stairway.

I knew I was late, so I slipped behind a pillar near the sitting area. Mavis Boyle was still sorting mail, and Gimp was collecting the trash behind the desk. I scanned the desk for Hawkins. Then something sharp tapped my back. I turned and saw old Hank staring up at me.

"Who's after you?" Hank said. He was always pestering me to play hide-and-seek.

"Nobody," I whispered. I put my hand over his mouth. "Just a game I'm playing with Hawkins."

"He ain't here," Hank said. "But I'll play."

"Maybe next time Hank." I turned away and looked for Hawkins.

"You said that last time. I wanna play." Suddenly, he slapped my back. "You're *it*, Eddie."

Before I could say anything, he waddled off across the lobby.

There was still no sign of Hawkins, so I stepped around the pillar and approached the desk. Mavis looked at me over the top of her glasses. "You're late, Edward."

I stepped behind the counter and put my arm around Mavis; in the crook of my arm, I felt the hardness of the hump on her back.

"It's only a few minutes," I said.

"Late is late," she said. With her small precise steps, she walked over to the pigeonholes and sorted the last of the mail. "And those minutes are important when they're mine."

"I can't see getting upset over a few minutes."

"You kids infuriate me." Mavis picked up a bundle of fresh towels and tossed them at me. "You may think you're being smart, Eddie, but Mr. Hawkins will get somebody else."

"He's never sober long enough to know what's going on," I said.

"That's none of your business. Your job is to be here on time."

It was obvious Mavis was getting worked up over nothing. "You're right, Mavis."

"I like you, Eddie, but there's only so much any of us can do for you. And Lonnie here," she said nodding to Gimp, "is in no position to cover all your mistakes."

"What'd I do now?" Gimp said. "Hi, Eddie."

"Nothing," Mavis said. She pointed to a bundle wrapped in brown paper under the counter. "Here's your fresh sheets, and make sure they get only one set."

"Got it," I said.

"There's plenty of change. And don't let nobody talk you out of a double room if they're alone."

"Unless they pay for it," Gimp said.

"Won't do that again," I said.

"Anything else comes up, ask Lonnie."

I started to walk away.

"And Eddie," Mavis said, "you and Lonnie keep a sharp eye open for any drinking in the lobby."

"We won't stand for any of that," Gimp said.

"Don't look good finding Hank sleeping off his wine in the lobby."

Having made her point, Mavis nodded and walked to the door. "Good night," she said, and showed us her back in one swift move.

Gimp picked up his weed basket. "Well," he said, walking toward the door, "something you need, just holler."

The tail of Gimp's work jacket was hung up on the neck of a pint bottle in his hip pocket, and I could see the bathroom key chain sticking out.

"Gimp, you seen the key to the john?"

Twice Gimp had locked the bathroom keys in the bathroom after slipping in for a few pops of 'ointment' for his bad knee. Both times he had to take the door off and give Hawkins an explanation. "It should be up there," Gimp said.

"It's not. Hawkins is going to hit the fan."

"It must be there." Gimp dropped his basket, stared off in deep thought, and then started slapping his pants and jacket. I heard the muffled clank of his ring hitting glass, followed by the jingle of the keys that he proudly produced.

"Had me there for a minute," he said.

Gimp picked up his basket and gave me a sharp nod on his way to the front door. "I got weeds to pick up," he said. "I'll see ya later for some checkers."

The large IBM clock above the mail slots was the curse of the night shift. It seemed like the clock worked just fine during the day but slowed down after dark. The night shift gave me a lot of time to think, but too much thinking got depressing.

I kept busy with tasks spread over the night. I would vacuum the lobby and later take my time dusting the window sills and furniture. By nine I had the Coke machine refilled and the chips, peanuts and candy bars restocked under the glass counter. The only advantage to working the desk was having access to the magazine rack. I learned to read anything and everything on the night shift.

That night Gimp saved me from the latest issue of *Modern Romance* when he fell down the stairs. Coffee cups, checkers, board, and Gimp were scattered on the landing. He never let out a sound when he hit, which made me think he might be hurt this time. When I got to Gimp, he reeked of booze. I rolled him over and stared down at his wide, silly grin. "Ready to play, Eddie?"

"You all right?"

"Ripped, ready and roaring to go."

"You better run an inventory on yourself. That was a nasty fall."

Gimp sat up slowly and rubbed his chin which was red from scuffing the rug.

"Smarts right here," he said. Gimp breathed an odor of whiskey, onions, and garlic. "Don't even feel the bum knee."

"You're lucky, Gimp. Anybody else would've broken their neck."

I helped him down the stairs, seated him at the small table behind the desk, and then went back and picked up the checkers and coffee cups. I no sooner sat down than he filled up our cups with Wild Turkey.

"Maybe we shouldn't drink any of that tonight," I said. "I don't want Hawkins walking in on us."

"Don't worry," Gimp said, "nothing will happen."

I looked quickly around the lobby.

"See?" Gimp said. "Now, let's play some checkers."

I hated board games, but I couldn't say no to Gimp. I thought of Gimp as young and somebody's son. Did his parents know how he had ended up? It was sad to think of all the things Gimp might have been. I swallowed the whiskey in one gulp and shuddered at it's bitterness.

"They leave the turkey feet right in the stuff," Gimp said.

I finally jumped one of Gimp's men, and I felt good until I saw he had set me up. Gimp jumped three of my men and grinned broadly at me. I was down to five men, and he had lost only three. After he got his first king, it was all down hill for me. Gimp cornered my last man, and I surrendered. I checked the lobby again and drank another cup of whiskey.

"Nice warm-up," Gimp said.

I took two bags of nuts from the snack shelf. "You had that game mapped out from the first move, didn't you?"

"Funny how whiskey makes you hungry," he said.

"I didn't stand a chance."

"Why is that?"

"Beats me."

"You're suppose to know those things. You're a college boy."

"Not anymore, Gimp."

"You finished already?"

"Things were moving too fast. I jumped off the assembly line."

"Know what you mean," Gimp said. "I quit the sixth grade and went working the mines at fourteen. Good experience when I came out West looking for gold."

"I didn't know you were a prospector."

"No reason you should."

Gimp poured more whiskey while I reset the checkers.

"Where did you prospect?" I asked.

"California. Spent some time in Nevada. Then I came up north here with a buddy, and we poked around Gold Bar and Monte Cristo for awhile. Most everything was mined out except the rocks."

"A real gold miner," I said.

"But I ran into enough of a slide to end my prospecting," he said, slapping his bad knee.

Gimp drank his whiskey and poured more.

I had no feeling in my tongue. I poured water in my cup. "Ever find any gold?" I asked.

Gimp laughed. "Some. But not enough to mean much. I did save this," he said. He pulled a leather string away from his neck. Attached to it was a chunk of metal. "Quartz gold," he said, "but a fine specimen."

"So that's what it looks like," I said. "Sure doesn't look like much."

"Well, it ain't," Gimp said.

"At least you tried," I said. "That's what I'd like to do."

Gimp took another drink and stared up at the clock. Then a grin came over his face. "I did go after it, didn't I?"

"And you found some of it, too." A proud smile crept over Gimp's face, and for the briefest moment, the hardness in his face seemed to disappear. It was an unmistakably pleasant sight. He repositioned the last of his men and smiled again.

"You ready for another game?" he said.

I nodded.

Gimp made his move. I stared at the board.

"Do I sound drunk?" I asked.

"No more than me."

"Good. I felt like I sounded real drunk." My head felt numb inside and out, and I stared at the checkers a long time before I made each move. Gimp seemed to be moving slower, and he blinked his eyes a lot. At least I thought it was Gimp. He took two of my men, and I didn't care. I didn't care about anything except how light and airy my head felt. Then the front door opened.

I jumped up. I knew Hawkins was checking up on me. It turned out to be a sailor looking for a room. I was so glad it wasn't Hawkins, I considered giving him a double room.

Gimp grinned at me every time I looked back at him. The sailor leaned over the counter and sniffed. He wasn't too sure what was going on. "Smells pretty drunk in here," he said.

"You oughta smell it from where I am," Gimp said.

The sailor smiled. He picked up his towel and wash cloth. "Say," he said, "you guys look pretty smart. Where's a guy get a woman around here?"

The sailor looked at me, and I looked at Gimp.

"Same as any other place," Gimp said.

"And where's that?"

"The gettin' place," Gimp said.

"Say again?"

"Right between the legs," I said.

The sailor gave us both hard looks. He snatched his bag off the floor. "Just what the world needs," he said. "Two more fucking assholes."

Gimp stood up. "Try Dook's or the Wheelhouse. Always a few strays in them places."

We finished two more games of checkers, and Gimp made it four wins in a row. I had no strategy at all. I just pushed those little red markers from spot to spot and marvelled at how many times Gimp frog-hopped my men. My head felt padded with horsehair, and I was enjoying the numbness when the front door opened again. I didn't move until I heard Hawkins' voice and an even louder woman's voice.

I quickly grabbed our cups and started for the bathroom, but tripped over my chair. Gimp grabbed my arm, keeping me from falling. When I regained my balance, Gimp palmed a moist object in my hand. I didn't pay it any attention until after I had emptied our cups in the bathroom sink and had come back to the table. By then the smell of garlic was quite strong.

"What the hell's this for?" I whispered.

Gimp pointed to his mouth and continued chewing.

"You can't be serious."

Gimp rolled the garlic mash around his mouth until he got it balled up between his lip and teeth. Hawkins and his lady friend were still arguing in the doorway.

"Just chew it," Gimp said. "Garlic eats up the smell of the whiskey."

I stared at the garlic.

"Just eat it, Eddie."

The front door slammed, and I ate the clove of garlic. The first bite brought tears to my eyes. As Hawkins and his lady approached the desk, I chewed harder and faster. My mouth filled with garlic-soaked saliva, and I swallowed just as Hawkins reached the counter. He pointed his thick finger at me.

"This here is the guy, honey."

Hawkins was fat and sloppy, and he reminded me of a sea cow.

"Eddie here took it on himself to tempt the clergy one night, honey. I would've loved to seen the look on that reverend's face when Wiggles came in."

He turned to the woman. "You know Wiggles, don't'cha honey, over at the Crow's Nest? Imagine her walking in on a priest in her bed?"

"It was an accident," I said.

Hawkins wrinkled his face. "What the hell smells?" he said.

"It's pizza or spaghetti," the woman said.

"The Mafia check in tonight?"

"Just a sailor," I said.

"Him you can put in with Wiggles. She's a little late on her rent." Hawkins spun the register around and looked up at me. "You sick or something?"

"Not me," I said.

"You don't look so good," Hawkins said.

"Looks good to me," the woman said.

"What do you know?"

"His hair's cute," she said.

"Cute my ass," Hawkins said. "Looks like a goddamn fairy. Get a haircut, Carr!"

"Most fairies I've seen," Gimp said, "got short hair. Not much longer than yours."

"What are you saying, you old drunk?"

"A point of fact," Gimp said. "Just a point of fact."

"Well, the point of fact is you're a drunk and replaceable."

"Come on, sweets," the woman said, clutching Hawkins by the arm. "Let's call it a night."

Hawkins turned to Gimp. "So what do you say about that?"

Gimp rubbed his scuffed chin. "All work is the same means to the same end. It's between you and me who decides when I find a new means."

"Oh yeah?" Hawkins said. He turned to the woman. "What the hell does that mean?"

"Let's call it a night, lover boy," the woman said.

She led Hawkins to the stairs and looked down at us, smiling.

"Get a haircut!" Hawkins bellowed. "I mean it, Carr. Or— you're fired!"

Gimp and I listened to Hawkins' voice fade down the upstairs hallway until his apartment door slammed shut.

"He won't remember a thing tomorrow," Gimp said.

My stomach felt like it was being rung like a sponge. Everything about me smelled of garlic. Gimp ran ahead of me and lifted the toilet seat. I kneeled down and waved Gimp away. Suddenly the storage closet door flew open behind me and crazy Hank popped out.

"You're still *it* Eddie," he said. Then he slapped me on the back. Hank hobbled out of the bathroom, laughing to himself. After that I stared into that rusty toilet bowl for what seemed like forever.

7

Sherman Clay was Bremerton's only music store, and like Olberg's Drug, that summer it became a gathering place for the young people in town. Musicians came to the store for instruments and supplies, and they would often try out new guitars, like the Rickenbacker twelve-string or the violin-shaped bass, upstairs in the practice room. Morrie Stans, the owner, was a pudgy good-natured man who liked us when we were buying but when we weren't, he would scream and threaten us for hanging around and "depreciating" his merchandise. I walked into Morrie's the day after I dropped out of college, to pay off the bill on my drums. "It's a great day, Morrie," I said.

Morrie looked at me over the top of his glasses and smiled painfully. "Sometimes this is a place of business with paying customers."

"Well, today I'm paying." I laid three twenty-dollar bills on the counter.

Morrie looked at the bills, and then quickly slapped his hand over them. "Eddie, all the picks you've *borrowed*, and the drumsticks and guitar strings I've *donated* on account—and now *real* money?"

"You know Morrie," I said, "this place wouldn't be the same without you."

"I know I'd be better off without you and your friends."

"You don't mean that."

"Yes I do."

"That's a shame," I said. "I like you, Morrie."

"Well, don't like me. I've got enough problems."

Morrie peeled my sixty dollars off the counter.

"The drums are mine now—clear and legal, right?"

Morrie examined my account slip then wrote PAID IN FULL across it.

"Anybody upstairs?" I asked.

"Bret and Mooch. Scooter Hayes is up there and a few others. Tell that Mooch I've got an inventory of everything up there. I swear I'm supporting that thief."

I scooped a pair of drumsticks off the counter and went upstairs.

It was standing room only in the practice room that overlooked Pacific Avenue. A dozen people were squeezed into the small room. Only Scooter, wearing his army dress greens and with his head shaved, looked out of place. I felt embarrassed for Scooter in his uniform, so I walked over and sat down next to him.

"What's with the suit?" I said.

"I'm leaving today," Scooter said. "I was hoping you would stop by."

"Something wrong?"

"Just ready to go."

"Seems like you just got back," I said.

"You can see me and Henderson any time now. They've got our picture up in the enlistment office," he said.

"I like the real thing," I said, and lit a cigarette.

Bret looked over at Mooch and then picked out a chord on the guitar and sang:

He hid under tables and abandoned all task,
Knew what was coming, that nothing would last . . . .

"That's right," Mooch said. He bummed a cigarette. "What's the sense of anything when it can all go tomorrow?"

Bret and I looked at each other. We'd heard it all before. Scooter stood up and brushed off his uniform.

"I've got a ferry to catch," he said.

"Already?" I said. "I just got here."

Scooter smiled and shook his head. "I've got to go."

"How about I ride over with you?" I said.

"No, that's all right."

"I've got nothing else to do."

"It's up to you," he said.

Scooter shook hands with everyone, and I followed him out the door. Morrie was just finishing up with a customer when we reached the foot of the stairs, and Scooter asked for his bag from behind the counter.

"That time already?" Morrie said.

"Time to move on," Scooter said.

"Well, you take care." Morrie shook Scooter's hand.

"Sure thing," Scooter said. "Thanks."

Scooter slung his duffle bag over his shoulder, and we headed for the terminal. We climbed to the second deck of the ferry and sat outside. The sun was warm, and the smell of low tide hung in the air. The wind stiffened when the ferry pulled away, and the air smelled of diesel smoke as well as salt. The ferry seemed empty, devoid of young people and shoppers going to Seattle, and Scooter was uncommonly quiet as we watched Bremerton grow small in the distance. Only the huge shipyard crane loomed large against the sky.

"Wish there were some girls on the boat," I said.

"Who needs them?" Scooter said, staring shoreward.

"Girls are always nice." Scooter didn't respond. "What's got into you?"

"Nothing. Just—who needs them?"

"You always liked seeing girls on the ferry. Something's wrong. Did the army turn you weird?"

"Let's talk about something else."

"What else is there?"

"Forget it, Eddie." Scooter and I had always been able to talk, and we had never disagreed on the importance of girls. He had only been gone five months, but something had changed.

"You've just been away too long," I said.

"No, Eddie. Been back too long."

Scooter walked to the railing. Then he said, "You haven't seen the way they look at me. Friends know me and know they liked me once, but it's like I've died and come back. It's like I don't exist."

"Sure you do."

"You know what Jeannie said about my fingers?" Jeannie had been Scooter's girl for almost two years. "She said they were hard."

"What's wrong with that?" I said.

"Hard—from learning how to kill."

"What's she know, Scooter?"

"She knows, Eddie. Everybody knows."

The ferry turned so the Bremerton crane disappeared behind us as we approached Waterman Point.

"Funny," Scooter said. "I couldn't wait to get home. It's all I've thought about for months. Now I can't leave fast enough."

"*I'm* glad you're back."

"I'm not here, and I'm not there, Eddie. I'm nowhere." He looked away and then turned back. "Know something funny, Eddie?"

I shook my head.

"I don't really want to go. Kind of scary, Eddie. Never felt this kind of scared before."

"You'll be all right," I said.

"Yeah, sure."

"If it was really bad, everybody would be going."

Scooter smiled and then stared blankly ahead. He didn't say anything for a long time.

"I really do like women, Eddie."

"Hell," I said, "I knew that."

The ferry rounded Waterman Point and moved into the channel to avoid the exposed rocks through Rich Passage. Scooter took out his wallet and checked his plane ticket for the departure time.

"Remember this?" Scooter said. He held his wallet open to a badly worn picture of astronaut Alan Shepard.

"Sure. That's your man."

"First guy up there."

"The same year Maris hit sixty-one homers."

"Kennedy said we'd be on the moon in ten years."

"A great year," I said.

There was a pause. "What went wrong, Eddie?"

As long as I had known Scooter, he had dreamed of being an astronaut. He loved science; his bedroom walls were covered with star maps and National Geographic paintings of planets, and when he talked of space, he got so excited you'd have thought space was a girl's name. When everybody else was saving money to buy a car, Scooter saved for his first telescope. He had applied for the Air Force Academy but wasn't accepted, and he knew it was impossible to become an astronaut without being a pilot. Then the army drafted him. "You going to try the academy again?" I asked.

"Might be too late," he said.

"Working on helicopters should mean something."

"It's not flying a jet."

"What happened to the guy who wanted to fly to the moon?" I said.

Scooter turned to me and grinned. "He's flying to Vietnam."

Downtown Seattle, framed by its two tallest structures, the Space Needle and the Smith Tower, came into view as the ferry rounded the south end of Bainbridge Island, and grew larger as we passed Alki Point. The air horn blew, and Scooter and I stretched.

"I don't know why I said all this," Scooter said. "Forget what I said out there."

"We all get scared," I said. "You'll be all right. You're the one who told me you can be whatever you imagine."

"I stole it from Kennedy."

"It's still true. Don't worry," I said. I put my arm around his the neck. "You'll be back and better than ever."

Scooter punched me on the arm and then lifted his duffle bag. It was hard to name what was wrong with Scooter. He was afraid, but there was something else. He was like people you knew who had mono. Scooter looked beat, and for the first time since I had known him, he made me depressed.

I told Scooter I couldn't go out to the airport. Short of money, I said. We didn't talk on the ramp or through the terminal. On Alaskan Way Scooter flagged a Graytop.

"I guess this is it," he said. "Sure you won't ride out with me?"

"Positive."

"I'll pay."

"I can't, Scooter."

The cab pulled up, and the driver opened the trunk. Scooter tossed his bag in and shook hands with me.

"It's funny how a little talk loosens a guy up," Scooter said. "Makes you want to talk more."

"Next time you're home."

"Forget about me spouting off, okay?" he said.

"Sure."

The cabby honked.

"See ya, Eddie."

"See ya, Scooter."

Scooter waved, and I waved back. I thought of a dozen more things I could've said. And they would have been good things, but as the cab moved farther away, I knew that none of them would have been true.

8

Toshi's apartment glowed yellow from the inside and bright light sprayed out into the darkness. A chorus of off-key voices sang *HAPPY TOGETHER/SO HAPPY TOGETHER,* only to be drowned out by loud screams and laughter.

As I approached the apartment from the beach, I saw two figures on the patio. At first they were speaking normally, but suddenly their voices turned sharp and intense. I stepped behind a hedge to wait for a break in the conversation. The girl was tall and slender, and her head was bent down toward a glass she held.

"I just thought we meant something," I heard her say. Then her voice turned soft. "I really thought that."

"We *do* mean something." I immediately recognized Danny's voice. "Things are just different," he said.

Through a space in the bush, I saw him put his hand around the girl's neck, but she pushed him away.

"*We* are different, Sara," Danny said. "That's why I said that. You always said you wanted honesty."

"I didn't want to hear *that*," Sara said.

"We've been good for each other," Danny said. Sara turned and looked away. "Hell, you're the nicest girl I know."

"Don't call me *nice!*"

I heard someone laugh down the stairs behind me, and I started to step onto the walkway when Danny spoke again.

"You're really different from other girls," he said. "Can't we be friends?"

Sara laughed. "For some reason I thought we were more than that. But I can see I was wrong. It's not the first time."

The couple down the stairs came into sight. I cleared my throat and stepped out from behind the hedge. I looked straight ahead.

"Eddie!" Danny yelled. "Thought you'd never show up."

I stopped. Danny tried to bring Sara over, but she pulled free and went inside.

"Sorry to bust in on you."

"We were through anyway," Danny said.

"Looks like a good party."

"The hearty ones are still here," Danny said as we walked across the patio. "You've met Toshi, haven't you?"

I shook my head.

"Maybe next time. He passed out an hour ago."

The apartment was hot and humid from all the bodies pressed so closely together, and the air smelled of smoke, perfume, and beer. Most people were crowded in the middle of the room, but there was a steady flow in and out of the kitchen.

Danny closed the door behind us, and immediately eyes from all over the room focused on us. Danny started pointing to girls and calling out their names.

"That's Veronica. There's Becky. Down here we have Joyce. Joyce, this is Eddie."

I smiled, and Joyce went back to her conversation.

Danny stepped over a guy with a crew cut and kissed a dark-haired girl.

"Eddie, this is Loy. Toshi's girl."

Danny continued pointing out girls around the room, yelling so loudly that I got embarrassed. I looked for a familiar face. Everyone I saw was a stranger, obviously college friends of Danny and Toshi. None of them were people I would have known on my own. The guys struck me as either science majors or shoe salesmen, and as good looking as some of the girls were, they seemed silly the way they laughed at everything. Girls who laughed at everything left me cold. Finally I heard a familiar voice.

"Eddie! Hey, Eddie!" Jack was sitting in the far corner next to a girl with wild red hair. He put his arm around her and smiled proudly.

Danny squatted down next to Loy and reassured her that it was no reflection on her that Toshi had thrown up and passed out. He kissed her, and then kissed her again—the second time with conviction. Danny missed no opportunity to give of himself in a girl's moment of need.

I moved toward the kitchen because it was the least crowded room. I stepped over a couple embraced on the floor, dragging my butt over the guy's head. He was so busy massaging his date's chest that he didn't say a word. I grabbed a beer from a plastic cooler and sank into obscurity.

The only thing I liked about big parties was that there was always something going on. A girl getting stroked in a corner, loud music, women dancing, and fights. The worst thing was that it took at least four parties before you got to know anyone interesting other than the one or two people you already knew. After four parties you had something in common, and you were acceptable as someone new to know. Since this was my first party with this crowd, I had a lot of time on my hands.

I was on my fourth beer when the front door flew open. For a moment everyone hushed. Then Joe the Squid appeared with more beer. Cheers followed. Behind Joe was Margy Vasina. I turned away until I thought it was safe to turn around, but when I did, Danny's girl, Sara—clutching a cat—was staring at me.

"I'm looking for wine," she said. Her eyes were swollen and puffy, and I just stared at her a moment. "It's red wine," Sara said. "Have you seen it?"

I followed her eyes as they darted around, and I was struck by how pretty she was. Her hair was cut short, and she didn't wear any make-up. She wore a white oxford shirt over a pair of tight powder blue chords.

"Well," she said, "have you seen it or not?"

"There should be some somewhere," I said.

I opened the refrigerator and shoved bottles aside looking for something red.

"Anything's fine," Sara said.

I grabbed something in a green bottle, and when I turned around Margy was standing next to Sara, smiling at me.

"Hello Eddie," Margy said.

Joe stepped behind her. "How about I trade this warm beer for a cold one?" he said.

Sara cleared her throat. "My glass of wine?"

"Coming up," I said.

"Nice party," Margy said. "I'm glad there's somebody here I know. Are you alone, Eddie?"

"I'm working the hotel tonight."

"Tough break," Joe said. "There's a slow tune, Margy. Let's hug up."

"See ya," Margy said.

I watched Joe lead Margy into the living room. When they started dancing, I handed Sara her glass of wine. She thanked me and was about to leave when Danny came up and put his arm around her. "Just the girl I've been looking for," Danny said.

Sara lifted Danny's hand off her shoulder. "No more, Danny."

Danny put his hand back on her shoulder. "Sara, this is my good friend Eddie."

"Eddie Carr," I said.

"Thank you, Eddie Carr, for the wine."

"Eddie here saved my hide the other day," Danny said. "He's a real quick thinker."

"That's nice," Sara said. "Some of us are a little slow to care." Sara turned out of Danny's grasp and walked away.

Danny smiled, and I shrugged my shoulders.

"I've got a favor to ask," Danny said, in a slightly hushed voice.

"What favor?"

"Sara. She's a little upset. She needs to be with someone."

I looked at Danny warily. "What's wrong with her, Danny?"

"Nothing. She's just upset."

"Something *is* wrong with her," I said.

"E-d-d-i-e," Danny said.

"Nobody pawns off a good-looking girl unless there's something wrong with her."

"We just don't agree on things."

"Sounds too simple."

"The truth, Eddie. She's a good kid. Good-looking, great sense of humor. And a nice body."

"If she's that good, why me?"

"You're a friend, and you saved me from that big gorilla."

"You're all heart, Danny."

"I'm not asking you to marry her. I just want her to be with someone and have a good time."

"She wasn't too friendly a few minutes ago."

"That was me," Danny said. "She'll warm up. What do you say?"

I gave Danny a hard look, but before I could say anything, he slapped me on the shoulder and smiled.

"Knew I could count on you."

I saw Sara near the front door talking to another girl. A moment later she went outside still clutching the cat. For the next few minutes, I watched her through the kitchen window. She remained alone holding the cat and looking out into the night. I couldn't keep from looking at her. Finally I poured another glass of red wine and went outside.

"Thought you might be thirsty," I said.

Sara looked at me blankly.

"It's me, Eddie Carr. Remember?"

"I remember." She looked back toward the apartment. "What is taking her so long?"

"Who?"

"You can get back to the party now." Sara's knees buckled slightly, but she quickly straightened up. "I'm perfectly fine."

Sara looked like she was about to cry, when her knees buckled again. The cat slipped to her side where Sara pinned it with her elbow.

"I think you're choking the cat," I said.

"Just never you mind. I know what I'm doing."

Sara was leaning at a severe angle trying to hold herself up while wedging the cat between her elbow and hip. The cat hung at Sara's side, kicking with its hind legs. I grabbed the cat. Sara stood up, and I handed the cat back to her.

"You can tell Danny Peezor his plot has failed. I can stand on my own two feet without him."

"Why don't you sit down before you hurt yourself?" I said.

"Me?"

Her knees collapsed, and she hit the decking hard, the cat still pressed to her side. At first she looked startled. Then a sleepy smile crept over Sara's face.

"Where is that Gloria?" she said.

"My place is just down the stairs," I said. "How about some coffee?"

"I'm going home," she said.

Sara clumsily got to her feet. She wavered, and the longer I watched her legs, the less I believed she could walk on her own. The cat didn't look like it would survive the trip either. I put my arm around Sara and convinced her to walk off some of the wine. I got her to take deep breaths as we walked around the porch, and she belched twice.

"I'm so embarrassed," she said.

We circled the patio three times before Sara stopped and leaned against the door. She reminded me of a big, little girl, and just as I leaned forward to kiss her, she opened her eyes. "Would you get my coat and purse?"

She described her things, and I propped her up against the building.

"Thank you," she said and closed her eyes.

I went inside and dug through the coats and shoes and bags by the kitchen table until I found Sara's ski jacket and purse. When I got outside, Sara was sitting on the ground, her head on her knees.

"Here's your stuff," I said.

Sara slowly raised her head. I lifted her up and helped her with her coat. She fell back against the building and stared at me blankly.

"Well," she said, "good night, Eddie," and she slid straight to the deck.

I crouched down. "Where do you live?"

"I can get there myself."

She stood, collected all her strength, and stepped out with a goose step and then corrected her gait to shorter, more guarded steps. Twice Sara drifted off into the laurel only to right herself on the stairs. At the top she walked in a circle, apparently getting her bearings, before she walked off toward town. I was sad to see her go. A moment later she reappeared, this time walking in the opposite direction.

I grabbed my beer and hurried up the stairs. I caught up with Sara in the middle of the block.

"Lost by any chance?"

Sara crossed in front of me. She wandered across a small patch of grass in front of an apartment building and stumbled back onto the sidewalk.

"Mind if I walk along?"

"It's a free country. You can walk all the way to Alaska if you want."

I walked beside her while she meandered from the parking strip, across the sidewalk, onto a lawn, and back onto the sidewalk, all the time clutching the cat at her side. Then Sara wandered off onto a little walkway to a pink building.

"Enjoy Alaska," she said.

Before I could say anything, she missed a step on the stairs and fell flat on her face. I ran over and took the cat from her.

"You all right?"

"Oh, damn it!" she said, sitting up.

I sat down next to her and dusted the dirt off her knees. Sara buried her face in her hands. "I can't do anything right tonight."

Sara opened her purse. "I *really* don't feel very good," she said.

I grabbed her keys. "Up we go," I said and helped her up. "Which apartment is yours?"

She pointed toward the second floor, and I gently guided her up the stairs. Outside her door there were six white saucers lined up in a row. Seven or eight cats of various sizes and colors sat at the far end of the balcony. At the door Sara took the cat from me and looked it straight in the face.

"Now you just get in line," she said, setting the cat down. She opened her door, turned on the outside light, and grabbed a bag of cat food from inside the door. She filled up the saucers, and the cats rushed the plates, overrunning the newest arrival. Sara watched them a moment and then stepped inside and slammed the door. A second later the door opened.

"Good night, Eddie Carr." She started to close the door again, but I stopped it with my foot.

"I'd like to see you again."

"No, thank you," she said.

"Not even over coffee?"

"Good night," she said and closed the door.

I waited a moment for her to open the door. Then I heard the click of the door lock. The new cat on the porch was pacing behind the others doing just as Sara had instructed: waiting in line for his turn at what was left on the saucers. I stole a couple chunks of food from a saucer and laid them in front of the new cat. He didn't even look up. New guys need all the help they can get.

9

The music at Toshi's was still blaring, but I couldn't decide whether I wanted to return or not.

"You look lost, Eddie." I turned and saw Margy Vasina behind me. She looked very relaxed.

"Waiting for Joe?" I said.

She shook her head. "He's inside discussing the words to songs, and I got bored. You give a girl a complex standing over there." Margy patted the railing, and then caressed it with her right hand.

I walked up to her, and she wrapped her arms around me and kissed me. I pushed away, but she kissed me again, and this time her tongue darted furiously after mine. I didn't want to start anything, so I just stood there. Margy wrapped her arms around me tighter and pressed herself against me.

"Let's go, Eddie," she whispered. She kissed me again. "Come on, Eddie. Please."

She reached down and touched me, and the touch of her hand cleared my head of everything but her. I didn't want to go with Margy, but while my head said NO my body said YES.

"I need you, Eddie. I need you now." My cabin was not lit, but in the bedroom Margy quickly pulled off her sweater, and blue filaments of light danced in the dark. I could see the silhouette of her full breasts and round hips. She slipped out of her pants and unbuckled mine. She brushed her cheek against my thigh, lowered my pants, pulled me down to the bed and rolled me onto her. She dug her heels into the mattress, pressing her body against mine. She gasped and sighed deeply. I forgot everything except the sound and the feel and the taste of Margy. She twisted under me and cried out. Her nails were sharp blades, and in pulling up to avoid the pain, I only succeeded in stimulating Margy more. She screamed, writhed more violently, and pulled me against her harder, but I resisted. Suddenly, Margy exploded in violent contractions. Screaming, she buckled and collapsed on the bed, dead quiet.

I lay there motionless, relieved she was still. Her pupils were rolled back, only the whites of her eyes exposed. I touched her hand. It was cool.

I whispered her name, but she didn't respond. Her chest wasn't moving. Her skin felt clammy. I scooted away from her and paced the room. The longer I looked at her, the more concerned I became. I dressed quickly. I shook Margy once more, but she didn't respond. I ran up the stairs to Toshi's to find Jack.

I burst through Toshi's front door and looked around the room for Jack, but I didn't see him. Danny ran in from the kitchen.

"Where's Jack? Where's Jack, Danny? I need him."

"Last time I saw him he was headed for the bedroom." A moment later I turned on the light in the back bedroom. Jack rolled over and squinted at me. The redheaded girl pulled the blanket over her.

"Jesus Christ, Eddie!"

"Come on, Jack."

"I'm not through," Jack said.

I tore the blanket off the bed. The girl squealed and ran out of the room with the blanket around her.

"Now look what you did," Jack said.

"I think I've killed her," I said.

"You sure killed it for me," Jack said.

"I'm serious. I think Margy's dead. You've got to come help me!"

He stood up and slipped on his jeans. "Are you serious?"

"Dead serious," I said, pacing. "We were on the bed—you know—and she started screaming and hollering. Then she stopped breathing. Come on! Forget your shoes!"

I clutched Jack by the shirt and pulled him out the bedroom door.

Down in our cabin Jack and I stood like mourners at the foot of my mattress just staring down at Margy's naked body.

"It's worse than I thought," I said.

"You've really done it, Eddie."

"Don't say that." I knelt down and put my ear to Margy's chest. "Is she breathing?"

"My ears feel plugged up," I said. "You listen."

"I don't know about touching a dead person."

I grabbed Jack by the shirt and shook him. "Just check. It was an accident. I didn't know you could kill somebody doing that."

Jack slowly lowered his head. "This is weird, Eddie."

"Just listen."

I paced the room. "Why me? I don't even like her. It was her idea. I didn't even want to sleep with her. You gotta believe me, Jack. It's the truth."

"Shut up," Jack said. "I hear something."

"Is she breathing?"

"It's real faint."

I fell to my knees. "Are you sure?"

"It's not much, but there's a pulse."

"Oh, thank God. I swear I'll never sleep with another girl again."

Jack pulled the blanket over her, and we tucked it under her, and put her head on a pillow. Still Margy didn't move.

"Thanks Jack. You saved my ass. I thought I'd killed her."

Jack shook his head. "Some stud."

I sat back and leaned against Jack's bed, feeling embarrassed but relieved. "She's really out," Jack said. "What did you two do?"

"Nothing."

"It was one of those French things, wasn't it?"

"No! She just started jumping around. Screaming. Then she went out. I'll probably have scars on my back."

"Well, Eddie, you're either real good or real bad."

"It was nothing. I swear. It was nothing."

At Jack's suggestion we rubbed her feet and legs and arms until Jack felt a stronger pulse. Then her head moved, and she moaned. I immediately felt better.

When I started feeling good about Margy, Joe the Squid became a problem. Margy had gone to the party with him, and it would be a problem if he found her in our place. Jack quickly saw the dilemma. Joe was a friend, but he wouldn't stay that way if he found Margy with us.

We tried waking Margy, but she wouldn't come to. Jack suggested we dress her and take her to Joe's place. There was no doubt in my mind Jack was a genius.

Dressing Margy was a challenge. Neither of us had ever dressed a naked girl before, so we tried it as a team, doing our work by touch. We left the lights off, so no one would drop in. Jack held up Margy's legs while I worked her panties on. Then he helped me with her jeans. It wasn't until we started on her jeans that we found the dark working against us.

"You screwed up," Jack said.

"No, I got the button here in front."

"The panties," he said. "The cotton part goes on the inside."

"Well, hell, I'm not taking them off. Nobody's going to know but her."

Wrestling Margy's pants over her hips was like slipping a narrow bag over a wide log. Through all the jostling and rolling around, Margy never came to. She mumbled and moaned but nothing more.

Once her jeans were on, I worked on her tennis shoes while Jack took care of her bra. You could tell Jack was a fisherman the way he worked the bra cups like a pair of nets under her breasts. But once he had them netted, we had a struggle with the straps. After some twenty minutes we had Margy in a reasonable condition to be moved.

Jack checked outside, and when all was clear we carried Margy along the walkway from our place to Joe's. Like most of us, Joe usually left his door unlocked. I balanced Margy on one knee and pushed on the door, but it was locked. I lost my balance, and I dropped my end of Margy. She moaned, but she didn't wake up. I grabbed Margy's feet again, and we tried the front windows.

One window was ajar, so Jack held Margy up while I raised the window. I crawled inside and grabbed Margy's shoulders. Suddenly, Jack pushed her at me all at once, and I fell over backwards, knocking Margy's head on the window frame.

"Eddie," she moaned.

"What the hell are you doing?" I said.

"There's somebody on the beach."

"Well, back up!"

"I can't," Jack said. "Pull her in."

"E-d-d-i-e?" Margy moaned. "M-y . . . E-d-d-i-e."

"Not Eddie," I said. "This is Joe."

"Oh J-o-e. You don't sound like J-o-e."

Jack lifted and then pushed Margy through the window, and the three of us ended up on the floor.

"J-o-e?"

"Yes darling," Jack said.

"Shut up!" I said. Jack and I got up and dragged Margy into Joe's bedroom and placed her on the bed. We covered her with a blanket, and then climbed back out the front window.

When we returned to our place, we just stood in the dark kitchen for a minute and shared a smoke.

"Some stud," Jack said.

"This is enough to turn a guy against sex."

"That's easy for you to say. You cut me short." He held his cigarette to his watch. "Maybe there's still time to catch Donna."

"Oh shit! What time is it?"

"Still early."

"The real time."

"Quarter to one."

"Goddamn it! The hotel!"

"I'd say you're late."

"If Hawkins is there, I'm canned. I'll see you later." I opened the door.

"Aren't you forgetting something?" Jack said.

"What's that?"

"Wearing shoes might make a better impression."

I grabbed my shoes and socks from the bedroom and put them on outside. I caught up with Jack on the stairs.

"Just tell Hawkins you were saving a girl's life," Jack said, as I ran past him. "He wouldn't can you for that."

10

When I woke up the next morning, I thought my being fired had been just a dream, like the taste of rum in my mouth and my sore stomach muscles. Then I rolled over and saw the splatter on the bedroom floor. My worst fears were confirmed. I had been sick, and Hawkins had fired me.

Suddenly there was a knock at the door.

"Hooooody whooooo! Hooooody whooooo!"

I opened my eyes and listened.

"Hooody whooo to you in there."

"It's Flex," Jack said, bolting out of bed. "I told you he'd show up."

I heard Jack open the cabin door, followed by a girl's scream. I immediately thought of Margy and pulled the covers over me.

"My God, Jackson! Where are your shorts?"

"Come on in," I heard Jack say. "Eddie, it's Flex and Lolly. Well, come on in. It's cold with the door open."

"Not on your life," Lolly said. "I don't want you exposing yourself all over me." I stepped into the kitchen, rubbing my eyes.

"Dear God!" Lolly said, looking at me. "They're both naked."

"Lolly," Jack said, "this is Eddie, our third roommate. Eddie you remember Flex?"

Lolly still had her back to us. I nodded and shook Flex's hand. He was a weight lifter, short with highly developed arms that bowed out from his chest.

"This place has gone totally naked," Lolly said, turning to Flex. "Maxwell, can't you do something?"

"It's their place," he said.

"Well, you can do something," she said.

"I suppose so."

Flex smiled and took several long, deep breaths, slowly pumping his arms out from his side, like he was working an imaginary bellows. Then with a deep inhale, he expanded his chest. Two shirt buttons clinked to the floor. Jack and I applauded. The first time I met Flex, Jack got him to smash a beer can between his forearm and biceps. It was a neat trick.

"Damn it! Maxwell. I told you no more of that." Lolly picked up one of the buttons. "You sew this one on!"

"You said *do* something."

"I'm warning you," Lolly said. "No more popping buttons."

Jack went into the bedroom, wrapped a blanket around himself, and brought me out a dirty towel.

"We're going to need some beer," Jack said to Flex. "Moving you in will be thirsty work."

"You're gonna love it down here," I said.

"Well," Lolly said, "we're not going to have time for beer today. Are we Maxwell?"

"Yeah, that's right," Flex said. "We're on our way to see her folks. Some lunch thing."

"A luncheon, Maxwell."

"Deviled ham on crackers and scrawny sandwiches with no crust is a lunch *thing*."

"So what's the occasion?" I asked.

There was a pause.

"Well," Lolly said, "Maxwell has some good news. So we're celebrating."

Jack scowled, looking from Lolly to Flex. "You two aren't getting married, are you?"

"Not yet," Lolly said.

"That's a relief," Jack said. "We're not set up for mixed company."

Lolly glanced around. "This place is barely ready for the Stone Age."

"There's that wit of yours again," Jack said.

"I've joined the army," Flex blurted out.

The cabin went quiet, and Jack's face froze. "You've what?"

"I enlisted. But before you . . ."

"Of all the crazy, fucking things to do."

Lolly stepped between them. "He's not crazy," she said. "It's what we want."

"I knew this had to be your idea."

"It was mine," Flex said. "So yell at me."

"Why, Flex? Why do this to me?"

"It's not you," he said. "I had to do *something.*"

Lolly clutched Flex's arm. "We're all very proud of him."

"Proud my ass!" Jack shook his head. "He's not stupid enough to do this on his own. It takes a real idiot to join the army when guys are getting shot every day, off in a goddamn place we never heard of."

"I'm putting in for Germany," Flex said.

"They promised him that," Lolly said. "So—he'll be safe."

"Safe!" Jack yelled. "I don't believe I'm hearing this. They'll promise you anything. How many times did they pull that on your old man? And yours, Lolly? And mine? Hell, nothing they ever say means anything. It's a con, Flex. A goddamn dog and pony show. And you—of all people—bought a ticket."

"I didn't expect you to understand," Flex said. "I just wanted you to hear it from me."

"And that's suppose to make me feel better? You could've said something *before* you signed up. Maybe I could've talked you out of it."

"That's why I waited," Flex said.

"So you never had any intention of moving down here."

"I was thinking things through."

"All those plans we made. So I find us a place. And you do this. Boy, what a sucker I was."

"Things change," Flex said.

"But not friends," Jack said. "Friends stick together and keep their word."

"We were just cut out for different things."

"Maxwell's going to apply for officer's school," Lolly said."

"Six months ago it was owning a gym. Now the army?"

"When you moved out," Flex said, "things changed."

"Don't lay this on me," Jack snapped.

"I'm doing what I think's best. My family's all been army. Seemed like something I'd be good at. Runs in the family, I guess."

"Well, I put a stop to it in mine," Jack said.

Lolly gave Jack a hard look. "Not everyone is *blessed* with your flat feet. And for your information, Jackson Hill, I know all about you jumping off the garage roof. I wondered why you were doing that all the time. You may have fooled your father, but not me."

"So here's a dime," Jack said, "call somebody."

"You haven't heard a thing I've said, have you, Jack?"

Jack turned, and when he started to walk away, Flex grabbed him by the blanket and spun him around.

"Now you listen," Flex said, "or so help me, I'll drop you right here."

Jack tried pulling against Flex's grip, but Flex held him firmly and then slowly let go. Flex walked to the windows, his back to Jack.

"I'm glad you and Eddie found this place."

"It was for the three of us," Jack said. "That was the plan."

"Your plan, Jack. Hell, I was just coming along because I didn't have any plans."

"What about the gym?"

"A dream. Not a plan."

"You could have it. You're strong as an ox."

Flex turned and shook his head. "I don't want to be an ox, Jack. And I don't know the first thing about business."

"Go to school and learn, like Eddie."

I cleared my throat. "I dropped out, remember?"

"So Flex drops in."

"I was lucky to get out of high school," Flex said. "Twelve years of school and what can I do?"

"More than march around and get shot at. You deserve more, Flex."

Flex laughed. "I deserve what I got—like everyone else. And for me, Jack, that ain't much."

Jack stared at Flex and then looked over at Lolly and me. I thought about the rent and wondered how just the two of us were going to make it each month. Suddenly, Jack threw a beer bottle into the living room. The bottle shattered and part of the front window fell out.

Flex and Lolly were wide-eyed.

"We should be going," Lolly said. "We'll be late."

"Jack," Flex said.

"It's okay," Jack said. "If this is the way it is, then so be it."

"I just wanted you to know," Flex said.

"This is really what he wants," Lolly said. "It's nothing personal. Maxwell just had to make some plans. You can see that, can't you?"

"Sure. I can see that." Jack headed for the bathroom. "I'll meet you outside."

"So, when do you leave?" I asked Flex on our way out.

"December," he said. "I got one of those ninety day delay programs."

"I would've liked Maxwell home for both Thanksgiving and Christmas," Lolly said, "but Thanksgiving will be fine. I can hardly wait to see him in a uniform."

Flex stopped near the bulkhead and looked around the beach. "This is really an all right place," he said.

"No mansion," I said, "but it's home."

Jack came out of the cabin still wearing his blanket and joined us on the grass. He was smiling.

"All this good news calls for a proper send off," he said. "A real sizzler before you go."

"Only if I'm invited," Lolly said. "I don't trust you, Jackson Hill."

"Wouldn't have it any other way," Jack said, winking at me.

"I'd like that," Flex said. "Like that a lot."

Lolly walked to the bulkhead. "The view *is* nice."

Flex looked at Jack, and as their eyes met there was a moment of unspoken affection that brought a smile to Lolly's face. The longer nothing was said, the more embarrassed I felt, and the harder it was for me to say anything.

"Hooo-dy who?" Flex said—tentatively.

Jack grinned. "Yeah, sure, Flex. Hooody who!"

"Come on Maxwell," Lolly said. "Mother's going to blow a fuse if we're much later."

Jack and I waited until they were out of sight before stretching out on the grass. The sky was overcast with high, thin clouds that let through enough light so it was still bright.

"That joining up shit is something else," I said.

"Trading all *this* for the army."

"Can't see it myself."

"Lolly's got her eyes set on bigger things," Jack said.

"It takes two."

"Not with Lolly. She can be ruthless. She's the only girl Flex has ever dated. And she's kept it that way."

"I wouldn't mind keeping her for a night," I said.

"You and Flex both."

"You're kidding."

"Three years now.

"He must be a wreck inside," I said. "How's he do it?"

"How do you think he got that body?"

We lay there on the grass, talking up the virtues of girls we knew and comparing exploits. It was hard to trust any guy with telling the exact truth. You never knew for sure just how far the facts had been stretched. The important thing was in the telling and the challenge of outdoing the other guy with a little twist of duration or feat of seduction or the significance of an anatomical wonder. Ultimately, we found ourselves back on the subject of Lolly, and what a jerk Flex was for putting up with her when there were so many pastures to be mowed. Jack looked a lot better after we had skewered Flex.

We left the grass and walked back toward the cabin. It was spooky seeing someone you knew caught in little things that could ruin him. It was bad luck, we decided. In our own way we tried to ward off the curse with chest beating and high talk. We felt better for it, but that feeling gave way all too easily to more immediate problems. Problems like money—and how to get it.

11

Old bone is brittle. A very fine powder that defies brushing covers bone long left to the elements: the more you brush it, the more dust you create. The dust fills the scoring in your fingertips and makes everything feel velvety smooth.

Every time I washed my hands after a day's cleaning, I knew I was washing away part of the Indian woman. And this detail work—performing many small tasks to create a larger whole—was quiet work you did alone. Success or failure did not depend on anyone else. It was just you, the bones, brushes, and a skeletal chart to point the way.

Fall arrived on a Saturday—September 17th to be exact—and the first thing I felt was the change in the air: cool, thin, and static. I could smell the kelp and small decayed crustaceans on the beach. On the hillside there was the thick smell of sod and alder smoke, and the scent of wild blueberries and overripe blackberries.

Around noon there was a heavy knock on the cabin door. I went to the back door and peeked through the curtain. Sara stood on the porch. She wore jeans, tight on her legs, and high black boots that made her seem leggier than I remembered. I opened the door.

"Am I interrupting you?" Sara said, and followed my eyes to her legs. "Is there something—wrong?"

"No," I said. "Do you want to come in?"

"It's nicer out here," she said. "Did you see all the birds on the beach?"

I closed the door behind me. Sea gulls were huddling around a dark mass near the water. I helped Sara down to the beach, and several gulls flew away as we approached them.

The baby seal hadn't been dead long. It's skin still had a soft sheen. Tiny whiskers stood erect from its upper lip.

"It's a pup," I said.

The gulls danced away from the carcass, but kept their eyes on us.

"The poor thing," Sara said. "I hate seeing things like this."

I poked the pup's skin with the toe of my shoe.

"What do you think happened?" Sara said.

"Something got it," I said. "Right there." I pointed to the missing chunk of flesh.

"But what?"

"Something bigger."

"What should we do?" she said.

"I don't know."

"Do you think its mother knows?"

"She's probably missed it."

"That's so sad."

"I'll find something to move it."

I found two slats under the cabin. The pup was about six feet from the water, and while the pup was small, it was dead weight. We pried our sticks under the head and tail and rolled the pup toward the water. A pungent stench rose when we moved the carcass, and Sara jumped backed. Finally we pushed the pup into the water. It floated for a moment. Then the tide slowly pulled it into the current, leaving a faint trail of oil on the water.

"Good work!" a voice called out.

Motherbright was standing on her porch. Her bright, white dress stood out sharply against the blue house.

"Know her?" I asked Sara.

"We've talked a few times."

Then Danny stepped out from behind Motherbright. Sara immediately looked out over the water.

"Are you sure we shouldn't have buried it?" she said.

"I'm sure," I said. "Want something to drink?"

"No thank you."

We went up to the cabin. I grabbed a beer from the fridge for myself and then joined Sara on the deck. She was sitting on the arm of the big chair.

"I really came by to thank you for seeing me home from Toshi's."

"My pleasure," I said.

"I used to come down here a lot," she said, "when the cabin was vacant. It's one of my favorite places."

"Mine too." I lit a cigarette. "Danny sure looks different with his goatee."

I told Sara about Danny being dismissed from Olympic College for failing grades and that his aunt had stopped supporting him. She didn't seem surprised. We watched the sea gulls, still floating in a group but further out into the narrows now. We both knew what they were doing, but neither of us said anything. We just watched and listened.

"Eddie," Sara said, softly. "Do you think I'm pretty?"

I looked at her blankly.

"Now that's a stupid question," she said. "Just forget I said that." She stood up. "I'm always saying the wrong thing. I better go before I make a bigger fool of myself."

"Don't go," I said.

She took a Kleenex from her pocket and wiped her nose.

"Probably the seal pup," I said. "Dead things'll do that."

"No," she said. "It's just me."

"Not Danny?"

She looked over at me. "It's always somebody. Nothing seems to last."

I was quiet while she wiped her eyes again.

"I bet I'm a sight," she said.

"Do you think I'm handsome?" I asked.

Her face froze.

"I mean—even just a little?"

For a moment Sara's eyes got wide. Then she slowly nodded her head. "Well," she said, "now what?"

"If I had any money," I said, "we could go to a show."

Sara smiled. "There's really nothing playing I want to see."

I told her about a lake out of town with an island in it—that it was a great place for a picnic. She said she liked the idea, and we agreed to go on her day off.

"Until Tuesday," she said.

I watched her from the porch until she was out of sight. Then I sat down in the big chair and watched the tide slip out further. The sea gulls remained in the same place on the water, and their cries were soft in the distance. For the first time in awhile, I felt on top of the world.

12

On the stairs I met Danny, and he invited me to lunch at Olberg's Drugstore. We had no sooner sat down in a booth when he told me he was giving up his apartment and moving in with Motherbright. He was smiling broadly like a Cheshire cat.

"But this weekend?" I said.

"You won't believe the place," Danny said. "She's changed everything so it doesn't even look like a regular house. It's so damn *blue*, Eddie."

"I've seen the outside."

"I mean the inside. There's nothing square in there. She's got this parachute for a ceiling. And it's all round-like inside. It's like being inside something that's alive."

The waitress set down two orders of burgers and fries in front of us, and we attacked them like ravenous wolves. When the waitress turned away, Danny filled his coat pocket with packets of sugar, jelly and crackers from the counter. A trick we picked up from Mooch.

"How you doing for money?" I asked Danny as he divided his take.

"Two tennis lessons next week and that's it."

"What are you going to do?"

Danny grinned. "You know me, Eddie. I always land on my feet. If there's an easy way to make money, I'll find it."

"Like what?"

He looked around. "I'm not suppose to say anything."

"Come on," I said.

"Promise. Not a word?"

"Promise."

"Motherbright says that something big is coming soon."

"Like what?"

"She hasn't said, but it's got to be something big."

There was a loud yell behind us. Jack Hill and Tony Bingham, one of Jack's oldest fishing pals, came toward us with their fishing poles and tackle boxes.

"There you are," Jack said.

"The mighty hunters return," I said, and slid over.

"And with a masterful plan," Jack said.

"First, what's for dinner?" I said.

Jack opened his fish basket and withdrew a string of four beautiful trout. He laid his catch on the table. Almost immediately our waitress was standing over us.

"All right," she said, "get those fish off my table and back where they belong."

Jack looked at Danny and me. "Come on," she said, "I mean it. Right now!"

"I'll do my best," Jack said.

"In the basket," she said.

Tony grinned. "They're a little sluggish," he said.

"It's tough when you're out of your element," Jack said.

"I noticed," the waitress said. "In the basket."

Jack finally complied.

"So what'll you have?" she asked.

"Nothing for me," Tony said.

"How about you, Kingfish?"

"I just came in after my fish," Jack said. "You doing anything tonight?"

The waitress smiled painfully. "Try again when you're old enough."

"How about Monday then?" he said.

The waitress scowled and walked away.

"She's got no sense of adventure," Jack said.

"So what's this plan of yours?" Danny asked.

"Easy money."

"Doing what?" Danny said.

Jack leaned back in the booth and picked at his nails.

"Well," I said, "what the hell is it?"

"Dogsharks."

"Dogsharks?"

"I thought you were going to say Bangor," Danny said.

"Bangor?" I said.

"Heard they might be adding extra shifts loading ammunition."

"Think I'm joking about dogsharks, don't you?"

I grinned.

"Got it straight from Merle at the tackle shop. I saw the poster. The state is paying a fifty cent bounty on dogsharks."

"Now that's America," I said.

"Do you know how many dogsharks are in the sound?" Jack said. "Millions."

"What's fifty cents on a million?" Tony said.

"They're everywhere," Jack said. "Like rabbits. It's easy money, believe me."

"How easy?" Danny said.

"I'm talking spare time. At the right time."

"And when is the right time?" I said.

"When the moon's full."

"Jesus," I said. "Here it comes." I slid out of the booth.

"I'm serious, you guys. Fish feed at night. And they love the full moon."

"You had me going there for a minute," I said.

"Negativity," Jack said. "I come up with an easy hustle for money, and all I get is negativity."

"Well, I'm game," Danny said.

"Fifty cents a fish?"

"All we can catch."

"Sounds good to me, Eddie," Danny said. "What's to lose?"

"You're just damn lucky we need money," I said. "And this better not be one of your damn wild hairs."

"It'll be easy," Jack said. "I'll get everything we need and work out something with the barge."

"What barge?" I said.

"*Our* barge. It's perfect. It'll get us off shore, and everything will be fine. Trust me."

13

The next morning I was sitting on our front porch, reading the Sunday paper I'd swiped from Frog's doorstep, when I heard Jack call my name. This was followed by "What's to eat?" from Mooch. The front window opened, and Jack's head popped outside. Mooch opened the other window and sat on the sill. He was wearing his leather aviator's cap and goggles. He also had a gray lump of something in his hand, and his mouth was full.

"Hi, Eddie," Mooch said. "You reading?"

"Mooch, you're getting smarter all the time. What the hell are you eating?"

"I don't know. It was just laying on the stove. Want some?"

I shook my head.

"Don't blame you," he said. "It's a little dry. Got any milk?"

"No!" I said. "And stay out of the kitchen, you cretin."

"I ain't no cretin. Say, Jack, you got a smoke?"

Jack held out his cigarette pack, and I went back to the paper.

"Say, Jack, did you tell Eddie what we figured out?"

"We must be nice to Mooch," Jack said. "He came through with some rope for us."

"What—to hang ourselves with?"

"The barge," Jack said.

"You mean he stole it."

"I didn't steal it," Mooch said. "I found it outside the shipyard fence. I know where there's a pulley, too."

"What we need now," Jack said, "is transportation."

"Like my car?" I said.

"Wouldn't look good walking through town with a navy pulley."

"Told you he'd do it," Mooch said. "Let's go."

Jack looked around the corner and turned back to me. "Somebody's looking at our address," Jack said.

Mooch hopped down from the sill and squeezed through the railing, ready to drop to the beach.

"If it's the law," Mooch said, "you haven't seen me."

"So—you just *found* the rope!" I said.

"You know how cops are," Mooch said. "They look for you whether you've done anything or not. What's he doing?"

Jack looked again. "He's just standing there. He's got a sack."

"Probably the evidence," Mooch said.

"What evidence?" I said.

"*The* evidence. They've always got evidence when they come looking for you."

I walked up behind Jack and cautiously looked down the side porch.

"It's okay," I said. "That's my dad." It had been over two months since I had seen my father. There had been hard feelings about my moving out, and he was the last person I expected to see. He stood rigidly at the door, his back to me.

"Well," I said, approaching him slowly, "this is a surprise."

He whirled around and held out the paper sack. "Your mother sent these," he said. "Shorts and socks you forgot."

"That wasn't necessary," I said.

"Your mother—she wanted you to have them. You know how she worries."

I smiled. "Can I get you a beer?"

He looked pained and shook his head.

"Come on," I said. "Just one."

He nodded, but without looking at me. "Great," I said.

I started for the door when I saw Jack and Mooch looking around the corner at us.

"That's Jack," I said. "My roommate."

Jack smiled and gestured. Mooch grinned and waved.

"The other one's Mooch. He lives in a truck."

"I see."

Jack and Mooch came out from behind the corner. "I think Mooch and I'll go take care of that business, if you'll just give me your keys."

I handed Jack the keys. "I'll just meet you at the dock," I said.

Jack shook my father's hand and left. Mooch started off the porch and then came back. "You look like a nice father," he said to my dad. "Not all fathers look like good fathers, but you look like a good one."

My father looked bewildered.

"Mooch," I said.

"It's true, Eddie." He turned to my dad. "Family is real important, sir. I lost mine in the blast."

"The blast?" my father said.

"Yeah, the big blast," Mooch said.

"Okay, Mooch."

"Sure, Eddie." He shook my father's hand. "If you and Mrs. Carr ever decide to adopt someone, Eddie knows where to find me. I'd be honored."

My father stared expressionless at Mooch.

"You'll be the first to know," I said. "Jack! You want to help Mooch to the car?"

Jack grabbed Mooch and pulled him from the porch.

"He's harmless," I said.

My dad looked down at his hand. "I want to wash this."

I led him to the kitchen sink. I retrieved two beers from the fridge. There was no towel, so I handed him a T-shirt from the table. My father came into the living room behind me. His shoes crackled as they peeled off the sticky linoleum.

"The cleaning lady's been sick," I said.

"Pigs live better than this," he said.

"It's home."

"You had a home," my father said.

He paced the room, kicked clothes aside. "You didn't come down here just to deliver a sack," I said.

He stopped in front of the window and looked out. "Your mother doesn't understand what went wrong."

"Nothing went wrong," I said.

"Hair down to your ass. Garbage everywhere. Hanging around with goofballs. And you say nothing's wrong?"

"If something went wrong," I said, "it went wrong a long time ago."

"You're not a kid anymore, Eddie. You're nineteen. And it's time you started acting like an adult."

"The truth is I don't feel like one. Nothing adult interests me."

My father stared at me with a stolid, pensive look pasted on his face. He seemed very old and tired. "So you're just going to stay here—like this?"

I shook my head. "No. I'm going to California."

"California!"

"I want to play music," I said. "Soon as I get some money, I'm going to California, with some other musicians."

My father walked to my drums. He slowly dragged his finger across one of the heads.

"Tell me, Eddie. Are you great on these?"

I thought for a moment. "I wouldn't say great. But better than most."

"Better than most," he said, and smiled. "It takes talent, Eddie, real talent to make it as a musician. Being better than most is never good enough."

"I should've known you'd say that."

"Good musicians are a dime a dozen. I knew a lot of good musicians who never made it. Most of those that stayed at it are sweeping up after the great ones."

"So no one should try?"

"You want to know the truth?"

"Sure."

"I don't think you've got it. Simple as that."

"Thanks for the confidence."

"I'm not saying that to hurt you, Eddie. I just don't want you to get hurt thinking you're something you're not."

"Sounds like you want me to quit—like you quit."

He turned sharply and looked at me and said nothing. He knew what I meant. When I was young, I listened to him play his saxophones behind his closed bedroom door. He usually played at night and Saturday mornings. It was always a treat hearing him play "Mood Indigo" or "Impossible You". Sometimes, when he really felt great, he would play "One O'clock Jump" or "In the Mood", and I would sneak down the hall, crack his door, and watch him swinging and playing in the corner of the room.

Then it stopped, and his horns stayed in their heavy black cases in the closet. One Saturday he took them out to the car, and when he came home later, he didn't have them. That was the first time I ever saw him drunk and the first time I remember hearing him swear.

"You want me to quit, don't you?" I said.

"I don't want you to make a mistake," he said.

"You told me you only fail when you never try."

He didn't say anything.

"You gave up something you loved, and you haven't been happy since. I don't want that to happen to me."

"What the hell do you know about what happens to people?"

"I know you hocked your horns," I said.

"I didn't play them much," he said. "They just took up space."

"That's bullshit. And you know it. You hocked your horns because somebody didn't like you being happy."

"Things changed," my father said. "I had responsibilities."

"You gave up! You loved those horns, and you quit 'em. I swore I'd never let that happen to me."

He stepped across the short space between us and slapped my face.

"That doesn't change anything," I said.

"I didn't mean that."

"I'm still going to California. I'm going to play music."

"Wait until *you* have a family."

"If that's what a family does to you, then I don't want one."

"I feel sorry for you, Eddie. You're living in a dream world, and you're headed for a fall." He walked to the door and stopped on the porch. "I've said my piece. If this is what you want, then do as you please."

"I want to do it."

"This'll tear your mother apart, you know. She wanted me to ask about Thanksgiving."

"I haven't thought that far ahead," I said.

"You let her know. She'd like to see you."

I nodded, and he turned and walked off the porch.

I went inside and sat down at the kitchen table. The side of my face still burned. I emptied the paper sack onto the table. Socks, T-shirts, and some tied letters fell out in a heap. Expired car insurance and an official notification of my withdrawal from Olympic College were the highlights. I tore them both up. I wouldn't need either of them in California.

14

When I reached the Second Street dock, Jack and Mooch were working near a large fallen madrona tree a ways up the beach. When Mooch saw me, he lifted a large wooden pulley lashed to the tree trunk and smiled proudly.

"Ain't this a beaut'?" Mooch said.

"Really something," I said.

"Makes you feel important working with big equipment."

Jack led me away from Mooch. "Check this," he said. "It's going to be perfect."

The landfill jutted fifty feet from the hillside, stood forty feet high, and was made of boulders and slabs of concrete. Jack stood on the rocks and waved me on. I climbed up to him.

"Well," Jack said, "there she is."

Below I saw a small wooden barge, half submerged. Blackberry vines snaked over it, and much of the planking was missing. A large rusted cable laid coiled around one end and disappeared into the rocks. It was worse than I had imagined.

"You want to fish off that?" I said.

"Ain't she great. And she's all ours."

"It doesn't even float," I said.

"I've already checked that out," Jack said. "She floats on barrels. The sunk barrels are missing their plugs. All we do is wait for low tide, let the water drain out, then plug 'em up. It's simple, Eddie. I got Mooch working on plugs now."

I sat down on a rock and shook my head. "I don't believe this."

"Come on," Jack said. "Use your imagination."

"It would take all the imagination in Bremerton to picture that thing floating."

"There's that damn negativity again. Think positive, Eddie."

"I'm thinking about staying afloat."

"Believe me, Eddie, what's left of her is as solid as a brick."

"A dollar says it floats like one, too."

"Come on," he said. "Seeing is believing."

The barge was about fifteen feet wide by twenty feet long with a short lip-beam around it. Jack jumped up and down on the decking. The holes in the deck were the size of doorways, and a line of green showed where the tide had been stopping for years. It was old and gray and waterlogged.

"So. What do you think?" Jack said.

"I think you're crazy."

"Just like that?"

"It's not even a barge," I said. "It's a float used between ships in moorage. And I think its floating days are over."

"You think we've got the choice of the fleet? We take what's available. And this is it. That is, unless your old man brought your inheritance in that brown bag."

"Leave him out of this."

We climbed off the float. On the way back, Jack explained how the three of us could pull the float off the rocks once her barrels were drained and replugged. Then, he said, it was just a matter of waiting for high tide to float it around the fill to the beach where we would hook her up to the pulley. He tried to make it sound routine.

Mooch was sitting under the madrona tree, checking himself out. His flight goggles were down over his eyes, and he was soaking wet. The front of Mooch's pants was open. He looked like he had lost something and was trying to find it through his zipper.

"Mooch!" Jack yelled. "You ever been caught playing with yourself?"

Mooch looked up, startled. "Nope. Never."

"You have now," I said.

"I ain't doing that," he said. "It's these damn things here."

Jack and I stopped. "What things?"

Mooch squeezed something off his skin and held it up between his fingers. "These things," he said. "They're biting the hell out of me."

"Crabs!" Jack yelled. "You got crabs!"

Mooch looked astonished, and we backed away.

"How'd you get all wet?" I asked.

"Tried drowning them," he said. "Guess maybe they can breathe underwater."

Mooch picked another crab off himself and popped it between his nails. Jack and I backed further away.

"How have you survived this long?" I asked.

Mooch grinned. "Easy," he said. "I'm one of the gifted ones. Like them seers in the olden days. Guys that went around seeing things that nobody else saw. They were really connected. In touch with invisible forces."

"When did you realize you were—gifted?" I said. "Roughly speaking."

"Oh, I know exactly, Eddie. One thirty-five A.M., August the sixth, 1945. My birthday. In the beginning there was the bomb."

"Oh, Jesus," Jack said.

Mooch stared up the beach. "Everything was dark. Then the Man said, 'Zap 'em with light!' and he parted the waters. I felt the waves."

Jack and I turned and started walking up the beach.

"Hey!" Mooch said, "I'm serious." He ran up next to us. "That's the way it is. I'm in touch with things. Big things. Listen, Eddie. I saw it in your old man today."

"Saw what?"

He stopped me. "Mutation."

"I told you not to encourage him," Jack said.

"Your old man grew up with dynamite putting little holes in the ground," Mooch said. "But with us, Eddie, one flick of the switch and we're the hole. Don't you see it?"

I looked at Jack, and he shrugged his shoulders. We walked. Mooch ran ahead and walked backwards while he continued his train of thought.

"Life's just a big game," Mooch said. "Nothing means anything anymore except—when does it all end?" Mooch suddenly grabbed me by the arms. "Jesus, Eddie." Mooch stopped. "This is bigger than I thought. The bomb is God."

15

On Tuesday I drove the Beast to Sara's apartment and honked the horn. Sara came down the stairs and ran to the side of the car. "I'm impressed," she said through the window. Then she chipped off a piece of bubbled paint.

"Put all my money into the mechanics," I said.

She smiled and tried the door, but it was stuck. I reached over and tried the inside handle.

"Obviously not *enough* money," Sara said.

A car drove up behind me, and the driver honked his horn. I set the hand brake, put my leg up on the seat, and kicked the door. I kicked it again and this time it flew open, knocking Sara on her butt onto the parking strip.

"Sorry!" I shouted. I felt my face turn red. "You all right?"

The guy behind me blew his horn again. There were three cars behind him now. Sara quickly slapped the dust off her shorts, grabbed the wicker basket and got into the car. Horns echoed louder behind us.

"Good to see you," I said. "Hold on."

I held the Beast in park, revved the engine hard, and then slammed the shifter into drive. The Beast lunged forward, and

Sara flew back against the seat. A blue-white cloud engulfed the string of cars behind us.

"I love a fine machine," Sara said.

We crossed the Manette Bridge and headed north on the Brownsville Highway. The stores and gas stations ended just past Clare's Marsh, and small farms with horses and milk cows appeared, dotting the sloping grasslands. The sun broke through the high clouds and warmed the sweet smelling air. At Cluge's Pond near Gilberton, I slowed down. Here, I pointed out to Sara, was a good swimming hole in the summer and great place to sled in the winter when it froze over.

I turned onto the Central Valley Road, and the thick stand of woods that surrounded the pond quickly gave way to more farm land. Not far up the road, Sara had me stop where a lone horse stood grazing next to a fence. She took a carrot stick from the wicker basket and walked to the fence.

"I used to ride a horse just this color at camp," she said. "His name was Rusty."

I stroked his forehead while she fed him the carrot.

"One summer," she said softly, "he stepped in a hole, and the owners put him down."

"That's too bad," I said.

"I never went back to camp. Now every time I see a beautiful bay, I like to think it's Rusty. He always liked carrots."

I stroked the horse's neck. "I hardly think this is Rusty."

"How do you know?" Sara said.

"This horse is alive."

"Rusty had a soul," she said. "Who knows where they go."

I smiled.

"Don't you think horses have souls?" she asked.

"Never really thought about it."

"Well, you should," she said.

"Why?"

"I don't know. Maybe it's all we really have. If we hurt other things, they might be someone you once knew."

"Like horses?"

"And cats and dogs."

"So what is it?" I asked.

Sara took a deep breath. "Maybe it's feeling. Some kind of affection. I'm not sure. But anything that can express affection and can be loved just has to have a soul."

"Is that why you feed all those beach cats?"

"It's not funny, Eddie."

I dropped my smile.

"I know it might sound silly," Sara said, "but it's serious. I've thought about it a lot. You understand, don't you?"

"Sure. I just don't know enough about souls to know."

We both stroked the horse and then returned to the car. For the next five miles, we stayed on solid ground; we shared all the things we thought were wrong with people we knew. At Island Lake the park was quiet. We stared out at the water which was smooth and very blue. The island was reflected clearly in the water.

"This is perfect," Sara said. "My first cruise to an island."

Sara carried the basket, and I carried the beer. We walked the narrow dirt road marked, "RESIDENTS ONLY". My friend Tom still lived on the lake with his parents, and he had told me on the phone he would leave the boat in the front yard. We took a shortcut through his yard and found the rowboat on the grass. Sara sat in the stern, and I pushed us off. During the ten minute ride, we didn't speak but maybe ten words. Sometimes we looked at each other, but for some reason I felt too awkward to speak, and we continued to smile and look around at the water and the trees. Near the island, the wind blew warm and soft. Sara closed her eyes and tilted her head back, exposing her face to the warmth of the sun. I leaned forward and kissed her. She bolted and almost knocked me out of the boat.

"Sorry," I said.

"Why did you do that?"

I thought for a moment. "To get it over with."

She shaded her eyes with her hand and twirled her neck chain. "I'm sorry I jumped," she said.

"That's okay," I said.

I brought the boat around a point of exposed rocks and rowed hard until the boat hit the sand. I climbed out, tied us off, and then unloaded the basket and the beer. Sara stepped out, and before I could turn and start up the rocks, she kissed me. It was a quick, brief kiss. "The second one is kind of awkward too," she said. "I feel better now."

"That's good."

"Besides, I didn't want you to think I didn't like it."

We walked hand in hand toward a grassy slope near the crest of the island. Pine trees broke up the direct sunlight and shaded the ground. The trees were widely spaced and the underbrush sparse. It was easy to see in all directions. The main trail had several narrow paths angling off on either side. The air was scented sweetly with warm huckleberries, wild strawberries, and fermenting pine bark.

"When I was little," I said, "I used to think this island went forever. You had to walk completely around the lake to see it all. Now I can see water in every direction. It's like the island has shrunk."

Sara smiled. "It's just that you've grown, and you can see more."

I made a slow 360-degree turn. "It was an all day adventure just circling the island," I said. "When it was over, you felt like you'd been somewhere. I think it was better when I couldn't see everything."

"I like it just fine as it is," Sara said. We walked down to a small clearing, laid out the blanket and the lunch basket. I opened two beers. The sun was hot and bright. Sara closed her eyes and leaned back again. I moved to kiss her once more, but she opened her eyes.

"Stay right there," she said, pulling a camera from her purse. "Can I put my arm down?"

"But stay the way you were," she said. "I want that picture."

"Right this minute?"

"Now don't move." Sara aimed and shot. "There!"

She opened the basket and stacked the quartered tuna fish sandwiches neatly on a paper plate around a pile of green olives. She pulled out a small bowl of potato salad, dusted red with paprika, and a container of apple wedges. Finally she produced two homemade oatmeal cookies.

"I think that's everything you said you liked," she said.

When I had swallowed the last bite, I told her it was the best lunch I had ever eaten. Sara made fun of herself for being too traditional, because she liked to cook and sew. She told me her mother wanted her to take an interest in her clubs, and her father wanted her to become a nurse.

"I love them both," she said, "but it wouldn't be me. I hate idle chatter, and people dying would be too depressing."

"What about the animals at the vet's?" I said.

"That's different," she said. "Those little creatures can't do for themselves."

Sara's family was wealthy—had been for generations—and well-placed, but her manner was unaffected. She was not a snob and in no way displayed the fact that her family had money. I liked her sense of humor and sensed she knew a lot but did not flaunt it. I told Sara about my dream to go to California and how I wanted to be a musician. "You'll do it, Eddie," she said strongly. "I know you will."

"How do you know?"

"You can have anything you want if you want it bad enough."

"But not everybody gets what they want."

"Only those who don't want it bad enough. I believe you really want to play music, and if you're willing to sacrifice for it, you can make it."

"No one's ever told me that before," I said. "Do you really believe that?"

"You can't help who you are inside. No one can. We're all going to be what we are until we die. Then maybe we'll end up like Rusty. Doing the same thing in a different form."

I followed Sara down to the lake. Near the two large rocks, she washed our plates, and I wiped them dry. I found it hard to understand why Danny had left her for anyone else, including Motherbright.

"I feel like getting wet," Sara called up to me. "Care to join me?"

She unbuttoned her shirt and took it off. She unzipped her shorts, and my heart started to race. She was wearing a white two-piece bathing suit, and while the result wasn't what I thought it was going to be, I still couldn't stop from staring at her slender figure. She looked just beautiful.

"Come on," she said, walking into the water. "It's warm."

"I didn't bring a suit."

"You're wearing shorts, aren't you?"

"I'll be right down." The lake was shallow for five or six feet until it dropped off abruptly. I walked out to my waist and then sat on the rock ledge, chest-deep in the lake. I watched Sara floating on her back, her small breasts just breaching the surface.

"This is wonderful," Sara said. She swam onto the ledge next to me. A chain she wore fell out of her top. On the chain was a gold ring and a small silver medallion with the letter "T" on it. Sara pushed them back inside her top.

"What's his name?" I asked.

"It's not what you think, Eddie."

"Tim? Tom? Toby?"

"Just some things."

"A ring and an initial are just things?"

"Can't we just enjoy ourselves?"

"Sure," I said, abruptly. "I should have known."

"There's nothing to know," she said. "It's not what—"

I stood up and dove into the lake. I knifed straight down, hit something hard, and felt a sharp pain in my nose. I panicked and thrashed wildly. I pulled and kicked until I reached the surface. I heard Sara's voice, but my head hurt, and I couldn't keep my mouth above water. I heard Sara again and felt my face running warm. I wiped at what I thought was water and saw the blood on my hand. I heard a splash behind me and felt a pull around my chest.

"Kick!" Sara yelled. "Kick!"

I moved my legs and felt us move through the water, but I couldn't open my eyes for the salty blood filling them. A moment later we stopped, and Sara stood up. I let my feet drop and felt the slimy weed bottom, and with Sara pulling me, I lunged and fell face first into the knee-deep water. Sara dragged me, and I crawled and then collapsed on the sandy grass. A steady rill of blood trickled down my cheek, and I gasped for air.

"Lie still," Sara said. "I'll be right back. Don't move."

When Sara returned, I was still gasping. She dabbed a wet cloth over my face, and I winced at the pressure.

"How bad is it?" I said.

"Two good cuts, but nothing too deep."

"Thought I was a goner," I said.

"You really scared me," Sara said. "When you came up, all I saw was red. Lie still for a minute," she said. "You've got good blood. Give it a chance to clot."

As Sara patted a cloth over my face, I sensed it was a mass of cuts. She opened a small box of Band-Aids—the tiny ones—and stuck them around my face. The necklace with the ring and pendant swung over me while Sara applied the last of the bandages. I couldn't take my eyes off it, and the longer I watched it, the madder I got.

"Who is this mysterious T?" I said.

She grabbed the pendant and held it still. "Look! It's a broken cross."

I saw a rough edge where the metal might have been broken. "And the ring?" I said.

She worked on my nose and then told me about Tal's going away party she had gone to the week before. They were old friends—close—like brother and sister. But at his going away party, she said, he was different.

"Tal never had a serious bone in his body. I liked that about him. Then, at the party, he said he loved me, and he gave me these." Sara held up the chain. "Along with his grandfather's watch."

"Just like that?"

"He said he wouldn't need them to kill communists. I didn't know what else to do with them."

My nose and forehead hurt. I touched her hand.

Sara smiled. "I'm always getting mixed up in crazy romances." She looked away and then back at me. "I like you, Eddie. I just want something normal."

I took Sara's arm, pulled her to me, and kissed her. Her eyes and face softened. I kissed her again and held her close to me and felt her heart pounding hard against her chest. I lay back with her tight against me. Her skin was warm, her breasts firm. I rolled Sara onto her back and her lips darted over my neck and ear, and as we moved to kiss again, our noses collided, and I bolted in pain.

"Eddie, I'm sorry. Here. Let me see."

The pain shot up my nose, and my eyes watered immediately. One of the Band-Aids came undone, and when Sara removed it, the cut began bleeding. Sara quickly dabbed it with the damp cloth.

"I'm really sorry," she said.

"I'm all right."

"I should've been more careful."

"Guess it's deeper than we thought."

Sara removed the cloth. "I think we'll just leave this one open for awhile."

"Got a mirror?" I asked.

Sara dug in her purse and produced a small compact. When I looked in the mirror, I was ugly. The rows of tiny Band-Aids made my face look like a line of miniature railroad ties.

"I look like Frankenstein," I said. "All I need is a rod through my neck."

"And some orthopedic shoes," Sara said. "The Band-Aids will help the healing."

"This is your plan to keep other girls from looking at me."

"It was a long shot," she said.

Sara dressed herself and kissed the top of my head. I tried kissing her, but she immediately stood up.

"We tried that once," she said. "Let's give your face a chance to heal." Sara laughed.

"What's so funny?" I said.

"You're the handsomest guy I know, Eddie Carr, and the scars won't change how I feel."

"Scars!"

"I'll meet you back at the boat, Mr. Handsome."

"What scars? You said they'd heal."

Sara was waiting for me in the boat, looking quite proper.

"That was a hell of a way to end a picnic," I said.

"It's the best way I know," Sara said, "of not ending something nice."

We said very little on the way to town. When we stopped in front of her apartment, Sara leaned over and kissed me. We broke, and she kissed me again. I moved toward her, but she opened the door and slid out.

"Thanks for the lovely day, Eddie Carr."

"That's it?" I said.

"I'd like to stop while we're ahead, Eddie."

"What do you mean?"

She waved at me. I watched her climb the stairs, and I waited for her to come to the window of her apartment, but she never did. I slowly pulled away, confused and disappointed, but not disheartened.

16

I arrived at the Second Street dock according to plan. The full moon was above the Cascade Mountains in the east and cast a white shard of light over the sound so that I could see the end of the barge on the beach. Jack, Danny, and Mooch were huddled around a gas lantern. Jack was instructing Danny and Mooch how to bait hooks. He was talking fast, pronouncing each active verb loudly. He was wired. Then I heard Margy's voice, followed by Joe's laugh. Jack called my name.

"It's about time," he yelled. "Where you been?"

"Taking diving lessons I bet," Mooch cackled.

I gestured to Joe and ignored Margy and the two girls beside her.

"Mooch, you're a funny guy," I said, slowly approaching him at the lantern. I shaded my eyes to better see what strange thing he had on his head. At first I only saw the corrugated hose dangling over his face, and then I saw the whole mask. "What the hell's that contraption for?" I said.

"Gas usually," he said, "but I can't stomach the smell of fish."

"Do you guys *really* know this gooner?" Danny whispered to me.

Jack and Mooch walked the length of rope tethering the barge to the madrona tree and checked the pulley. Danny studied his fishing pole, and I hauled gear to the barge. I heard the footfalls on the gravel, but continued loading the barge.

"Don't you say 'hi' to old friends anymore?" Margy was staring at me with that tight, baby doll smile of hers. Her girl friends stood behind her.

"What are you doing here?" I said.

"This is the guy I was telling you about," Margy said to her friends.

"It *is* long," said the taller of the two.

"I wanted Willis to grow his long," the other said, "but his dad won't let him."

"Just came by to see you, Eddie" Margy said. She stepped closer and asked for a cigarette. She put it to her mouth, slowly running her tongue over the filter. "Got a match?"

I lit my lighter, and in the bright flicker of light, I saw her nipples sticking out through the wide mesh of her sweater.

"You trying to burn me?" Margy said.

I looked up and raised the lighter just as Joe approached us. "Good to see you Joe," I said.

Margy stepped back and put her arm around Joe.

"Thought we'd stop by in case you guys needed help," Joe said.

"From the looks of things," I said, "we'll need all the help we can get."

"Also have a favor to ask you guys," Joe said.

"Shoot!"

"Keep an eye on Margy for me. I've got standby duty this weekend, and Margy's going to stay at my place. Just wanted you guys to keep an eye on things. You know, make sure she's okay."

I looked over at Margy. She smiled and squeezed Joe.

"Well," I said, "I'm going to help Danny move this weekend. Not too sure I'll be around much."

"I know," Joe said, "just whenever you're around. No big deal."

"Sure, Joe. Whenever we're there we'll keep an eye on things."

"I won't be any trouble," Margy said. "But sometimes, being alone at night gets scary. Maybe I could cook you guys dinner one night."

"That's okay," I said. "I'll probably be eating over at Sara's most of the weekend. We're kind of an item right now." I looked over at Margy to make sure the point registered. "But whenever we're around, Joe, you can count on us. And Margy, if there's something you need and we're not home, the door's always open. Just help yourself."

"Thank you, Eddie. I'll remember that."

Jack walked by carrying the last of the gear to the barge. "Well," he said, "let's shove off."

"Yeah, let's go," I said. I whispered to Jack, "Before we get Margy as a roommate."

"Got you covered here on the beach," Joe said. He headed up toward the lantern with Margy.

"What's with Margy?" Jack asked.

"Joe wants us to watch Margy this weekend."

"He doesn't know," Jack said.

"Well," Danny said, "once they've had it from killer Eddie, there's no keeping them away."

"Why is it," I said, "that it's always the ones you don't care about who never go away?"

"Pure animal charm," Danny said. "Got it pretty bad myself."

We climbed aboard the barge, and Jack took command. "Unlash the rope, Mooch. Danny, grab a pole."

"Margy can move in with me," Mooch said, loosening the rope.

"For some reason," I said, "I can't see Margy living in the back of a panel truck."

"Besides," Jack said, "you've already got Amy Swertz."

"Amy's okay," Mooch said, "but her face ain't clearing up like she said it would. It's getting worse."

The barge slowly slipped away from the beach. On deck there were long poles, the pulley tether, and there was a big can full of rocks tied to a rope. I noticed a list to the port side, even when Danny, Mooch and I were on the starboard side. I discreetly looked for life preservers, and then went up front and confronted Jack.

"What do you mean you forgot them!" I yelled.

"I can't remember everything," Jack said.

"Well, what'll we do if this tub takes a dive?"

"Don't worry," he said. "She's as solid as a rock."

"Well, your rock is leaning," I said.

The port side was three inches above water.

"That's age," Jack said, "not structure. Keep poling."

The gravel bottom dropped off about twenty feet out, leaving Danny and me nothing to push off of except an occasional large rock. The barge drifted straight out, but so slowly that the only way to detect movement was by watching Mooch let out rope. To the east the moon was higher above the mountains. The only sign of movement around us was the shimmer of moonlight on the bay. We drew closer to a set of old pilings. Jack threw a rope around one and tied us off.

"This is it," Jack said. "Tie your end off, Mooch!"

Mooch lashed the pulley line and came back to the stern. "Now what?" Mooch said.

"We bait up," Jack said, "and reel the bastards in."

"Just like that?" Danny said.

"Told you it was simple."

"Damn," Mooch said. "Making money is getting easier every day." Mooch had second thoughts when Jack handed him a bucket of bullheads and told him to cut some bait. "Do I have to?" Mooch said, wincing at the sight of dead fish.

"Are you sure your mother had any kids that lived?" Danny said.

"Oh, yeah!" Mooch said. He pulled his mask over his face, thrust his hand into the bucket and dropped a bullhead on the deck. With a flurry of quick cuts, Mooch had five chunks of bait scattered in front of him. "Take that!" Mooch said.

Jack rigged a drop line with six hooks set about four feet apart. He secured it to the high side of the barge and put Mooch in charge of it. Danny and I were also positioned on the high side for more ballast, and Jack stood up front. For almost forty-five minutes, there was just the quiet and stillness of waiting.

Suddenly, Danny's reel whined, and his pole flew from between his legs and skidded across the barge.

"Bingo!" Jack yelled. He handed me his pole and went to help Danny. No sooner had he left than his bait was taken. I stuck my pole between my knees, and with a hard jerk on the line, I set Jack's hook. I yelled for help, and Mooch came over and took my pole.

"Get the net!" I yelled. "Get the damn net!"

Mooch wedged my pole into the decking and returned with the net. He started pulling my line in by hand. The dogshark broke the surface about three feet out and drenched us both.

"Net!" Jack yelled. "Get that net over here, Mooch!"

"Got one over here," I yelled back.

Mooch leaned out. The dogshark closed in, and Mooch slipped the net under it, and with both hands dragged the bulging net aboard. Mooch lifted his mask and jumped up and down.

"Fifty cents, you guys. Our first fifty cents!"

I cautioned Mooch about the dogshark's poisonous tail barb and helped him retrieve the hook. Another shark came flying through the air and hit Mooch on the side of the head.

"Jesus Christ!" Mooch screamed. "Get 'im off me, Eddie! Kill 'im, Eddie. Kill 'im!"

Jack clubbed it several times with a small baseball bat, and then slit its jaw with his knife, and after a few tugs the hook was out. "That's all there is to it," Jack said.

Mooch shook and shivered. "They give me the willies."

Within an hour, dogsharks lay from one end of the barge to the other. We stopped counting after fifteen. Fish guts floated on the deck, and the planking was becoming slippery. Our shoes and clothes were soaking wet.

Suddenly I heard Mooch yell "WHOA!"

I turned in time to see him go over the side.

"They got me!" Mooch gurgled. "They got me!"

Danny and I pulled him to the barge and tried lifting him from the water, but his clothes were caught on a drop line hook. Several dogsharks were thrashing on the line.

"Owwwwwww! They're eating me alive! Get me out of here!" Mooch spit out water. "Get 'em off me!"

Danny and I held Mooch by the arms. Jack reached for the drop line.

"This sonofabitch is heavy," Jack groaned. "Might have us a squid."

"Oh God," Mooch hollered. "Get me out of here."

Jack pulled Mooch to the surface. I gripped the line and held it against the barge. With a knife I cut the leader holding Mooch's leg, and then Danny and I pulled Mooch out of the water and onto the barge.

"Somebody want to give me a hand?" Jack yelled. He was still holding the line, trying to stand up.

"I never want to see another fish," Mooch said. "They damn near got me."

"Eddie!" Jack yelled. "Grab the net. This one's running like a salmon."

"So you got something big?" I said.

"I'm serious, Eddie. He's big, fights like a king. Here, feel 'im."

I grabbed the line and felt the heavy jerks. "Could be anything, couldn't it? Bottom fish or something?"

"That's salmon," Jack said, "and he's big."

The line was fifty pound test, but it could take a larger fish if he didn't get his teeth into it. Jack unrolled his shirt sleeves and pulled the cuffs down over his hands like gloves. I did the same, and we both grabbed the line.

"That's more than fifty pounds of fish," Jack said. "The only way he's coming up is from exhaustion."

"What about us?" I said. "Hell, I'm beat."

"It's a waiting game," Jack said. "Whoever gives up first loses."

"Right now," I said, "I don't really care. Whatever it is can stay down there."

Jack looked at me. "The hell it can!"

The line slowly moved out from under the barge and headed straight out from us. Jack straightened up as the line rose.

"He's getting tired and mad," Jack said. "He wants off."

"Really think it's a big salmon?"

"I know it is." Jack's eyes were fixed on the water. "I've been here before, and I don't want to lose this one."

Danny came over and squatted between us. "Your buddy over there is going to catch pneumonia if he doesn't get dry. Maybe we ought to head in."

"Are you kidding?" Jack said. "Mooch! How you doing, buddy?"

"F-f-fine," Mooch said, shivering. "Lit-tle cold th-though."

"See," Jack said. "He's all right."

"Come on, Jack," I said.

"If we start back now, I could lose this guy."

"I'm a little cold myself," Danny said. "I could use a long hot bath."

"Bath hell! I'm talking about a prize salmon."

"Then lets drag him in," I said.

"No way," Jack said. "One wrong twist of the line and he's history."

While Danny and I argued for going in, the drop line rose up near the surface followed quickly by a series of violent splashes about ten feet out.

"See. I told you," Jack yelled. "I told you it was a salmon."

"All I saw was a splash."

"Didn't you see how big he was?"

Danny shook his head. "Too dark."

"Well, I saw it," Jack said. "Sixty, seventy pounds if he's an ounce. Thick in the belly." Jack stared at a swirl of water eight feet out. "You ain't getting away this time, you big bastard."

"What are the odds?" I said. "There are millions of fish out there."

"Hey, you guys?" Mooch called out.

"Hang in there, Mooch," Jack said. "You'll be dry soon enough."

Suddenly there was a shift in the slope of the barge, and Danny slipped face first onto the deck. Jack looked around.

"No bouncing," Jack said. Mooch sat on the bow beam, huddled in a ball. "All the papers will want a picture of this one," Jack said.

"Say J-J-ack. E-ddie," Mooch said. I looked back, and Mooch pointed across the barge. "We're s-sinking," he said.

The three of us turned and saw the port side underwater. Dead dogsharks were floating off the side.

"Jesus!" I said. "We're going down!"

"No we're not," Jack said. "Grab the fish."

Danny slipped in the sloshing water and fell into a pile of fish. Jack and I gripped the starboard lip and monkey-walked to the stern to untie the barge from the piling and raise the anchor. Jack got Mooch to unlash the pulley line and start pulling us in. "Joe!" Mooch yelled. "Hey Joe! Pull us in!"

I was leaning over the stern, raising the anchor, when we started to move away from the piling. Jack was pulling some of the dogsharks back onto the barge while Danny tried keeping the others aboard. "Just cut the anchor!" Jack said. "Too much drag."

I held the bucket of rocks suspended off the bottom and started cutting the rope. I leaned back while cutting to keep the anchor from dragging on the bottom. Then suddenly the rope snapped. I flew backwards, down over the port side, and into the water.

Everything went cold and then black. I clung to the rope and kicked and pulled until my head broke the surface. Jack was leaning over the stern—screaming—his arm outstretched. There was too much water under me, and with the tides I knew it would be all over if I lost my grip. Then I saw Danny and Mooch next to Jack, but the water in my ears muffled their voices. My arm muscles burned, and I felt fear and the cold taking away my strength. I took a deep breath and relaxed my arms. Then, slipping beneath the water, I pulled myself up the rope and lunged for the barge. My fingers clutched wood, and someone grabbed my elbow, and I felt myself slowly rising from the water. My knees knocked the bottom of the barge. I kicked toward the surface. I found a foothold and clung to the stern beam until Jack and Danny rolled me up onto the deck.

"Spit it out!" Jack said.

I took another deep breath and coughed up more water.

"Don't do that again," Mooch said. "Scared the hell out of us."

I shook my head and coughed.

"He's all right," Danny said, and I nodded.

My first thought was life. Then Sara. The day at the lake seemed so far away, but I clearly saw her face in my mind's eye. I was so cold, I couldn't move. Off in the distance, I heard rocks scraping the bottom of the barge. The stillness that followed was abrupt. Then voices. I sat up when I heard cheering, but I only saw Margy at the front of the barge.

"Eddie," she said. "Are you all right?"

I felt strangely apart from everyone and everything around me.

"What happened?" she said.

I stared blankly at Margy in the flat darkness of night and then saw Jack running toward me.

"The drop line," he hollered. "My salmon!"

I slowly got up and staggered over to the side of the barge where Jack was pulling in the line.

"I knew it," he said, throwing the line into the water. "The sonofabitch is gone."

"You sure?" I said. I could barely talk with my teeth chattering.

"Of course I'm sure," he said. "There's nothing on the line." Jack sat down on the deck, his head in his hands.

I looked at the barge covered with dogsharks. "At least we got the rent," I said.

"That's twice I've lost him," Jack said.

"It was probably a different fish," I said. "What are the chances of catching the same fish twice?"

Jack glared at me. "I know what was on that line. If you hadn't gone over the side, I'd have him now."

"If this damn tub hadn't started sinking, none of this would have happened."

Danny stepped in. "Knock it off you guys. What's done is done. We got all these other fish."

"They're not fish," Jack snapped. "They're garbage. Where's the glory in landing garbage?"

"Is that fish worth your friends?" I said.

Jack stared out at the dark narrows. I helped Mooch cut off the tail fins of the dogsharks. Jack joined us, but he didn't say much. He was still mad.

Mooch began vomiting over and over into the water. Joe sat down and helped us. Margy stood next to me with her back to the fish. "I'm glad you're okay, Eddie. You didn't look too good at first."

"I'm fine," I said, even though my bones felt frozen. I moved away from her touch. "Maybe Joe could use another beer."

"No, I'm fine," Joe said.

"Can I get you something, Eddie?"

"Yeah. There should be another coat somewhere. Maybe you could find it for me."

"Sure, Eddie."

Margy walked up the beach.

"I think she's still got a soft spot for you," Joe said.

"Margy?" I said. "Are you kidding. She's just trying to help."

"I count forty-three," Danny said.

"Not much more than twenty bucks," I said.

"Garbage!" Jack said.

"Let's see," Danny said. Four of us, for what, about four hours. And twenty bucks. That works out to about a buck and a quarter an hour."

Mooch wiped his chin. "I didn't need to know that."

"I can borrow a few bucks," Jack said. "We'll make rent."

"I do better than that on the street," Mooch said.

"We need a better scam," I said.

"There's scuttlebutt in the shipyard," Joe said, "that Bangor's going to three shifts."

"So, what's that mean?" Mooch said.

Joe stood up. "It means they can't load the ammunition fast enough to keep up with the shooting. I hear the money's good."

"How good?" I said.

"Seven—eight bucks an hour."

"Beats the hell out of fishing."

"I've got eighty-seven days left," Joe said. "If the shooting lasts beyond that, I just might hire on myself and make some real money."

I threw my last finless dogshark into the water. It floated for a moment, lifeless in the moonlight. The beacon off Point Herron swept across the bay, and in the arc of light, I saw the carcasses of more than a dozen dogsharks floating on the tide.

Jack stood next to me. "Kind of eerie," he said.

I shook my head. "Makes you wonder."

"A lot of mouths to feed out there," Jack said. "With this bounty, we've just made it a little easier."

"Thanks for pulling me out of the water," I said.

"The narrows is treacherous. It takes what it wants. When it wants. Whatever survives has to be tough."

"Like your salmon?" I said.

"Like anything."

17

I arrived at Sara's at exactly 7:30 for the dinner date we had arranged the morning after our great dogfish disaster. I swallowed the last of a beer at the bottom of the stairs to her building and walked up to the second floor. Beside her door there were two empty gallon wine bottles next to the cat plates. Sara didn't seem like the type to consume that much wine, but I quickly found out differently.

"Is it that time already?" she said, gripping the open door. She hiccupped and grinned, touching her wine glass to her lips. I nodded, and she just stared at me, smiling.

"Dinner," I said. "Remember?"

"Sure," she said.

"Can I come in?"

"Sure."

"Now?" I said.

"Oh God. I'm sorry," she said. "Of course. Come on in. I don't know what got into me. I got off work early, and I've been racing around in circles. Please excuse the place. I'm really a better housekeeper than this. Can I get you something? A beer? Some wine? That's a wonderful shirt, Eddie."

She shut the door, and we both stood silent. The apartment smelled of fried potatoes. Sara grinned. "What did you say you were drinking?"

"Beer!"

There were framed pictures of all sizes on every wall. Some pictures were enlarged, but most were color snap shots hung in neat displays. Her walls were like a giant walk-through photo album. Sara brought me a glass of wine. "So. What'll we toast?" she said.

"Warm food."

"To warm food," she said. I took a sip, wishing it was beer, and Sara emptied her glass.

"Can I help with anything?" I said.

"Everything's under control. Five more minutes. Make yourself at home."

I looked at the photos. "Lots of money tied up in pictures," I said.

"I never thought about the money," she said.

"Are all these people friends of yours?"

"You just never realize how many people you've known until you nail them to the wall."

"Who's this?" I said. "You have a lot of him."

"That's Tal. You know, the watch and the cross."

"Looks like the type who's into Time or Religion."

"Why's that?"

"Doesn't look like anybody I'd know."

I had seen the picture of her and Danny on Danny's wall. The one on Sara's wall was just of Danny.

"Nice one of Danny," I said, and quickly regretted it. "As far as pictures of Danny go."

"I don't hate Danny, if that's what you think."

"Never crossed my mind," I said.

"I *was* mad at the time, but I'm over that now. It was just as much me as it was Danny. We have to get on with things and not dwell on the past."

Smoke was coming from the stove door. "Sure I can't help with something?"

"Oh God!" Sara said, and she ran into the kitchen. She opened the oven, and smoke billowed out so thickly that for a moment I lost sight of her face. I opened the apartment door and two windows, and then helped Sara to the door where we watched until the casserole stopped smoking on the stove.

"Go ahead and sit down," Sara said. "It'll just be a minute."

When Sara finally sat down across from me, she mustered up a proud but shaky smile, and we both stared at the dish between us. There were only a few faint traces of the charcoal crust remaining.

"Smells—interesting," I said. "I'm starved."

"You're not just saying that, are you?"

"Not me. What is it?"

"Tuna surprise. It's usually my safest dish."

"Tuna fish?" I said. The mention of fish made my stomach quiver.

"And noodles," Sara said. "We lost the potato chip crust, but some of the flavor should still be there. Some more wine, Eddie?"

"Yes, please. Just—bring the bottle."

I ate my modest portion of tuna surprise so slowly that the last bite was cold.

"That was really something," I said.

"Did you really like it?" Sara said.

"Couldn't eat another bite." I took my plate to the sink, and ran the dishwater. "I'll just start the dishes."

We spent the early part of the evening drinking and talking about ourselves and our families. She asked about brothers and sisters, and I told her I missed not being allowed to see my younger brother Cliff because I had left home. Sara, I learned, was an only child, and unlike me she had a good relationship with her father. It was a relationship, she said, built on support and honesty. Sara leaned across the table.

"I suppose you want to sleep with me?"

The wine I was drinking caught in my throat, and I coughed. Sara reached over and slapped my back until I stopped.

"Are you all right now?" she asked.

"Fine." The word squeaked out. "You come straight to the point, don't you?"

"Should I take it back?"

"No," I said, and I kissed her.

From Sara's bedroom window, I watched the beacon light off Point Herron for a few moments as it swept the dark waters of the narrows. Then I joined Sara for the night in her lilac-scented bed.

18

Danny's apartment was cluttered with boxes and paper sacks, and it smelled of food and burnt rope. Only his Nazi flag still hung over the bedroom door. Danny was in his kitchen staring at two boxes. There was a red tennis shoe in one box and a brown wing tip in the other.

"You know," he said, "a pair of shoes is more than a pair of shoes."

I nodded.

"Shoes are universal and significant. Just look at them! They're separate. Identical, yet opposite parts of a whole universe. They're made as a pair, sold as a pair, bought in pairs, worn in pairs, and dumped in the trash together. It's hideous!"

"Disgusting," I said.

"Their whole existence depends on the other matching shoe. If one goes bad, they're both gone. I mean—it's their lot in life. One shoe is nothing in the world without the other."

"Just shoes to me," I said.

"But that's just it. Shoes are the stamp of our society. With our little feet stuffed neatly inside them, we hoof down those glorious streets of life. Just bodies in shoes."

"Don't you have any cold beer?" I said.

"It's pairs, Eddie. We've been raised on pairs. A sock without a match—we throw it away. One worn-out shoe, and we buy a new pair. No wife, and you're a leper. No big career plans— you're a failure. Everything is connected to some separate but opposite match. And so the flow goes on and on. On and on."

"So?"

"It's all so simple," Danny said. "It's funny." He lifted his pant legs. He had a brown wing tip on his right foot and an old red high top sneaker on his left.

"A pair is just a pair," Danny said, "but a red shoe and a brown shoe is bigger than any pair. Nobody knows what you are. Over here I'm Mr. Business, and over here I'm Mr. Casual. This is so me, Eddie, it's scary."

"I like it," I said.

"It could change the way people think, revolutionize the shoe industry. Just think. No more pairs. Till holes do us part. A brogue and a slipper. Wall Street in night shirts. Any old shoe will do. No more being locked into the trap of shoes that match. We're free, Eddie. Our feet are free at last. Jesus, Eddie, we can be anything we want. It'll be a whole new way of life—where nothing adds up."

"To what do we owe this discovery?"

"I owe it all to indecision," he said.

"To indecision," I said.

Danny remained in this frame of mind all during the move. While we sorted his belongings, Danny kept finding things that would send him down memory lane. At one point a pair of wrinkled tennis shorts elicited the epic of Maxine, his first tennis student. He pointed out a faint round impression over the fly and explained how Maxine, his tennis student turned lover turned memory, had inadvertently caught him between the pockets with a net slam.

"She dropped me like a folding chair," he said.

"True romance."

"Painful affection," he said.

"What happened?"

"Negative vapors," he said. "Poor Maxine. Pain is a painful experience that I prefer not to experience."

Danny loved to talk about girls the way Jack liked talking about fishing. There was always the strong sense of affection in Danny's talk of girls. He always used their names instead of "she" and always had a hint of a smile as he shared a story. I could never recall Danny saying anything bad about the girls he had known. It was always the good things he remembered, even with Sara.

Where indecision had earlier spawned Danny's theory of pairs, decisiveness quickly determined which of his possessions would survive the move. Danny decided not to keep anything connected with bad memories. He saved some of his clothes, his tennis racket, and, of course, his Nazi flag. Everything else went in what Danny called "the cleaning away of the strangely distant." That evening we hauled Danny's things to Motherbright's. The sun was low to the west, and the hillside was brown and green. The exception was the cool blue light that spilled from Motherbright's out onto the vines and shrubs. I felt apprehensive as I approached the cabin with Danny, yet something about it deeply attracted me: the play of hazy, blue light that seemed to make the cabin glow, and the hint of danger—the unexpected—in Motherbright, even though I had no definite reason to fear her.

Danny stepped inside the blue house and called out, "Anybody here?"

There was no answer. I followed Danny into the kitchen, and my eyes strained against the dim, heavy light. The strong glow reflected off the blue walls with such intensity that I had to keep my eyes low, glancing up for short intervals.

"Gave me a headache my first time," Danny said. "Now it doesn't bother me at all. Motherbright!" he called out.

The ceiling was like the tent of a desert nomad. There were several small, colorful rugs and many pillows of every size and color. Huge sheets sewn together hung like a draped canopy from the ceiling. Danny came into the room.

"Guess she's out." He went over to the record player and switched on some sort of oriental music. I fell into a pile of thick pillows.

"How's that feel?" Danny said.

"I could stay here forever," I said.

"Sorry," Danny said. "The position's filled."

The doors and windows of the house were round. Their frames had all been altered inside with curved wood and molding. The entire cabin—the color, the pillows, the draped ceiling, the curves—had an airy, but compelling quality. Danny led me to the bedroom. We had to stoop through the doorway to enter the small room, also draped with a cloth canopy. It was in the rear of the cabin, butted up close to the hillside where it received very little light. Danny flicked the wall switch, and a soft, violet-pink light filled the room. The floor was wall-to-wall mattresses covered with blankets, brightly colored Indian bedspreads, one long round pillow and several small ones.

"This is the ultimate," I said.

"It feels as good as it looks," Danny said.

I lay down. Danny sat with his back to the wall.

"I feel like a new man, Eddie. Around Motherbright, everything feels different. She's turned me around."

I thought about Sara.

"This is big, Eddie. I mean, real change."

I sat up. "Like what?"

"I feel there is something big out there for me that I haven't felt before. It's even bigger than women, Eddie."

"Must be serious."

"It's everything, Eddie. And it's nothing. I feel on the edge of something."

"Sure you're not getting sick?"

"How about—consumed?" A soft voice filled the room. "Consumption, Danny, is a sickness."

Danny and I looked up. Motherbright smiled from the doorway. She wore jeans under a flower-print dress. Her long, brown hair fell across her shoulders. Motherbright's eyes were hard to look away from.

"Don't get up," Motherbright said, stepping in. "This room was meant for company."

"Danny was just showing me around. I've never seen anything like this." Motherbright smiled willingly. "People dream about comfort. I prefer to live it."

I nodded my head.

"Dreams," she continued, "require action or they're empty. My house is full."

I wondered if I was missing something? Despite the floor covering of mattresses and the bedding, the room was sparse. The walls were bare. There was no bureau covered with the tiny bottles and jars normally found around a mirror in a woman's room. There was only one table large enough for the small bed lamp, a book and an ashtray between the mattresses. "It's all here." Motherbright said.

"Maybe you can use a few of Danny's posters," I said.

"The unadorned wall is a canvas for the mind."

I looked at Danny.

"See?" he said.

"You both look thirsty," Motherbright said. "Some tea, perhaps?"

Danny nodded.

"I'll take a beer if you've got one," I said.

"Make it two beers—for now," Danny said. "We've got a lot of boxes to move."

The day's light was fading, and from the kitchen window I could see the narrows and the cabins down on the beach. A light appeared to be on in our cabin, but I knew how light reflected off the water.

"Something of interest?" Motherbright said, coming up beside me.

"Just the view," I said, "and the colors. Sometimes at night this blue out here comes in through our bedroom window. It feels like morning."

"I like living in the colors I feel," she said. "I was immediately struck by this shade, Celestial Fire."

Danny came up and stood between us. "I never thought of fire and blue going together."

"Next time you're near a fire," Motherbright said, flatly, "look closely at the deeper flames. I think you'll find them quite blue."

Danny shrugged.

"Frog, our manager, told me once he would burn this place if it was his."

"He said what?" Danny said.

"Said any place this color ought to be burned to the ground. Then he told me to get a haircut."

"He's living in the dark ages," Danny said.

"Panic always strikes hardest those who are least able to adapt. You see him everywhere," Motherbright said. "He's a very sad man. Afraid of all the things he doesn't understand."

The oriental music pitched loud and then twanged and quavered. Motherbright excused herself and left us. Danny told me nothing would change, but I already saw the difference. His clothes were wrinkled, his hair ragged around the edges. A month earlier he would have looked immaculate. It wasn't that I cared about his shirts or his hair or whether he talked about tennis or women, but they had always been important to Danny, and when the important things in a friend's life start falling away, you take notice, and you wonder. He constantly spoke of Motherbright and almost always used the word "we". Motherbright had left Danny a note. He smiled at the part he didn't read to me.

"Motherbright says it's tea time," he said.

"I'll pass on the tea and take a beer."

"This isn't that Lipton crap." Danny opened the fridge and removed a small metal mixing bowl and put it on the stove. "This is Mother's Brew, and there is no brew like Mother's Brew. Believe me."

The green liquid began to steam, grew darker, and finally boiled. Danny poured us each a cupful. "One important rule," he said. "Nothing is said about this outside of here. Agreed?"

I shrugged in half-hearted agreement.

"Okay," Danny said, holding his cup up to me. "Here's to the future."

I looked at him warily. "Is this an Ex-Lax trick?"

"No tricks."

"If it is, I'm gonna shit all over your shoes."

"This is better than a six pack of beer."

"Then you drink first," I said.

Danny agreed and sipped his tea. I waited and watched a moment to make sure he hadn't faked a drink, and when I was sure, I took a taste. It was bitter, strong, and tasted like burnt rubber.

"Isn't that nice?"

"This is the worst shit I've ever tasted."

"Taste isn't everything. Drink some beer."

"Here," I said. "You can finish mine."

"This'll do me fine," Danny said.

"Then dump it. This stuff belongs in a transmission."

"Can't. Rule Number One. Never waste Mother's Brew."

I drank the cup. Then I quickly washed the bitter aftertaste in my mouth with my beer. I looked through Motherbright's records. I took the record of oriental music off and put on The Byrds' *Mr. Tambourine Man* album. I was familiar with that, and the music made the strange surroundings seem a little less foreign.

"How do you feel?" Danny asked. "Fine. Why?"

"Just checking."

I lay back on the pillows and listened to the music. My eyes darted around the room.

"How about you?" I asked.

"Just fine."

"Well, I guess everybody's fine."

"I guess you're right," Danny said.

"Fine, fine, fine. Everybody's fine. I like that. Could be a Beach Boys song. Fine, fine, fine till your daddy takes your T-bone away. Yes sir, I like that a lot."

Danny grinned.

"What's so funny?" I said and chuckled.

"Nothing."

"Good. We don't want to be laughing at nothing. Nothing is too serious to laugh at."

"I like that," Danny said.

"What?"

"Nothing is too serious to laugh at. I like that."

"What's it mean?"

"Who cares? It's right."

"Jesus," I said. "You're right. Meaning is irrelevant if something is right. When it's right, you'll know it. So meaning doesn't mean anything unless something is wrong."

"And who wants to know the meaning of something that's wrong?"

"You're right," I said. "Who cares? Who cares? Who cares?"

There is a place far back in the crease of life, where all seems clear and bright and meaningful, where the purity of thought is surpassed only by its complexity. Never have so many impressions shaken hands with one another in an effort to bind together all that has passed, all that is present, all that lies beyond us into a single, usable thread by which all that is immaculate is bound as one. In such an event, all is brought to bear on the moment where memory becomes life. Patterns unfold and emotions dance. Faces, once rooted in place and time, become splotches of fleshly paint swashed behind the eye. All is memory in the spring of rites.

My brain felt like it was being kneaded by strong fingers. There were brief moments between the spaces in Danny's words where my head seemed to elevate and then contract and expand. My mouth dried up, and the beer did nothing for it. The cabin became a fuzzy, disoriented cavity. Danny's boxes, strewn around the room, removed the feeling of openness there had been earlier in the day. Box pillars now crept up the walls like life-size bar graphs. The room now was uncomfortably crowded. Then everything became connected. Nothing seen or heard in the room felt separate from anything else. The music fit between the blue walls. Voices draped over us, and the lyrics went straight to the back of my head.

"It's the Flow, Danny."

"I know," Danny said. "So, what do you think?"

"I think those boxes are going to take over if we don't do something."

"They *are* menacing."

"They don't fit."

"I've always hated boxes."

"I've always hated hating boxes."

"The paradox of boxes."

"Menacing."

"Can't move without them, and you can't move within them. Bad condition. In the epidemic stages at this very moment," Danny said.

"Negative flow, Danny."

"Never seen it so bad. What would Louis the Pasteur do?"

"Attack the bastards."

I stood up and felt two hundred pounds heavier. I staggered, and Danny laughed loudly. I plodded over the pillows. I began to laugh too, until there were tears in my eyes. I fell head first into a tall stack of boxes. Danny stood there as if light-blinded, and watched it fall. Pennies spilled across the floor. I wanted to apologize, but Danny started to laugh again. I laughed with him. It made sense.

"Ever heard a prettier sound?" Danny said. He stared at the mess of pennies, papers, golf tees, and toilet articles on the floor. "Or seen a more beautiful picture?"

"Kind of takes your breath away."

"It's the flow, Eddie."

"It's you all over the floor."

"A 'me' painting," Danny said. "That's what it is. But it needs some green over here." He threw a green shirt near the pennies. "Just look what that does," he said. It added a green shirt next to the brown pennies.

"What goes with green?"

Danny looked at me. "Hell, anything goes with green."

I took a pair of blue cords from another box and threw them next to the fan of notebook paper where they seemed necessary for balance.

"I was just going to add that," Danny said.

I reached into another box and pulled out a framed picture, and without looking at it, I handed it to Danny.

"This, without a doubt, belongs out there," I said.

Danny stared at the picture. "Oh, yes," he said. "The one that Sara missed."

"Let me see." The picture was of Danny and Sara sitting in the kitchen nook of his old place. Sara was smiling, and I liked her picture. Danny walked over the green shirt and the fan of paper. He set the picture up next to a can of shaving cream so that it faced us.

"So you and Sara are really an item?" Danny said.

"We like each other."

"You don't just like someone like Sara. She requires everything or nothing."

It was hard focusing my thoughts. There were too many things racing through my head, each one a separate track seemingly cut off from all the others. Danny began pulling things from boxes: a hat, a potato peeler, a colander, photographs. He dropped them on the kitchen floor and giggled with every new addition. The floor quickly became a patchwork of color, fabric, plastic, and objects round, flat, and lumpy. Danny finally lifted an entire box, dumped its contents on the floor and laughed.

"Mere trinkets," Danny said.

I followed his lead by emptying another box onto the floor. Danny knelt down into the mess and spread the objects around like he was frosting a cake.

"Trinket, trinket, little star, how I wonder who you are."

I dropped my box and stared down at Danny. "I don't feel so good," I said.

I sat in the corner of the kitchen, staring blankly at all the wonderful shapes and patterns. I tried closing my eyes, but the spinning was so strong I had to force myself to sit up straight. My back felt like it was made of rubber, and I felt myself slowly slide down onto the floor.

"You're wrecked, Eddie."

"I know." I was lying out flat on the floor, my head propped up on the wall molding and my chin flush against my chest. "They got my radiator."

"I'll put on a different record," Danny said. "That should bring you back."

I watched Danny get up, giggling to himself. I couldn't move my head any further. My eyelids felt as heavy as coffee mugs, and I couldn't move off the floor. The connection between my head and body was gone, like the "loving feeling" with the Righteous Brothers on the stereo. I had lost the moving feeling, and I didn't really care. My feet were stuck into the colorful wash of everything Danny owned, and the image felt very important. But my heavy eyes outweighed everything, and I couldn't go on.

19

The touch of the hand on my leg felt distant, like some event in history reaching out and pulling me from sleep. The repeated touch along my leg grew in intensity until I opened my eyes to Motherbright standing over me.

"Welcome to the future," she said.

My thoughts refused to come together.

"Looks like you both had a good time."

Danny came over and stood at my feet, rubbing his eyes. "Eddie took it hard," he said. "One minute he was helping with the boxes, the next he was crapped out in the corner. Just too much fun. Right Eddie?"

I nodded and sat myself up.

"I mean, how much fun can one guy have," Danny said.

"I feel like I've had it all," I said, and stood up. "I have to go."

"Go where?"

"I feel like going home."

"This is home," Motherbright said, her hand still brushing my ankle. "You can stay here."

"I feel like being in my own bed, thanks."

"Sure you're all right?"

"Just tired. Real tired."

I stood up feeling groggy and very disoriented. I propped myself against the wall until my sense of balance returned enough for me to walk home. I felt embarrassed, and my mind was set on getting home.

"Danny'll go with you," Motherbright said.

"No," I said. "Goodbye"

I stepped out, and it was pitch dark. The night air was cool, and it felt like a piece of Saran Wrap draped over my face. I hobbled down the stairs thinking only of sleep. I opened the front door of my cabin and immediately felt safe inside the kitchen. I started to turn on the kitchen light and then decided against it and walked straight into the bedroom. I unzipped my boots, kicked them off in the direction of the closet, sat down hard on my mattress, and fell back. Just being on my own bed made me feel better, but that sensation of ease quickly turned to fright with the whisper of my name.

"Hello, Eddie."

I bolted straight up off the bed and scooted across the floor until my back hit the wall.

"It's okay, Eddie. It's me, Margy."

"Jesus Christ, you scared the hell out of me. What the hell are you doing here?"

"You said the door was open."

"Well, it's—it's—what the hell time is it?"

"The last ferry left some time ago."

"You don't belong here."

"I came over earlier," Margy said, "but nobody was here. So I thought I'd be a surprise."

"I don't need surprises." My eyes slowly adjusted to the darkness. Margy was sitting up on the bed holding the blanket up under her arms with one hand. She brushed her hair back from her face.

"Eddie?"

"I really don't feel like talking," I said.

"I'm not here to talk," Margy said.

She drew herself across the bed toward me, and against my better wishes, I didn't move.

"You've got me all wrong, Margy. We're through."

"You don't like me, Eddie?"

"That's not it."

"Maybe you'd like me better this way." Margy rose up on her knees, her chest arched, and she slowly sat back on her heels. She combed her fingers through her hair, and the blanket that had been around her fell to her waist. "Better?" she asked.

"Don't, Margy."

"But, I want to, Eddie. I've wanted to all night."

I started to stand. Margy touched my knees, and I felt her breath on my face.

"I need you," she said. "Some people belong together."

"Margy, there's nothing between us."

"Yes there is, Eddie."

"No. There is someone else," I said.

"Not right now," she said. "Not when we're alone." She straddled my knees. "And there will never be anyone else."

She clasped my hand and brushed my arm with her wet mouth. She pressed my fingers between her legs and took a deep swallow of air. Her body swayed from side to side. I pulled my hand away, but Margy gripped it to her. She squeezed her legs around my hand, and her thighs trembled.

"Come, Eddie," she said.

Then she placed my hands under her breasts and leaned back. She kissed my mouth, my neck, my ears. She unbuckled my belt and undid my fly-buttons and quickly—feverishly—held me with both hands. She did not let go but drew herself closer and brushed me between her legs, and then slowly pulled me to the mattress.

"Touch me, Eddie. Touch me all over," she said.

❧

The room was dark and still, and I was empty of all feeling but relief. Then I felt sick inside, and I couldn't look at Margy without hating myself.

"Eddie," Margy called out. I shuddered at the touch of her against my back. "Eddie, why did you move away?"

"You'd better leave," I said.

"It's too late, Eddie."

"Joe's place is just down the walk."

Margy kissed my neck. "The night doesn't have to be over."

"It's over," I said.

"What's wrong?"

"It was wrong from the beginning."

"You were fine, Eddie, if that's what you're worried about. It just takes me awhile, but we'll do better next time."

"No next time, Margy. This was it. There is someone else."

"I see," Margy said. Suddenly she was angry. "And you think it's that easy? Do you think I have no feelings?"

"Sex doesn't mean anything," I said. "It's over."

"No it's not, Eddie."

"It is."

"I was hoping for a happier moment."

"Excuse me?"

Margy pulled away. "I'm pregnant, Eddie."

"No," I said. "It can't be."

"It is, Eddie."

"How do you know?"

"A girl knows."

"How do you know that it's me?"

"I know."

"How do you know it's not Joe? You've been seeing him for over a month."

"I'm not a tramp, Eddie. Don't look so sad. It's not the end of the world. It's only a baby."

I slid away from her and pulled my knees up under my chin.

"I wanted you to know," Margy said, "so plans could be made."

"Plans?"

"The plans you make when a girl gets pregnant."

"This is too fast," I said. "You tell me you're pregnant, and now you want to make plans. I don't know what the hell's going on."

"I just want you to be as happy as I am."

"I'm not happy. I'm nineteen. You're telling me I'm a father? Hell, I don't even have a job."

"You're getting worked up over nothing," Margy said.

"You are chopping my life off at the beginning, and you call that nothing?"

My head swirled. I could see it all. Marriage. A kid. A steady job. The End. No California. No way out. Then—why me? I should've said no. Why naked in my bed? Then—if she wasn't pregnant before, she will be after tonight. You're dead, Carr— you're dead.

"Eddie, Eddie?"

"I am dead," I said out loud.

"Don't talk like that."

"I should've known better."

"Where are you going?" she said.

"Out."

I dressed quickly. Margy followed me to the door. "Don't go like this," she said. "Let me go with you."

I jumped off the bulkhead to the beach. The tide was up to the pilings. I followed the tide line to the Manette Bridge. Its concrete leg towered high and black against the sky. Its side span crossed overhead into an even darker night. The waves washed at my feet, water trickled down into the bed of the beach, and up above the wind fluttered leaves on the hillside. And there was the ever present whisper of rushing water.

The outgoing tide was running fast—beckoning—as it followed its age-old course. It washed defiantly against the bridge footings, hissing as it swirled and dropped off into the sucking holes invisible in the dark.

Climbing over the fallen tree above Jack's fishing hole, I tore my hand on a serrated limb, tripped over a rock, and fell face first into the sodden beach which gave way under my weight. I lay still. Far across the narrows I could see the old Indian site high above the beach. I pictured how the Indian woman might have stood on the far hillside, looking out into the dark. Maybe it was here—at this place—that her man had burned his fires into the dark. I lay there still at the water's edge. The tide flow hissed louder. I stood and slowly walked to the water. My body stiffened from the cold. As I moved out into the water, the rocks tumbled under my feet with the undercurrent pulling at my legs. Then the bottom dropped away, and I fell below the surface.

I touched the rock bottom and pushed off. I broke the water's surface, gasped and swirled below again. I reached for the bottom and rolled with the current. Fingers of kelp slipped over my face. The rush of water grew louder and louder, and then there was a brilliant flash of light, followed by the deepest chill, and the sound of water flowing.

The rush of water stopped. I felt nothing but the fullness of the air. Waves broke over me and rolled me over the rocks. I remember waking on the beach, thinking of the Indian woman's bones and the one place that felt safe. Without a second thought, I was gone from the beach.

❧

The smell of floor wax was strong, and for a long time I felt as if my head alone lay on the floor. My eyes searched the room for the other parts of my body. My right hand was warm, wet and bleeding from the wrist. In my other hand was the skull of the Indian woman—my fingers dug deep into the black eye sockets. My legs felt sore, and I tried to raise my head, but my neck was stiff. Behind me, a hinge creaked. Glass tinkled to the floor and then crunched under foot.

"Don't move! Police!" the voice said. "Don't move!"

⁂

Two men in white shirts, loosened ties, and rolled up sleeves paced in front of me. They asked the same questions again and again, and I knew it was real.

I heard the same questions later when I spoke with Dr. Ashburn on the phone. I apologized for waking her, but I had no answers for her either. I felt better when she promised to come down to the station right away. At 2:45 in the morning she was brought into the holding room, and I was told I was free until such time as the college decided to press criminal charges.

"I'm sorry about this," I said. "I really am."

My jeans were stiff from the salt water, and I waddled down the stairs.

"What exactly were you doing in the lab, Eddie?"

"I don't know. All I know is I woke up on the floor, and the police were telling me not to move."

"How did you get so wet?"

"The last thing I remember was being on the beach."

"Did you break into the lab?"

"I don't know," I said.

"The Dean isn't going to be happy about this."

"What did you tell the police?"

"That you were authorized to be in there but not at one o'clock in the morning. Eddie, did something else happen tonight?"

"I appreciate your help. You were the only person I could call. I'll pay for the window."

"The Dean will want to know why, Eddie."

"Tell him I have a history of blackout spells."

"Is that true, Eddie?"

"It could be."

"You were one of my best students Eddie, but sometimes an education can be wasted. I was glad you continued to work on the skeleton after you withdrew, but I don't understand tonight."

"I just don't know anymore."

"I have an early class. I'll tell the Dean something."

"Can I still work on the Indian woman?"

"Wait for awhile. Meanwhile, don't do this again."

"Yes ma'am. It won't happen again."

"Can I drive you home?"

"No ma'am. Thanks for vouching for me."

She left, and the night was suddenly still. I was free to leave, but nowhere felt like home. Bremerton was asleep. I walked to the rear of the Enatai Hotel where I still parked the Beast. The back seat was vinyl cold. My ears rang in the stillness, and I could still taste saltwater on my lips. I pulled myself up into a ball, and it seemed like forever before I fell asleep in the darkness—alone.

20

The historian Albert Dravis, in an interview, spoke of two Indians named Modac and Tolom, who fled the village of Tlintot in search of the Heart of the World. They were lovers, Dravis said, but lovers destined to never live out their love.

According to Dravis, the Skomish Book of Life spoke of the woman Modac and how her eyes held the beauty of life. Her hair was long and black, and like the stilled surface of the sound waters, it shimmered in the sun. Her beauty was so extraordinary that she was the object of every young warrior's desire. But Modac desired only Tolom.

In the village of Tlintot, as in the others on the sound, all warriors went to the deep waters to harvest fish. Tolom was strong and handsome, but unlike other tribesmen, he was not skilled in the ways of fishing. He fished with the others but yearned for more than fish.

The Skomish lived mainly off the fish they caught, but the sound waters were often treacherous, and the catch unpredictable. It was believed that the Keeper of the sound made the waters perilous and scattered the fish because the Keeper was unhappy.

It came to pass one day that there were no more fish in the Skomish nets, and the sound waters became dangerous. The waves rose high, and the tides pulled from all directions, capsizing many canoes. The next day the men went onto the waters as they did on the third and fourth days, and again no fish were caught. The Skomish tried to please the Keeper with songs and dance, but nothing calmed the waters or filled the Skomish nets.

On the fifth day the waters grew more treacherous, and in the turbulent tides that sunk two canoes, Tolom was lost.

When Modac learned of Tolom's fate, her heart was heavy, and the joy that had once filled her eyes vanished. Modac's life was empty without Tolom, and it was made worse that there were no fish to eat. Modac did not understand the ways of the Keeper, and for days she cried at the loss of Tolom and the hunger in her village. Then one day on the beach, Modac saw a shell necklace like one she had given Tolom, rolling in the tide wash, and she chased it into the shallows, but it eluded her grasp. She threw herself into the water, but the tide pulled the necklace from her. Modac cried out in anger. Suddenly her cries were stilled by a powerful voice from the water.

"Be not afraid," echoed the Keeper's voice. "I bring you no harm."

Modac was fearful. She started to run from the water but stopped when she saw the necklace. She reached for the shells, but again they were drawn from her.

"You are beautiful, and I long for happiness," the Keeper said.

Once again, Modac reached in vain for the necklace.

"We give you song and dance," Modac said, "but you take away our fish and our people. What is it you wish?"

"I want a wife."

"But you are not of flesh."

The Keeper spoke to Modac of why the waters churned and why the fish and Tolom were gone. But she was unsure of her belief in the Keeper.

"If only you will be my wife," the Voice said, "the tides will quiet, and the fish will return."

"And what of Tolom?" Modac asked.

"You will grant him life."

"But mine will be empty without him," Modac said.

"You can see him always and make him the best of fishers."

Modac wanted her people to eat and Tolom to live and so agreed to join the Keeper.

The Keeper kept his word. That evening Tolom washed onto the beach near the village, and Modac's heart was light with joy. The following day the waters stilled, the fish returned, and her people ate. Modac's sadness passed when Tolom returned, and for days they were happy.

Then one night Modac was awakened by the Keeper's voice. He reminded her of her promise to join Him. His voice made Modac's heart sad. She did not believe in the Keeper's voice, only that Tolom had returned, and she ignored the Voice. But the Voice did not pass.

Modac spoke of the Keeper to Tolom, and they agreed that the Voice was the Voice of their elder's belief, not theirs. But the Voice continued. To save themselves, Modac and Tolom left their village by canoe and were never seen again.

Modac and Tolom escaped the village of Tlintot and traveled by canoe in the dead of winter in search for their Heart of the World. They believed that a water route, like the blood running through their veins, would eventually lead to the Heart. For days and weeks they paddled the sound waters, following the shoreline until one morning a dense fog overtook the sound and obscured the spurs and headlands Tolom used for direction. Without visibility or bearing, they left their course to the tides that in time drew them into a channel. The tides and water streams grew in strength as the canoe was pulled deeper into the channel. Far into the narrows the waters surged and roiled and finally swirled with such force that the canoe capsized, throwing Modac and Tolom into the churning tides. Once in the water, the divergent tides pulled Modac and Tolom to opposite shores.

For days and then weeks, Modac and Tolom were separated in the blinding mist of winter. Tolom tried swimming the channel, but with each attempt, the tides turned him back. Both built fires on the shore, but in the heavy fog no light crossed the waters. After many weeks passed, they built no more fires and no longer tried to swim the waters. Modac and Tolom believed they had found the Heart of the World, where little is seen and all is felt. Alive they were apart. In death, they believed, they would rise together from different shores and meet in the highest place. Albert Dravis called that place Legend.

Even today the elders of the Skomish still speak of kelp on the water as the hair of Modac and a portent of good fishing. And the narrows of Enetai still churn violently where, at least some believe, the Keeper unhappily waits for Modac.

21

You ready to be normal?"

I tried pulling my arms free, but they were still pressed tight against my sides. "I know you're awake. You gotta come out sometime." I recognized Gimp's voice. "If you're through being crazy, I'll unbuckle you."

"I'm not crazy." I said through the sheet.

"Here, try some of this." Something cold and wet touched my face through the sheet. I winced at the smell of the whiskey. "It ain't going to bite."

"Where am I?" I said.

I heard Gimp's familiar slurping sound. "Happened to me many a time," he said. "I'd get so drunk, I'd lose myself. Wander off to God knows where and wake up in some strange place scratching my head. I woke up once on a parade float in Billings, Montana."

"Is it Thursday yet?"

"Thursday's gone," he said. "It's Friday." Gimp slurped again. "You want out?"

I shook my head.

"Then you ain't crazy." Gimp reached under the sheet and unlatched a buckle. My arms fell loose. "You're welcome to stay," he said, pulling the sheet back from my face, "but this is my bed. The couch is yours."

Gimp's room smelled like old musty clothes and mildew. The room was small and cluttered with clothes, TV dinner trays, and empty bottles. A yellowed picture, in an old wooden frame, sat on top of the dresser by the door. The couch was threadbare, and the table by the window held smudged glasses and newspapers. I stared at Gimp. I had never been to his room. Nothing in it indicated anyone was ever expected. He stood at the table with a cloud of cigarette smoke hanging above his head.

"Ain't a pretty place," he said, "but it's warm." He poured more whiskey into his glass. "Sure you don't want some ointment?"

I pushed the heavy leather belt off the bed onto the floor. "I have to go."

"I only used it because you were talking crazy and banging around."

I tried pushing myself up, but my arms were so weak that I collapsed on the bed, closed my eyes, and fell back to sleep.

≥≈

When I woke up again, it was dark outside with only the table light on. Gimp was sitting at the table, and the room smelled Chinese.

"Something smells good."

"There's some China food in those boxes."

I peeled back the sheet and slowly got out of the bed. My shirt and jeans were still starchy stiff, and I smelled of sea water. I stood at the sink and stared down at the food.

"Spooked five years off me," Gimp said. "How's the head?"

I touched the knot on my forehead and then spooned some chop suey and rice out of their cartons.

"You got a head like me," Gimp said.

"Don't remember anything," I said.

"Drunk lumps are like rings on a tree. Reminders of where you been in life. Hell, I been more places than I can rub."

The food was cold, but it tasted good.

"Ain't none of my business," Gimp said, "but you got a face long enough to step on."

I left the Chinese food and went down the hall to the bathroom. Radio and TV noise filtered out of rooms. I quickly closed and locked the bathroom door, and it was quiet. I closed the toilet lid and sat down. I heard shoes shuffle up to the door, followed by a loud hacking and someone rattling the door knob. I flushed the toilet and opened the door. Crazy old Hank stood in the hall grinning at me. He had forgotten his teeth again, and he was sucking his bottom lip into his mouth. I stepped out into the hall.

"You hidin' again?" Hank said.

"No, Hank, I'm not hiding."

"Then I'll be it," he said. "I'm the only one left." He stepped into the john and closed the door. The slide bolt latched from the inside. "It's all clear," Hank said, through the door. "Ninety-nine, ninety-eight, ninety-seven, ninety-six—"

I walked back to the room. "There's coffee in the thermos," Gimp said, without looking away from the window. I poured myself a cup and sat down at the table across from Gimp.

"What do you see out there?" I asked.

"Things I like," he said. "That old pine tree there and the water. The mountain too, though it's gone at night. Mount Rainier was the first thing I saw when I came here. Makes you feel small."

"Thanks for the food, Gimp."

"A man don't eat for a day, he's bound to be hungry."

I lit one of Gimp's Camels.

"Been kind of lonely around here at night," he said, "since you been gone. The new guy ain't much for company. Don't drink or play checkers. You ever tried playing checkers against yourself?"

"I miss those nights myself," I said.

"You working now?"

"I'm looking. You heard of any work?"

"Not around here. This new fellow is here temporary, he says, until he hires on at Bangor."

"I've heard the talk," I said.

"He goes down to the employment office every morning like clockwork."

"Does he know anything for sure?"

"Just what I told you." Gimp took a long drink from the pint and handed it to me.

I shook my head. "Can I ask you something, Gimp?"

"Shoot!" he said.

"You ever been in trouble with a girl?"

"Every woman I ever knew caused me grief."

"Like—in a family way?" I said.

"Can't say I have," he said. "Least not that I know of."

"I was afraid of that."

"But that ain't from a lack of indulgence. But that was when I had two good legs. Why?"

I looked up at Gimp, and without saying a word, he knew why I was asking.

"Well now," he said. "That's a horse of a different stride."

"It's bad, Gimp, and I don't know what to do."

"Sounds like it's already been done."

"What's a guy do?"

"Never a problem I've had to consider."

I told Gimp how far back Margy and I went, about her obsession with me and her staying on the beach with Joe the Squid. He laughed when I brought up how I thought I'd killed her. He listened to everything I had to say about Margy and me and Joe: the flirting, and her waiting for me in the cabin, and how good she was at getting what she wanted. Then he broke out into a horse laugh when I mentioned Sara.

"You're a real glutton for punishment, aren't you?"

"Sara's different."

"They're always different. Different until you see the sameness."

"Margy was naked!" I said.

"Just like that."

"Just sitting there naked on my bed. I screwed up, Gimp."

Gimp rubbed his chin. "All naked on your bed, huh?"

"I don't know what to do."

Gimp just smiled and shook his head. He didn't say anything for a long time. He gripped his bottle and pressed it to his lap, twisting his old fingers over the neck like it was some kind of crystal ball. The longer he remained silent, the worse my situation seemed.

"Have you talked to her doctor?" he finally said.

"I haven't even talked to her."

"If she's as playful as you say, it may not be yours."

"I already asked her that. She said Joe never touched her."

"Then again, maybe it is yours," Gimp said. "But a sailor has a young girl, and he never touches her?"

"Hell, I don't know what they did." I stood and walked across the room and leaned against his dresser. "First thing I'd do is see her doctor."

"That's it?" I said.

"They got tests."

"Hell, I thought you knew something. That's no answer."

"There ain't no answer," he said. "You think you just ask for answers and they appear?"

Gimp got up and came toward me. I tightened up. He brushed me aside, opened the small top drawer and pulled out a fresh pack of Camels. "Answers!" he snorted and walked back to the table. "If everything had an answer, life would be easy." He gestured to the yellowed photograph on top of the dresser. "The Yakima Kid there would be livin' on a mountain instead of under it. Now there was a kid with smarts. Sharper than a brass tack. He knew rocks. We were a team. The Kid had smarts, and me a hunch. We was close, and if there were answers, he'd be alive today."

"I just thought you'd know something," I said.

"It ain't much. But short of hitting the road at dawn, I'd look up that doctor. Then again, at your age I was kind of partial to hitting the road. I've never been one to linger over bad situations."

I went over to the bed and put on my shoes.

"You're welcome to stay," Gimp said.

"I better get going."

"I ain't no magician," Gimp said. "Things done are things done. I can't change 'em. If it turns out it's yours, there are doctors around that can fix that."

"Hell, Margy'd never do that, and even if she would, I don't have the money."

"Well—Highway 16 runs both ways."

Gimp snatched his bottle off the table and held it out. "You want one for the road?" I shook my head, and Gimp stared out the window. "Me and the Yakima Kid were going to be bigger than that mountain. We had some big plans. Then the mountain got the Kid and took my knee. He was like my own. I wanted an answer too."

I stopped tying my shoe and looked over at Gimp still staring out the window. He turned to me and then back to the window.

"I wish I knew more, kid. I really do."

22

I sat on the beach in the bright September sun listening to the whine of Jack's reel and waiting for Margy to arrive. The minus tide had pulled the sound far back into itself. The barge, which we now kept tied to the pilings under the cabin, was resting at the edge of the water with Jack sitting off the aft end. The low tide added ten feet of beach front—exposing jagged rocks, chunks of block cement, twisted iron rods, and sewage pipes.

Jack came back to the blanket and laid his cold, wet line on my chest. "You sure she's coming?" he said.

I lifted the chunk of bullhead off me. "She said she was."

"We oughta just split," Jack said. "There's nothing here. There are a lot of clubs where a good band could make money in Canada." Jack waited for a response, but I didn't say anything. "And the draft can't touch anybody up there," he added.

"The shooting over there isn't going to last that long."

"They got Scooter."

"They got lucky."

"What if Margy doesn't show up?"

"What if the world ends tomorrow?"

The toilet flushed from up inside the cabin, and a moment later Mooch boomed out, "Here she comes!"

I glanced up between the cabins looking for Margy, but all I saw was Mooch standing on the front porch hiking up his shorts.

"She's a whopper!" he yelled.

The gurgling sound of water came from way back under the cabin and then moved straight down from the bathroom into the beach. The pipe went quiet for a moment, and then where it emerged from below the gravel, water hissed and whooshed out the end. When the last of the water trickled down into the rocks, a tiny brown lump sat just outside the mouth of the pipe. About a foot farther down the beach, Jack's contribution held a comfortable edge.

"How'd I do?" Mooch yelled down.

"Not even close," Jack said.

"Try again," I said.

"Again? I must've beat him."

"Look for yourself."

"Don't touch a thing. I'll be right down."

Mooch was a tough, untrusting competitor. He came down and immediately went to the end of the pipe and inspected the results.

"That's the third time now," Mooch said. "What the hell is this?"

"Superior training," Jack said.

"Bull! It's because you go first."

"It's the sardines," I said.

"Sardines will walk all over crackers and bread every time."

Mooch screwed up his face and then inspected the results again. This time more closely.

"You think that's really it?" he said, poking the projectile with a stick.

"Bulk is the key," Jack said.

"You can't argue with the laws of physics, Mooch," I said.

"So if I was to physic more, I could get more distance?"

"Certainly. More fish and a lot more physic."

Mooch produced another twisted look where you sensed each of his brain cells battling with one another for a shot at clarity. He was just about to launch into something undoubtedly profound when Jack nudged me and pointed toward the cabin.

"I guess you're right," Jack said.

Mooch looked confused. "I didn't say anything."

I waited for Margy to walk to the beach, but for the longest time she remained out of sight. Jack kept looking at me, which made me even more nervous. Mooch squatted at the end of the pipe. Margy finally walked into sight. She wore a white skirt, tight yellow sweater, and shoes with tiny heels that caused her to wobble. I thought, what a shame she had to be Margy.

"Mooch and I will head up the beach," Jack said.

"Don't go—yet."

"Four is definitely a crowd."

"I haven't figured this out yet," Mooch said.

Margy stood and clasped her hands in front of her. "Hi Jack," she said, wincing at the sight of Mooch.

"You remember Mooch?" I said.

"I sure remember you," Mooch said.

"We were just going," Jack said.

"Don't leave on my account," Margy said.

"Okay," Mooch said. "I like your sweater. I wish Amy looked like that in a sweater."

Margy looked at me. "Do you like it, Eddie?"

"You look nice," I said.

"I wore it for you."

"You ever lived in a truck?" Mooch said.

"Let's go, Mooch," said Jack.

"Where?" Mooch said.

"I don't know. Grab your shit."

Mooch looked at the end of the pipe. "You've got to be kidding."

Jack picked up Mooch's shirt and pants off the beach and threw them at him.

Mooch turned to Margy. "If Eddie's not the father, I'll get rid of Amy and fix up the truck. It ain't a bad place, really. Hell, I've even got a toilet."

"Get him out of here!" I said.

"Come on, you gooner," Jack said, and he pulled Mooch away.

"What was that all about?" Margy said.

"Mooch has a very complicated mind."

Margy sat down on the blanket next to me, and I immediately felt removed from her. I could hear the sound of her voice, but it was hushed by the tide.

"Eddie, are you listening?"

"What?"

"I said I'm glad you called. I was worried when you didn't come back. I missed you."

"Things have not been good."

"I'm sorry if you're upset, Eddie, but I thought you should know."

"This whole thing is wrong," I said.

"Well, it has happened, Eddie."

"It won't make me love you."

"I believe that you'll love me in time and love me the way I love you, Eddie."

"That's not the way it works."

"I just know how I feel about you and how much I want to be with you. I can wait for you to love me."

"You really don't understand, do you?" I said.

"Don't you think it's possible to love me?"

"Not this way."

"But *this* is the way it is, Eddie."

I felt her hand on my shoulder, and I pulled away from her.

"I want to see your doctor," I said.

"My doctor? Why?"

"I want the test to know it's mine."

"You're the only one," she said.

"I want to know for sure."

"You make me sound like a liar."

"His name, Margy."

"Let's not talk about this right now, Eddie." She rubbed the back of my neck. "Can't we be happy today—drive somewhere, maybe?"

"All I want is to see this doctor. So what's his name?"

"I don't remember it right now."

"You don't remember your doctor's name?"

"It was a foreign name."

"A foreign name?"

"I certainly didn't go to our family doctor. My father has some very strong feelings about what's right and wrong."

"So do I. I'll get dressed, and we'll go to his office. You do remember where you went, don't you?"

I stood up. Margy looked up at me sadly. "Eddie—"

"I have to know that it's mine, so let's go."

"I can't, Eddie."

I walked around in front of her. "Margy," I said. "There is a doctor, isn't there?"

"Don't be silly."

"Then let's go," I said. I took her wrist and pulled her to her feet. She just stood there.

"I said, let's go."

Her eyes darted from me to the ground and back again. She put her hands over her face, turned away, and then started crying. I tried pulling her hands away from her face, but she fought me.

"Tell me what I'm thinking is wrong," I said.

She sobbed louder.

"Look at me," I said, "and tell me this hasn't been a lie."

She pulled her hands free of mine and covered her face again.

"There is no doctor, is there, Margy?"

"Stop it, Eddie!"

"There's no baby, no nothing. It's all been a lie."

"Stop it!"

"It's been a lie from the beginning, hasn't it?"

"I love you, Eddie. More than I've ever loved anybody."

"The cheapest word you know."

"Eddie, I've always loved you."

"Of all the fucking tricks!"

"Please, Eddie."

"I want to know why, Margy? I want to know how you figured this would work?"

"I don't want to talk about this."

She looked away. I grabbed her and shook her hard.

"Look at me, Margy, and tell me why you did this. You're not leaving until you do."

"You'd never understand, Eddie."

"You almost ruined my life. I want an answer!"

"Let go of me, Eddie. You've got all the answers. Figure it out."

"You're a whore, Margy. A cheap, sick—" Her hand caught me squarely on the cheek. Margy covered her mouth.

"Oh, Eddie, I'm sorry. I didn't mean to do that." I picked up the blanket and started for the cabin. "Please, Eddie." Margy ran up behind me and grabbed my arm. "I really do love you."

"Let go, Margy."

"Don't do this, Eddie. Please."

"I said, let go."

"You don't know what it's like. You're the only guy I ever wanted. I need you, Eddie. Please, don't leave me."

I walked away.

"I suppose your little blonde girlfriend gives you plenty?"

"Good-bye Margy."

"What's the matter? I'm not good enough for you?" I kept walking. "Or maybe I'm too good."

"You call it," I said over my shoulder.

"Can't make you feel much like a man."

I stopped and turned around slowly.

"You cut both ways," I said.

"I don't like losing what I want."

"I don't think anybody can give you what you want."

"Is that so. Why don't you ask Jack? Or Danny?"

"About what?" I said.

"I don't lose without taking something, Eddie."

"Well, I haven't got anything left for you to take." I walked away and left Margy standing alone on the beach.

"Don't go, Eddie." She ran up behind me. "Eddie! Eddie! You can't walk away from me."

I got to the bulkhead steps and saw Jack looking down at me from the porch.

"I don't forget," Margy yelled out. "Remember that, Eddie. I don't forget."

I threw the blanket over the porch rail.

"It wasn't anything, Eddie," Jack said.

"Shut up!"

"I didn't think it would matter."

"It does matter, so don't say anything."

"How was I suppose to know she'd try something like this? We're still friends, aren't we?"

I just looked at him.

"Danny was news to me," Jack said. "But hell, if it had been true, Eddie, we could've beat it. With three of us, who could they pin it on? You've got to believe me, Eddie. I was going to tell you."

"When?"

"Well—I don't know."

"After I married her?" I stared down at Margy. Her face was ugly with anger. I climbed up the bulkhead and started for the stairs.

"We're still friends, aren't we?" Jack said.

I stopped and looked back at him. "What is a friend, Jack?"

Frog, the manager, was standing halfway up the stairs, holding a pair of large hedge clippers, watching, and listening.

"My father knows things," Margy yelled from below. "You can't treat me this way. Believe me. Do you hear me, Eddie Carr? You'll pay for this."

I climbed the stairs without looking back. Frog stepped in front of me as I was about to pass him. He held his hedge clippers open in front of his chest. "What's all that screaming about down there?"

"Nothing," I said.

"Sounds like something to me." He rolled his cigar stub from one side of his mouth to the other. "You bothering that girl?"

I laughed.

"Don't get smart with me," Frog snapped.

"Everything's fine," I said.

"I don't like you, Carr. Or people yelling and screaming on my beach. What's going on?"

"She's upset."

He squinted at me and withdrew the cigar stub from his mouth, spitting a brown, stringy wad onto the grass. "I don't like troublemakers, Carr."

"No sir."

"I ran the winos out of here for causing trouble, and I'll run you—you hippies out, too. I'll do it! You better believe it, bub."

"Just a disagreement. That's all."

"Trouble down here'll get you out."

"Nobody's causing trouble."

"And I want to know about that barge down there," Frog snapped.

"What's to know?" I said.

"What's it doing there?"

"Just sitting there."

"Well, it don't belong there. It's an eyesore, and it's on my beach."

"Sorry, can't help you."

Frog's face was distorted with frustration. "I really don't like you, Carr." He stuffed the slimy cigar butt back in his mouth. I sidled by him. "Won't have it," Frog mumbled. "No, sir. Damn rousers!"

I looked back over my shoulder at Frog, and he looked away. "Nope!" he said. "I won't have it. Goddamn blue houses and troublemakers. I won't have it. No way, no how. Nope!"

23

I woke up in the hazy morning light that sprayed into the bedroom, thinking about my breakfast date with Sara. Life felt good. The heavy clouds that had drizzled earlier had passed, and the cabin was full of yellow light. I was brushing my teeth when I heard footsteps on the porch. There was a series of loud knocks.

"It's open!"

There was another hard knock on the door. When I opened the it, two men—one old, the other young—stood in the doorway. They both wore work clothes and heavy boots.

"An Eddie Carr live here?" the older man asked.

"That's me," I said. "Who are you?"

"You know Margy Vasina?"

My eyes darted from the older man to the young guy. "I know her. Why?"

"We wanna talk to you about her," the younger one said.

"Shut up, Leon," the older man said.

"If there's some problem," I said, "she lives with her parents."

"We know where she lives," Leon said. He put his hands on his hips and cocked his head. "We came to see you."

"I said shut up," the older man said.

"Oh, Daddy."

"I'll do the talking." The older man turned back to me. "You know," he said, "I hate talking through a doorway. Be better if we stepped inside. I like keeping my business private."

"This is fine," I said.

"Who asked you, hippie?" Leon took a step toward me, and I backed up.

The older man stopped Leon with his arm. "Damn it, Leon."

"What do you guys want?"

"We come to talk to you about Margy. Man to man."

Leon laughed. "Looks like man to fairy to me."

"Look. I'm already late. Check with Joe, two doors down. He knows about Margy."

Leon stretched his arm out toward me. I tried to shut the door, but he wedged his boot between the opening and forced it open. The older man pulled me onto the porch and pinned me against the cabin with his fist. "Move and I'll crack you like a nut." He held me against the wall until Leon came back outside.

"Ain't nobody else here, Daddy."

"What's this about?" I said.

"Inside," Leon's father said.

Leon pushed me by the hair into the cabin. "So this is how they live." he said. "And look-ee here. Drums. I always wanted to play some drums." Leon slapped the cymbal with his knuckles, and then thumped the tom and snare drums.

"Leon!"

"What?"

"Knock that shit off."

"I don't know who you are," I said, "or why you're here, but I think there's been a mistake."

"You got that right, Mr. Eddie."

The older man strolled over to the chair by the heater and lifted a pair of nylons from between the cushion and the armrest.

"Yes sir, Mr. Eddie. A big mistake."

Leon flexed a drumstick between his hands, watching me watch him.

"You see," his father said, "I'm old-fashioned. I like having things that make me happy. Sometimes they're for work. And sometimes they're for pleasure. Either way, what's mine is mine and nobody else's till I say so." Leon thumped a drum. "Now it's one thing for a man to walk off with my hand drill, use it, then bring it back fit and working. I say to myself, it must've been important, and no harm done. Same goes for taking my truck—like in an emergency."

"I don't—" I started to say.

"But let's say a fella takes up with my daughter."

"And my sister!" Leon snapped.

"Shut up!"

"Sorry, Daddy."

"Let's say this fella fancies himself some sort of smooth talker, and he figures he can rut any ol' field till he's had his fill and then just move on to a new pasture. Now that's fine if it's open range and nobody's holding title. But when the field is mine— well, that's something else."

"I think you've got this wrong," I said.

"Nobody treats my girl like dirt without hearing from me."

"And me, too!" Leon snapped my drumstick in two.

"You gotta love my Margy like I love her, before you even think about beddin' her."

"There's some mistake," I said.

Leon smiled. "And you made it."

"Riled my blood just hearing about it. That was my daughter you forced into bed, diddled, then dumped like a tramp." He looked away. "My God—where's the decency?"

"I don't know what she told you, but I never forced her anywhere. If Margy said that, she's wrong. I never wanted anything to do with her from the beginning."

Leon reached over, grabbed me by the shirt, and twisted the collar tight around my neck. "Something wrong with my sister?" Leon said, twisting my shirt harder. "Think you're too good for her?"

"No," I said.

Margy's father walked over and stood right in front of me, his hands on his hips."You see, we keep things in the family. We're what you call *close.*"

"Yeah," Leon said. "Real close."

"I don't like weirdos diddling my family. Don't like it at all. Lying. Then putting lies into my girl's head. Just so you can swing your stick."

"This is all wrong. I never—"

"My Margy wouldn't lie about a thing like this. She was in tears!" He stepped right in front of my face, and the sour smell of his breath was strong. "Do you hear me! Tears!"

Leon had my head locked forward, and all I could do was look straight into the old man's face. "Crying about getting married and sleeping with some—some hippie I'd never seen. That's something for a father to see and hear—a father who loves his daughter. Just looking at you makes me sick to my stomach. And me holding that girl in my arms, hearing all those tears."

"Hit 'im, Daddy! I got him. Hit 'im!"

"You're making a mistake," I pleaded. "You've got this all wrong. I never—"

"You never should've started on me."

Margy's father turned and paced nervously in front of me. I tried to wriggle myself free of Leon's grip, but when I moved, he twisted my shirt tighter.

"I've never forced Margy to do anything. I swear it."

"Don't boy! You're up to your ass already."

"Hit 'im Daddy!"

"It was Margy's idea," I said. "She was naked and waiting in my bed. That's the truth."

"Truth? Truth!" The old man swung up from the hip and hit me flush with his fist. My knees buckled, but Leon held me up. "That's truth!" he said.

"Hit 'im again, Daddy."

"Whataya say, Mr. Eddie? Want some more truth?"

"Real easy with two of you," I said.

"Oh, we got us a fighter."

"Some fighter," Leon said.

"Let him go, Leon."

"Hell no, Daddy. I like this."

"I said, let go of him."

Leon slowly loosened his grip on me and pushed me off.

"All right, big stick," his father said. "Swing, or I'll drop you where you stand."

"You've got this all wrong. Ask Margy."

"Shut up!"

"Ask her what she was doing back there in my bed when I came home."

"I said, shut your fuckin' mouth."

"Or about the Senior Party, the Rodeo Drive-in. Ask her about the Vaseline—"

Leon hit me from behind, and I fell to the floor. I covered my head with my arms, just before I took a kick in the ribs that knocked the wind out of me. "Git up! Come on, git up you sonofabitch!"

I gasped for breath.

"Git him up," the old man yelled.

Leon grabbed me by the shirt and tore my sleeve, lifting me off the floor. His father stepped up to my face and grabbed me by my hair.

"You have dirtied my daughter, dirtied my family, and you have dirtied me. I couldn't beat you enough to wash that away."

"I could, Daddy. I could."

"You hear me, hippie?"

I tried to wipe the blood from my mouth.

"Do it! Go on, scum. Do something! Give me a reason."

My mouth was full of blood, and I couldn't talk. "F-f-f-" I bubbled out, trying to clear my mouth. All I saw was the blur of the old man's arm flying up and a flicker of light, and then I felt a sharp pain in my nose.

"Say it!" the old man said.

I spit out a mouthful of blood on the old man's pants.

"Tough boy."

"Let me," Leon said.

My head snapped forward. Blood flew, and I fell to the floor. My face and neck were wet.

"You're just damn lucky I don't cut you. Fix you good. Make you and that girlie hair of yours match up right." The old man knelt down, grabbed my hair, and lifted my head. "If Margy's in any sort of trouble because of you, I'll be back. I'll come back and fix you. Fix you so no woman'll want you. You hear me?"

I couldn't move.

"You read me?"

I finally nodded my head.

"Come on," the old man said to Leon. "Let's go."

"That's it?" Leon said. "I didn't get to do anything."

"I said, let's go!"

I closed my eyes and lay still, listening to the sound of heavy foot steps. A moment later I heard a loud, resonant POP that sounded like a balloon being pricked. There was another grating POP that rattled my cymbal. Then I saw Leon rear back and put his foot through my bass drum. The deadened THUMP reverberated through the room, and my cymbal crashed to the floor.

"Here ya go, hippie," Leon said. A drumstick landed against my arm. "That should do it."

Leon's heavy boots rattled dishes in the kitchen. Slowly his footsteps receded off the porch. I lay on the floor for a long time, praying I wouldn't hear returning steps. I felt the skin on my face stretching and starting to swell up. I thought of scars and being deformed and told myself, never again. If I'm okay, I thought, never again, so help me Eddie. Never again, God Damn it! NEVER!

24

She is kneeling there on a bed of clay, eyes fixed to the west. Beside her are the dying embers of a fire. The setting sun glows on her twisted face. She sings a chant as she thrusts a long shell back and forth against the rocks to sharpen its knife-edge. Suddenly her chant turns to a wail, and the wail turns harsh, silencing even the birds until there is no sound but the staccato bursts of her frenzied breathing. She lifts the razored shell skyward and pulls it down, deep between her ribs.

Now she is only dry bones—a mix of dust and salt. I touch her. She tastes like the Earth.

ঽ

Her scream woke me. "What happened?" Sara asked.

"Don't touch me," I said.

"Okay!" Sara said. "But I'll be right back, and then tell me."

A moment later she was wiping my mouth, pressing a cold cloth against my eye, and I tried explaining what had happened. "Not so hard," I said.

"You better see a doctor."

"It'll heal," I said. "Careful. That whole side there hurts."

She gave me two aspirin with the water. "These should help."
I heard the bathtub faucet creak on, followed by the sputter of
water. "What are you doing?" I asked.

"Running your bath."

"I'm not dirty."

"It will make you feel better," she said.

I stood up, but I was too sore to stand straight. Sara unbuttoned
my shirt and pulled it off.

"I'll get the pants," I said.

"It might be easier for me," she said.

"You want to wait outside?"

"This shyness is a different side of you," Sara said.

"I can do it myself." I unbuckled my belt. "Out!"

"I'll be right outside the door," Sara said.

It took me at least five minutes to unsnap the fly buttons, inch
my pants and shorts down over my hips, and finally free my feet.
I stepped gingerly into the tub, wincing at the pain in my ribs
and was just lowering myself down when the room exploded
with light. My arms went out, and I dropped into the tub with a
hard splash. "You and that damn camera!"

"I thought you were already sitting," Sara said. "Are you all right?"

"No thanks to you."

"It's going to be a great picture, Eddie. You have a cute butt."

Sara left, and I lay back in the tub. The hot water felt good,
but each painful breath reminded me of Margy and how stupid
I had been. The throbbing of my lip and forehead strengthened
my vow to never let this happen to me again. Never. When the
water finally turned cold, I climbed out of the tub and dried off.
I tried to dress but stopped with the first muscle spasm. I put on
my robe and opened the door. The bedroom smelled of bacon.
Sara was sitting on my mattress. The bed was straightened, and
Jack's pillows were stacked against the wall. There was a cookie
sheet on the bed, with a plate of eggs and bacon on it.

"Our breakfast date," Sara said.

I hobbled to the bed, eased myself to the mattress, and leaned against the pillows. "I'm not hungry," I said.

"Just eat what you can."

I rubbed my arm.

"Cold?"

"I'm fine."

Sara handed me the cookie sheet and unfolded the blanket at the foot of the bed.

"I don't need that."

She pulled the blanket up over me and tucked it in around my waist.

"Eat," she said.

"I can't look at it."

"It's my cooking, isn't it?" she said.

"No. My body."

"You're not just saying that to make me feel good?"

"Would this handsome face lie?"

Sara held a piece of bacon to my mouth. "Just a little," she said.

"I'm really not—" Sara slipped the bacon into my mouth. I tasted the salt and chewed slowly. My jaw muscles were sore. Touching my teeth to the bacon was painful.

"That's better," Sara said. She brushed back a strand of my hair and looked more closely at my eye. "I still think you should see a doctor."

"Doctors cost money."

"I'll pay for it," she said.

"No you won't."

She held a forkful of egg to my mouth. I chewed it slowly. She kissed my ear. Her breath was warm. She kissed me again, and I held my lips to hers. She broke the kiss and put her arm around my neck and kissed my cheek. Then she went to the window, pulled the shade, and unbuttoned her blouse. She popped the snap on her jeans, slipped out of her pants, and crawled under the blanket next to me.

"I can't, Sara."

"Just hold me, Eddie."

I pulled her to me as best I could. She reached under the blanket and opened my robe.

"I can't," I said. "Really."

"Just lie still."

"I don't want this," I said.

Sara did many things that morning. Some to me, but more for me. For a short while, I forgot about the soreness in my body, the emptiness inside, even Margy and her family. Then I slept. Sometimes when I woke, Sara was holding my arm, sometimes she was touching my face. Once, when it was totally dark, when I must have appeared asleep, she softly whispered the words I didn't want to hear.

25

Will this tape work?" Jack said.

"I hope so." I crisscrossed strapping tape over the tear until there was a solid sheet of it covering the drum head.

"What if it doesn't work?" Tony said.

"Then I'm out of goddamn luck."

"Couldn't you borrow some money from your old man?" said Jack.

I laughed and then grabbed my side. I took the head to the drum shell, and once the head was even, I slowly tightened the tension nuts. Jack and Tony watched from the couch. Then the cabin door opened, and Sara came in carrying two packages.

"You've still got the color of a turnip," she said, kneeling down to inspect my face. "Can I see you for a minute?"

"Not now," I said, gently tightening the tension lugs.

"I bet you could con old Morrie into some new heads," Jack said. "He's an easy touch. Take Mooch with you. He can tap anybody."

"Forget Mooch," Tony said. "He's depressed."

"Probably started believing his own doom shit," I said.

"Nope," Tony said. "It's Amy."

"Oh, God," Bumper said. "She isn't—?"

"Worse," Tony said. "Her face hasn't healed up."

"How do you know Mooch is depressed?" I said.

"I ran into him yesterday outside the shipyard. He was watching a truck being unloaded. He said it was worse than he thought. Then he told me not to breathe the air around this dead pigeon in the gutter."

"I'd worry if he was any different," Jack said.

I tightened the tension rods another half turn until I heard the first sound of tape peeling. I waited, and when nothing else moved, I continued tightening the head. I made another half twist, and with a POP, the head split wide open.

"I told you it wouldn't work," Sara said. "You can't repair things that work on tension."

"Is that right?"

"Once it's torn," she said, "it's gone. Even I know that, Eddie Carr."

"Even I know that, Eddie Carr," I said sarcastically.

Jack lit two cigarettes and handed me one. "Well," he said. "Now what?"

"I don't know."

"We could find Mooch," Tony said. "Pick his brain for an idea."

"There isn't enough time in the world," I said, "to find an idea in Mooch's head."

Sara stood up. She motioned me to the kitchen, and I followed her. "I want you to see what I have," she whispered.

"Only if it's something slinky."

"I think you'll like this."

She reached into one of the sacks and removed two thin, square boxes. As soon as I saw the boxes, I knew what they were.

"They're right, aren't they?"

"Perfect," I said. "But why?"

"Can't go to California with holes in your drums." Sara looked at me. "You're not happy?"

"Now I owe you something."

"Don't ever say that, Eddie. There's no debt on a gift."

"I don't know what to say."

"How about just 'thank you'."

"Thank you."

She smiled and kissed me. "You're welcome, Eddie Carr."

26

On the last Friday in September, local people celebrate the founding of Bremerton. The shipyard has an open house, and there are tours of the ships in port. In the morning at the Sportsman Restaurant, there is a fund raising breakfast followed by a parade in town. Both political parties have picnics at Lofall State Park with free hot dogs, beer, games and speeches about Bremerton's past and future.

Each year the city fathers honor one achievement. The first one, in 1939, was the dedication of the Manette Bridge which joined the two sides of town. In following years there was the dedication of the 11th Street cherry trees, the ground breaking of Governor's Park, the christening of the state ferry named for the nearby town of Enetai, and the opening of the city's first and only parking garage. The city lost money on the garage for years because no car longer than a Renault Dauphine could negotiate the spiral ramp.

This year the mayor closed Pacific Avenue between First and Second Streets for the dedication of an ambitious memorial. The Founder's Society paid to widen the sidewalk outside the main gate of the shipyard and transform the area into a concrete park. Two cement benches were placed alongside a brass drinking fountain against a backdrop of pine trees. The day the memorial arrived on a flat bed truck fitted with a large crane, so many people turned out to watch that tavern owners near the shipyard gate ran out of tap beer. Other nearby businesses had to close early and registered complaints with the mayor's office. They were simply told that memorials had top priority.

The memorial was a five-ton anchor provided by the Navy from a scrapped carrier. The stone pedestal was donated by Evergreen-Washburn Cemetery. The Masons contributed the stonework and the inscription, "The Pride of Bremerton".

≈

I had helped uncover the skeleton earlier that summer, and now I wanted to complete the job I had started. On Founder's Day, instead of partying with everybody else, I went up to the campus and tried to get in the anthropology lab, but the door was locked and the lights off. Through the window I saw that the lab was clean, that the tables and chairs were neatly stacked. The skeletal chart and the boxes of uncleaned bones were gone. I looked in the adjacent labs, but there was no sign of the Indian project. Then something occurred to me. I ran across campus to the offices of the humanities department and caught Dr. Ashburn at her desk.

"I was just at the lab," I said, "and the skeleton is gone."

"The project has been shelved," she said.

"By who?"

"The Board of Directors."

"Dean Scoggins, you mean!"

"He's one of the directors."

"I should've known he'd do this."

"You knew there would be an inquiry about the incident," she said.

"It was Scoggins," I said. "He'd do anything to get back at me."

"It was the board's decision."

"No!" I said. "It was Scoggins' decision. I know it, and you know it."

"I'm really sorry, Eddie. I thought you knew."

"Now what?" I said.

"The project is going to Washington State."

"Why?"

"The Board decided it would be safer in Pullman."

"Safer!"

"Dean Scoggins brought up your—how can I say this? Your instability."

"That's a crock."

"He said you threatened him with a trophy."

"I just wanted my tuition back."

"You destroyed school property."

"I told you I don't know what happened that night," I said.

"The board didn't feel the project was safe here."

"They're wrong, Dr. Ashburn. They're wrong!"

&

Late in the evening after the Founder's Day ceremonies, the police arrived at the new park outside the shipyard and found the words "Sez Who?" sprayed over the inscription "Pride of Bremerton". They found Mooch perched on the anchor's crossbar, his clothes in a heap at the base of statue along with an empty box of chocolate Ex-Lax. The *Sun* reported that Mooch held two patrolmen at bay for over twenty minutes with two cans of white spray paint. When Mooch surrendered he was arrested for public nudity and defacing public property. At the cabin we talked about trying to raise bail for Mooch, but none of us had any money. Mooch was arraigned the next morning, and I was allowed to see him for ten minutes. In the Visitor's Room he sat at a table behind a wire screen. He wore green overalls and looked tired, but he smiled.

"Hi, Eddie. Got a cigarette?"

I gave the guard a cigarette, and he handed it to Mooch.

"Why'd you do it, Mooch?"

"It was the righteous thing to do." Mooch leaned toward the wire partition. "I felt the end of it, Eddie."

"The end of what?"

"When I saw that giant anchor, I knew what was happening."

"It's only a statue."

"But what's an anchor for? They're weights, Eddie. They keep you from going anywhere. What the hell does Bremerton need with another anchor?"

"Decoration, Mooch. That's all."

"It's more than that, Eddie. Did you see what color it is? Not black or white, but gray."

"That's normal for the navy."

"The color of a burned out fire. Ashes, Eddie, ashes. It's true, Eddie. You've got time to think in jail, and I've been thinking a lot since last night. I've got a purpose now."

"What's that?"

He looked around and leaned toward me. "Director of Corrections," he whispered. For a moment I thought Mooch had really taken a turn. "Things that are wrong have to be fixed, Eddie, so that's what I'm going to do. I'm going to correct wrongness. You want to help me?"

"I don't know, Mooch."

"We'll always have something to do. You must know lots of things that are wrong."

"What did the judge say?"

"Five days in jail."

I told Mooch I would check on Amy while he was away, and he liked that.

27

For the next two weeks, the early days of fall held the sound in prolonged twilight. We fished at Chico Creek, talked for hours in Olberg's, played music upstairs at Sherman Clay, shot pool at the Y, and partied late into the morning. There was always time to stand outside Dook's listening to Motherbright sing until one in the morning and then go to the Blue House for "tea".

We had plenty of time and energy, and we usually found enough money somewhere. But there were days when the springs wound down and time suddenly felt like a loaded gun pointed at your head. Who was going to score the Spam for dinner? Who owed us money that we could collect? Jack even sold some of his fishing gear at less than a fair price as a last resort.

The Beast was not only my sole negotiable asset, but also my ticket to California. But eventually, I couldn't afford to keep it in gas, and with only one forward gear left, I used the old Buick sparingly. When the Beast finally died in the parking lot of West High School, a piece of my freedom passed with it.

I sold the Beast off for parts, but the fifty dollars went as fast as it came. We had overdue electricity and gas bills. Jack physically restrained the gas man from disconnecting us until I paid the bill. The Beast bought us warmth and light temporarily, but we were fresh out of assets. After the bills, all we had left were dreams.

After Danny moved in with Motherbright, he was different. His hair got longer, his beard fuller, and his shirts were never ironed. He still liked a good time, but the things he thought were fun had changed. Gone were the tennis lessons, skiing, and the parties. Instead, he talked of "trips", emotional colors, and plants.

He bought an old "woody" station wagon with the wood-panelled sides that looked brand new. I had to go with Danny to pick it up because he didn't have a driver's license and he didn't know how to use a stick shift. Danny loved that "woody" and in many ways it became his home away from home. For the first week he owned it, he made no attempt to drive it. He would just sit behind the wheel and pretend. We took it out on the road the first time after I accidently stumbled onto Danny sitting in the driver's seat, gripping the wheel, grinning and making engine noises.

"Been waiting for you," he said.

"You look pretty silly Danny."

"I've always wanted one of these. Get in," he said, and slid over. I got behind the wheel and closed the door. "It's nice they still come with a chauffeur. Let's check out Nirvana."

That was the first time I had heard of the place. I knew of Scandia, Olalla and Indianola up north, but not Nirvana. Danny stared straight ahead and pointed out the windshield. "Let's find it," Danny said, and we were off. It turned out to be one of our last sunny days together, and we saw a lot of pretty country that afternoon, but for all the trees and wildflowers and girls on bicycles, we never found Nirvana.

One day, I took Danny to the park and taught him to use a clutch. It cost him a headlight and a crease in the right front fender, but it didn't seem to bother Danny because he had a motive. All he talked about was driving to San Francisco. He had given up beer and started carrying a vile of Motherbright's "tea" wherever he went. You could always tell when he was doing "tea" because the world would become totally hilarious. One day in town an old lady fell right off the curb in front of us, and Danny laughed hysterically while helping her up. People were clearly shocked and stared at us. I told the lady—loud enough for everyone to hear—that Danny was retarded, and when we got her across the street, she gave Danny a quarter. Danny thought that was even funnier.

Jack too spent more time at Motherbright's, while I was staying away more—at Sara's. He told me that Margy was showing up more frequently at Motherbright's, and that she was different from when I knew her. An inscrutable look came into Jack's eyes when he spoke of Margy and Motherbright at the same time. He said how nice Margy was, how different she seemed, and I reminded him what Margy had pulled on me.

"That was the old Margy," Jack said.

"I just wouldn't trust her, Jack."

"Nobody's asking you to. I see who I want, and I do what I want."

"I think you're asking for trouble."

"You take care of your romance, and I'll take care of mine." I dropped the subject, and we spoke no more of it.

❧

Waiting on the future worked hard on me. No matter what I thought about or envisioned ahead, Sara was always there. No one had ever stayed with me that long before, and I felt she cared about me. It was easy to be with her and feel good. I thought about the other girls I had been with and what had become of us. The loss of the Indian bones made things even worse. I often thought about the skeleton and the Dravis legend, and the young man the Indian woman was said to have lost.

The talk of war was on radio and television, and fears of a draft were whispered on street corners, in the booths at Olberg's, and upstairs at Sherman Clay. There was talk of Canada if things got too crazy, which made the rumors easier to ignore. We sensed that times were changing. But that fall—for a moment—we were young and we had an answer for everything.

28

Danny woke Jack and me at 3:00 A.M. with the news from Motherbright. Bangor was hiring. By 4:30 the three of us were walking through the empty streets of downtown Bremerton to the employment office. Jack and I were desperate, and Danny needed money more than he was willing to admit. We hated the idea of working for the government, but the pay was good, and we agreed that when we had made enough to carry us for at least six months we would quit. It was that simple. And the simplicity of it all made the whole idea feel more like fun than actually getting a job.

Outside the brick building on Burwell Street, there were already a couple dozen men lined up at the dark office. The men looked anxious and cold—their heads bent down like they had all walked too long in the rain without umbrellas.

"We're saved!" Jack said.

"What did I tell you?" Danny said.

"We're really saved."

Danny looked inside the dark window and walked to the front entrance. I walked up next to him and cupped my hands against the glass. Everything was dark inside except for two green EXIT signs in the rear. Then I saw a chalkboard on the wall above the waiting area.

Monday 8:OOA.M.
Bangor—250 Laborers. Hazardous
All Shifts. $7.55 Per Hour.

Jack moved next to me and pressed his face to the glass. "We've hit the big one, Eddie. It's the goddamn mother lode!"

By seven o'clock, I couldn't see the end of the line. At 8:00 A.M. the doors opened, and by 9:30 Jack and Danny and I had jobs loading ammunition. The only thing we thought about was the time it was buying us and all the money we were going to make. The three of us had something in common to celebrate. We drank several warm beers that Danny found in a box and made big plans for our money, before Jack and Danny left for a "tea" hunt.

Sara and I finished the celebration in her lavender scented bed overlooking the bay. I was very awkward that night, and it bothered me that I hadn't improved very much.

"You're so silly sometimes," Sara said. "None of this is that serious. You make me feel very good, Eddie."

"Sure."

"I like feeling you near me and having you hold me. That feels good. I love you Eddie."

"That scares me," I said.

"Like with Margy?"

"I don't want it to," I said, "but I don't want anything to happen. I couldn't take hearing I was a father again."

"I could never trick you, Eddie. And I would never force you to do anything. I want you to be happy."

Sara looked so pretty. I felt very lucky to have her, and I wanted to make her feel good. But I was afraid to try again, and I couldn't think of anything to say.

"You don't have to say anything," she said.

"But I want to."

"Then just say what you feel."

"You look great in the dark," I said.

"In the dark?"

I nodded.

"You still know how to sweep a girl off her feet, Eddie Carr."

"It's true. You are pretty in the dark."

"And in the light?"

"You look fine in the light too, but you're very pretty in the dark."

She pulled me toward her, and the touch of her against me made me want her more than anything else in the world. When I woke up the next morning, I was alone in her bed, and the room was washed in the gray light of day. A note Sara had left on the bathroom mirror read, "I love the silliest guy in the world." We were to start work that night, and I wanted to spend as much time with Sara as I could because Bangor was on a straight work schedule with no days off until there were no ships to load.

That afternoon I met Sara for her lunch break at Dr. Brinker's office, and after work we went to a Richard Widmark western at the Roxy theater. Afterward we went to Olberg's Drugstore where we each had a hamburger and a float. We didn't want to leave, so we drank coffee and made plans until the coffee shop closed. I still had an hour before I had to leave for work, so we took a slow walk through town to the ferry dock. The tide was high, and there was a strong breeze. I put my arm around Sara.

"I like you happy like this," she said." What are you thinking?"

"Picking berries as a kid. Waiting for the bus, so early in the morning, it was dark like this."

"I never did that," she said.

"The best part was always the going, not the picking. You never knew where you'd end up. Puyallup, Kent Valley, Bainbridge Island. You just never knew where you were going, and that was exiting."

"I'm glad you're excited," Sara said.

"I guess money does that. How about you?"

"I'm happy, Eddie. As happy as I've ever been."

29

The Bangor Ammunition Depot was situated ten miles north of Bremerton on the eastern shore of Hood Canal. It was a vast and wooded reserve, bordered by farms north and south. There were no street lights along the highway, just the occasional tiny square of light from a house along the road. The drive out to Bangor—our first night of work—should have taken half an hour, but we missed the Bangor turnoff. Danny's "woody" had no heater, and cold air whistled through it. I told Danny his first paycheck had to go for basic repairs, or we would never live to see a second check. Danny grinned and sipped from his vial of "tea".

He looked like a demented old lady the way he sank down in his seat, grinning through the wheel. The only lift Danny had was in his head. Twice I had to jar him from staring down at the lighted speedometer. When I checked to see what he was staring at the second time, the speedometer needle was lying lifeless on zero, and the fuel gauge was fixed on empty. There was no temperature registering from the engine, and our oil pressure was nonexistent. The "woody" ran out of gas about five hundred feet from Gate Three. Danny aimed the car off onto the shoulder, and we rolled to a stop.

"Imagine that," Danny said, grinning into the glow of the dashboard.

"What the hell's wrong with you?" I said.

"You ever wondered where color comes from?" Danny said.

"What time is it?" Jack said. He turned my wrist to see my watch in the dark. "We've got five minutes."

"Didn't you put any gas in the car?"

Danny smiled. "Amazing. All this green light and we're not moving."

"Cars run on gas not light," I said.

"It's funny," Danny said, "how you forget some things you've known for a long time until you need to know them again."

I turned to Jack. "He can't go in there like this."

"He'll be all right," Jack said.

A steady flow of cars rolled past us and stopped at the lighted gate. I opened the door and grabbed my lunch. Danny was still gripping the steering wheel.

"Danny, you coming?"

"I think light comes from our heads," he said.

He was still staring through the steering wheel at the dashboard. I walked around and opened Danny's door. "Turn off the lights, you goon, and let's go."

Danny punched off the headlights. He let out a sad sigh when the dashboard went dark. "Oh, it's gone," Danny said.

I pulled Danny out of the car. "Don't say a word at the gate," I said, "or I'll tear out your lungs."

Jack gave the guard our names while I kept Danny behind me. The marine checked us off the list, handed us our badges, and directed us to the pickup area. Jack and I walked away, and Danny went over and started talking to the second marine guard.

"I'm serious," Danny was saying when we came back for him.

"What is it you're serious about, sir?"

"The green lights don't mean anything," Danny said. "They're just for looks. If you could just get the car inside the gate here, everything'll be great."

"Sorry sir. We can't leave the gate."

"It wouldn't take you guys that long. A couple of minutes at the most."

The other Marine came over.

"Sir?" the second Marine said.

Jack and I grabbed Danny.

"He's real possessive about his car," I said. "It'll be all right out there."

"No it won't," Danny said. "I saw guys looking at it from here. They're after it. Soon as I'm gone, they're going after it."

The two guards looked at us suspiciously.

"It's okay, sergeant. Forget it. He's just got this thing about his car."

Jack and I eased Danny away from the guard shack and walked down the road. "I told you to keep quiet," I said. "You trying to screw us up?"

"I just wanted my car off the road. You guys are too tense. It's such a wonderful night."

"Come on," I said. "Move!"

Danny grinned again. "Where are we going?"

The pickup point was a large open field. Men were loading into a long covered trailer, so we climbed inside the trailer nearest us. It smelled of sweat and grease, and the guys in plaid shirts and stained overalls reminded me of Yardies I had smelled in town. The metal trailer rattled so loudly—once it started moving—that no one talked. Jack and Danny were next to me in the open doorway, and I could barely make out their faces bouncing from the rough ride. The only light came from the faint spray of headlights that washed out into the trees along the road. The night air was crisp and fresh smelling from the salal and salmonberries and pine pitch. I stared out into the darkness, thinking about Sara at home alone in bed, telling myself that Bangor was not the end.

After about twenty minutes on the winding road, the smell of salt and creosote got very strong and suddenly like a huge curtain had been drawn open, a bright orange glow lit up the sky. Our trailer rounded a sharp curve and two large freighters were right in front of us. They were tied bow to stern to a long dock, dwarfing a string of boxcars beside them. Yellow forklifts darted around the dock, and tiny figures walked the decks of the two ships.

Our trailer finally stopped near a white clapboard building, and we unloaded. Ship cranes raised and lowered cargo, and everywhere there was movement in what looked like a ghostly kingdom where the bright orange light made the night seem like day.

"It's so damn—infernal," Danny said.

I kicked Danny's shoe. "If you don't shut up," I said, "I'm gonna rip your fuckin' tongue out."

A group of older men glared at Danny. I self-consciously pushed my hair behind my ears.

"It's like gold," Jack said.

"I bet Lucifer lives here," Danny said. "Just look at this place."

"I'm not looking at anything except you. Can it!"

When the last trailer arrived, we were all led into a huge lunchroom in the main building. About a dozen men wearing orange hard hats stood at one end of the room. The dock foreman, a man named Bledsoe, introduced the six crew chiefs and the dock supervisors. A large red-bearded man stood behind Bledsoe with his arms crossed over his chest. A strip of tape on the front of his hard hat read "Tank". He was flanked by several other men looking the room over. The red-bearded man looked familiar: the way his hard, narrow eyes seemed to dissect faces. I knew the face but could not name it. He was introduced as Tank Jacobson, head rigger.

The navy fire chief lectured us on the rules about lighters, matches, and smoking on or near the dock area. The only authorized area for smoking was inside the red line painted around the operations building complex. Then the chief got straight to the point.

"This is hazardous work," he said, "and the reasons are obvious. There is more ordnance on this reservation than we expended in Europe during World War II. One screw up out there and everyone within ten miles of here will be dust on windshields in Seattle."

Bledsoe went over the times for breaks and lunch and days off: two fifteen minutes smoke breaks, forty-five minutes for lunch, and a day off when we were out of work. Then he told us to step outside for crew assignments. One by one, names were read in alphabetical order, and men quickly moved to their assigned crew areas. I was the first of us to be called, and I was assigned to Crew Three. A man named Wade was my crew chief. He was short and stocky, and he looked tough. Jack and Danny got lucky. They were both assigned to Crew Five. I asked Wade if I could switch crews to be with Jack and Danny.

"You get two breaks and lunch," he said. "You wanna hold hands, do it then."

Tank Jacobson was the rigger for Crew Three. We waited by the ladder while Wade gave Tank his instructions. Wade explained how he wanted loads brought in, and all the while Tank kept looking at me. He looked as confused as I felt. When Wade finished, he climbed into the hatch. I followed him, keeping my eyes on Tank. He stared down at me, and I wondered where I knew that face. Suddenly the boot on my fingers brought my attention back on the ladder.

The sound of hammering and electric saws in the hold was deafening. Sound reverberated off the metal walls so that it seemed like there were two hundred men working instead of four. At the foot of the ladder, I waited for the rest of the crew. Suddenly there was a loud metallic crack next to me. I turned around and saw a large

U bolt, about the size of a fist, on the deck. I looked up, and Tank was leaning over his levers, grinning down at me.

"Slipped!" he yelled, and then laughed.

I turned to the others, but no one said a word. Wade walked over and picked up the bolt. "Well," Wade said, "you girls want a personal invite, or you want to start earning your pay?"

Wade put me to work with the carpenters. We framed the packing rails that our cargo of the day, seven thousand 500-pound bombs destined for Subic Bay in the Philippines, would be rolled onto. I stayed with the framers until the floor was completely laid and then joined the "rollers" loading the bombs onto the rails.

As a laborer I was two arms and a back. You might build shoring for two hours and then haul lumber for awhile, and later roll bombs or unhook pallets. There were enough different tasks that a good crew chief could keep his crew from complete exhaustion or monotony by working them around. That didn't ever change the exhaustion factor. It just insured that you would be sore in more places than one.

When the lunch whistle blew, I was too tired to climb out of the hold, so I stayed below. I also wanted to avoid Tank's strange sense of humor. I ate half my lunch, and then fell asleep on a bomb rail. The whine of the electric fork lift woke me, and when I opened my eyes and saw that thing on my chest, I thought I had woken up in a nightmare. The body was the size of softball, and it was hairy—like a porcupine. I screamed so loudly that I scared myself off the rail and onto the deck. The tarantula flew off me, and I pulled up my feet. The spider didn't move. Everybody—including Wade—was laughing, and I felt stupid and embarrassed. The spider had been found dead in the hold: a remnant of the ship's previous cargo of bananas from Panama. It happened all the time, I was told. Rats, spiders, even a snake once. That was the first and last time I ever slept in a hold.

The object, Wade had told us from the beginning, was to get the job done right, as fast as possible, with the fewest problems. Wade was a working crew chief, and when he wasn't supervising, he rolled bombs and hauled lumber. He promised two cases of beer to the crew that loaded the most ordnance by the final whistle. That night those of us who were new started losing steam at about the same time, around four in the morning. Our backs went first, and then our arms and legs. My team lost the beer that first night.

After the final whistle, I found Jack and Danny at the time clock. Danny had already made arrangements for a ride to a gas station. We waited in the bus area for the next cattle car to the parking lot. We were sitting and comparing aches when Tank Jacobson and two of his friends approached us. Tank's metal hard hat was pushed back on his head, and he was chewing tobacco. His tight, little eyes were fixed on me. He turned to Jack and Danny, giving them a long, threatening stare. Then he turned back to me. I turned and looked away.

"Don't turn your back on me, faggot. I'm talking to you."

"Me?"

"You!"

"You didn't say anything."

"Then you ain't listening," Tank's friend said.

His other friend said, "When Tank looks, you listen."

Jack looked at me. "Let's go." We started to walk away, but Tank grabbed me by the arm.

"You walk when I say walk, not before."

"Hey," Danny said. "It's a free country."

"This here is Tank's country," Tank's friend said.

Tank turned from Danny back to me. "I know you from somewhere, and I don't like you."

"Don't know you from anywhere," I said.

"It was somewhere. A bar—"

"Not me. I'm not even twenty-one."

"It was somewhere," Tank said. "And I know I didn't like you."

"He's got some hair, don't he Tank?"

"You know my old lady?" Tank said.

"I don't even know you," I said

"You got something to do with my old lady. I ain't sure what, but I remember you from someplace. I never forget a face I don't like."

I also recognized Tank from somewhere, but couldn't place him. Tank removed his hard hat, keeping his eyes on me. When I saw him full face, I placed him. I looked at Danny who was standing sideways behind Jack, facing away from Tank, and I knew I was right. Tank knew me from the morning he had caught Danny in bed with his wife. I was the one he had really seen when I steered him away from Danny.

"Really," I said. "You've got the wrong guy." I looked over at Danny again, and his eyes were searching mine for what he feared I might say. "I've never seen you before tonight," I said. "A lot of guys look like me."

"Then we're in big trouble," Tank's friend said, laughing. "Sissies popping up like weeds. Come on, Tank. Let's get a few beers."

Tank aimed his finger at me. "You done something to me, and I can feel it. I don't forget nothin'. You just remember that, 'cause I'm gonna stay on you like ugly on an ape."

Tank's buddy eventually pulled him away to the waiting bus, and I breathed easier when they got on, and the bus pulled away.

"What the hell was that about?" Jack said.

"Ask Danny."

"Hey," Danny said, "what the hell do I know about gorillas."

"You know about this one," I said. I recounted his early morning sprint down Washington Boulevard and his leap into the hedge above the beach.

"I remember someone saying that married women have something special." I looked right at Danny as I spoke, but he remained silent. "Remember what that something special was, Danny?"

"Him?" Danny said.

"All two hundred and fifty pounds."

"Just goes to show you how times change."

"Not for him," I said. "Why didn't you say something?"

"Like what? 'Hey, Mr. Kong, I'm the guy you want to grind up'."

"Like anything to get me off the goddamn hook."

"Come on, you guys," Jack said. "We're all buds. The guy's just a goon. Nothing to get tore up about."

Danny refused to look at me. His eyes were soft and droopy. He looked very tired. Finally the silence was more than Danny could handle. "So what are you going to do?" he said.

For the first time since I had known him, I heard genuine concern. I slowly shook my head, my eyes still fixed on his. "I don't know," I said.

"You going to tell him?" Danny said.

"What do you think I am?" I said. "How in the hell do I know what I'm going to do."

The third bus roared down the hill in low gear, backfiring behind the wall of trees. Then it rattled over the railroad tracks and stopped behind us. Jack stepped between Danny and me.

"This guy's a jerk," Jack said. "There's always one that's got to shove the new guys around. If we just avoid him for awhile, he'll forget all about you and find somebody else."

"You think so?" I said.

"Sure. They always do."

"All right," Danny said. "Next time a husband wants to know, I'll do the talking. Okay? Whataya say, Eddie? A deal?"

"Next time there's a husband," I said, "don't run in my direction."

The bus driver blasted his horn. We climbed into the steel box, and a moment later the bus pulled away. All the way home I imagined Tank stalking me in an empty hold of a ship surrounded by Yardies giving me thumbs down. I had to do something—short of quitting—to protect myself. It was clear that the friendship I had assumed existed between Danny and me was just a phantom. And I didn't like the way that made me feel.

30

Bangor changed everything about us. For the next two weeks, all we thought about was sleep and payday. Every morning, over coffee and eggs at the Pancake House, we figured out on a napkin how much money we would earn—everything seemed possible when you had lots of money. Jack talked about buying a boat, and Danny dreamed of going to Mexico and lying for weeks in the hot sun. I thought about a new set of drums and a car that went both forward and backward.

I saw Sara a total of 4½ hours that first week. I kept telling myself Bangor was buying me time, even though I managed only a few minutes a day to think about California before falling off to sleep.

But by the end of the second week, we were adjusting. Jack started to fish again and to sleep at the Blue House, while I was sleeping over more at Sara's. When I came home in the morning, she was usually getting ready for work but would always start a hot bath for me. Since I had known her, Sara had not lost any of her shyness and would always dress behind the bedroom door. I never understood that. She was so pretty and her body so beautiful; it was a shame for her to hide. Then one morning that too changed.

I was in the tub. The bathroom door opened and Sara walked in with nothing on. She climbed into the tub and lay next to me. She was soft and slippery in the water, but I found enough energy that morning to love her. After that morning, her shyness passed. Where the tide wash on the beach had once been my time keeper, now Sara woke me at six. She lay next to me on the blankets and made me want her. I got better at making love, and we laughed when we were too serious about it. She cried, she said, because she was happy for the first time. It had felt good before but never so good that she wanted to cry. I didn't understand that because she always made me feel good, but I didn't say anything. It seemed important to her to cry, and I loved her very much.

ðª

At work many ships came and went, and the ordnance varied depending on the destination. One night we loaded bombs for Thailand, and three days later it was artillery shells and grenades for Da Nang, Vietnam. Crew-size changed about as quickly as the ships we loaded. A bull driver drove his forklift off the dock and caught pneumonia. Another man fell from a ladder and broke his back. My crew lost three men in the first two weeks. One man's hand was crushed under a bomb, the other two quit because the work was too hard. And crews moved from job to job depending on where the work was, whether it be in the hold of a ship or outside in the boxcars. In the holds you were out of the weather, but on the docks, when the temperature dropped to freezing and below and the wind blew in off Hood Canal, you were working against the ordnance and the cold. There was nowhere to hide on the dock, and Tank Jacobson was always watching me from his roost. When there was a train delay, we had to stand by and wait outside for the work to arrive. The wind and the rain and the chill were always there and so was Tank Jacobson.

ðª

"The team is how you last out here," Wade told us. We had fallen below his standards of production, and he didn't like losing his position of prestige. "No one does it alone," he said. "Teamwork is how the job gets done."

It didn't take long before you forgot that you were working with explosives and what mattered were numbers; they were our mark of existence. The number of boxcars unloaded, the number of pallets shipped, the number of crates stacked. Tonnage was everything and everything depended on the work of the whole, because it's what you are when you're part of a team.

Every crew posted its tonnage at the end of each shift and that's all you knew about the crews. You knew how good a team was by its tonnage, and Wade had a long-standing reputation for having number one crews.

The men who lasted were hard men. Men who worked hard, talked hard, and played hard. There was nothing familiar about these men. If you were new, you were a body and a name. A last name. You got close when it came to the work because you depended on each other but never so close that you could say you honestly knew someone. You really only knew the people you were lucky enough to know before you came to Bangor.

The night before our first payday my crew was working down inside a ship. It was pouring rain, and instead of going topside during break for a smoke, I stayed in the hold with most of the crew. Swartz, who was sitting on the forklift with Tanner and Mickleson, withdrew a pouch and passed it to the others. They took something from the pouch and started chewing it. Mickleson saw me watching, and the three of them came over to me.

"Have some, Carr?" Mickleson said.

"What is it?"

"Beachnut. Chewing tobacco."

"Never tried it," I said.

"It's easy," Swartz said. "Just put a handful in your mouth and chew it. Gives you a hit like a cigarette."

I looked at the brown leaves in the pouch, and they didn't look appetizing.

"All the *men* down here chew it," Mickleson said. "You are one of us, aren't you?"

Mickleson stuck the pouch in front of me. "Go ahead," Swartz said. "Try some."

I picked out a few leaves. "How big a man are you?" Mickleson said.

I took a fistful of leaves and stuck them in my mouth.

"Now just chew," Swartz said.

The leaves were moist and bitter, and I was afraid of getting them back in my throat, so I chewed them in front of my mouth. My mouth quickly filled with saliva, turning the leaves to a thick mushy pulp. In a few minutes, my mouth was full of bitter pulp.

"Now what?" I gurgled.

"You swallow it," Tanner said. "What else?"

"Swallow?" I said.

"Just like all the *men* do."

"Swallow?" I said.

"Swallow," Swartz said.

I gulped down the bitter pulp, and immediately my throat started to burn. Within seconds my stomach cramped up, and I doubled over. I felt lightheaded and started sweating. I tried to straighten up, and my stomach wrenched.

"You don't look so good," Swartz said.

"Maybe that was too much," Tanner said.

I hobbled to the far corner of the hold, dropped to my knees, and threw up. Every time I tried swallowing, the taste of bitter tobacco brought back the dry heaves. Tanner and Swartz came over to me.

"Sorry, Carr."

"It was just for fun."

"Yeah. You all right?"

The break whistle blew, but I couldn't move from the corner. I heard Wade asking Swartz and Tanner what had happened.

"He just got sick, chief," Swartz said.

"One minute he was fine," Tanner said, "then he was over here puking."

Wade squatted down next to me. "Are you all right, Carr?" I nodded and spit out more tobacco juice. I sat back against the wall and took deep breaths.

"What happened?" Wade said. He looked hard at Tanner and Swartz. "Somebody tell me what the hell happened." Neither said anything. "Well," Wade said, "do I call the medics down here?"

"Bad food," I said. "I feel better now."

"You sure?" Wade said.

"I'll be okay."

Wade slapped my back and stood up. He stared at Tanner and Swartz. "I'm glad this wasn't one of your tricks."

"Yes, sir," Swartz said.

Wade looked at Mickleson who sat on his forklift. It was still raining hard.

"Swartz," Wade said, "I want you to work the rigging." The rain poured down in sheets through the open hatch.

"But chief, I don't have rain gear."

Wade smiled and clapped Tanner on the shoulder. "When you're water-logged," Wade said, "Tanner here will spell you. Now let's get to work. I want our tonnage up tonight."

After work that night, Tanner and Swartz thanked me for not telling Wade what had really happened. I hated them for what they had done, but as it turned out later, it was good I had kept my mouth shut.

ஃ

Our first payday we drove to the Sportsman Restaurant after work for the Huntsman Special—four eggs and a 16-ounce T-bone steak that covered the plate. My seven hundred dollar check was more money than I had ever seen at one time in my whole life. Jack said he could never sleep with that much money in his pocket, so we woke up Joe The Squid and spent the morning drinking Jack Daniels mixed with Hires Root Beer. Joe never forgave us for what we did to his rug. We stayed up all day spending money like sailors on leave. Jack and I paid our November rent which was a week overdue. Frog sniffed the fifty dollar bill. "This better be good," he said.

"It is," Jack said. "We have jobs."

"I'm calling the FBI and having it checked."

Morrie down at Sherman Clay gladly took my money, no questions asked. I paid cash for a new cymbal, and he was so happy that he threw in two pairs of drumsticks—no charge. I'm sure he wanted me to think of him as a nice guy, but not make it too obvious.

I spent over four hundred dollars that afternoon on bills, rent and new records. I also took Sara to the Olympic Broiler that night for dinner. She got all dressed up, and I felt like a rich man spending money on everything I wanted.

The night after payday things changed for me at Bangor. I was working the boxcars, waiting for a late train to arrive with another load of bombs for Thailand. I was tired and cold, so I walked over to the main latrine to get out of the cold and have a smoke. I turned on one of the hand dryers and warmed up my hands. It was still cold so I turned on all the dryers. I went into a stall and sat down with a newspaper. It felt good to sit down and be warm. One by one the dryers shut off, but the room remained warm and quiet. A few moments later a blast of cold air blew in under my stall, and I heard voices. When I stepped from the stall, Tank Jacobson and his two friends were staring at me. One guy stood at the door, the other in the middle of the room behind Tank.

"Look what we got here," Tank said. He spread his feet and crossed his arms over his chest.

"Looks like somebody's confused. This ain't the ladies room."

"You lost, lady?" Tank said.

I didn't say anything.

"Maybe the cat's got her tongue," the guy at the door said. "Can't you talk, lady?"

"I've got to get back to my crew," I said.

"There's no hurry," Tank said. "I finally connected your face. It *was* my old lady." Tank walked around the large round wash basin in the center of the room. As he moved one way, I moved the other. His friends, however, cut me off. "Nowhere to run, lady. You did all your running the last time I saw you. It's time to face the music."

I looked for a way out, but there was only the one door. I backed up until I bumped into the toilet partition. I went into the stall and latched the door. Tank threw his body against the door, and I bounced back. He rammed the door again, and this time I flew back against the toilet. I propped myself against the door, but Tank reached over the stall and grabbed my arm. He banged the door open and knocked me into the toilet. I crossed my arms over my face and took a hit to the side of my head. Tank pried at my arms for a clean shot. I heard the front door open, and suddenly Tank's grip slackened. There were loud voices and through my arms I saw Tanner, Swartz, and Wade walking toward me. Mickleson stood by the door. Tank let loose of me and stepped out of the stall.

"Out of my way," Wade said. Tank was taller and bigger than Wade. "I said, out of my way!"

Tank stepped aside.

"Come on out, Carr," Wade said. I stood up and stepped out. "Don't look like he got to you," Wade said. "You still got your pants on."

"This is no business of yours, Wade. This is between me and the lady there."

"If you've got to have some," Wade said, "try a real woman. It might only take two of you."

I saw Tank tighten his fists. Wade pulled me away, and we walked for the door. "I told you before," Wade said, loud enough for Tank to hear, "never go to the head alone and never bend over for the soap. It drives 'em crazy."

"This ain't the end of this!" Tank yelled. "He can't hide forever, and you can't be everywhere. You hear me?"

The five of us walked out of the latrine and onto the dock. When I looked back, Tank and his two friends were standing outside the latrine watching us.

"Thanks for showing up," I said.

"This isn't the first time," Mickleson said.

Swartz glanced back over his shoulder. "First time in awhile, though."

Wade looked straight ahead as we walked. "I don't know what Tank's rub is with you. That's your business. If he's after you, he'll find you. We can't always be around."

"What should I do?" I said.

"Avoid him," Wade said.

"I tried that."

"Take him on, then."

"He's three times my size."

"You could always quit," Swartz said.

"I need the money," I said.

"Then you better keep your eyes open," Mickleson said. Something hard slapped against my arm as we walked. Tanner stuck the crowbar against my stomach. "Take this," he said. "Keep it with you."

I took the crowbar and looked over at Wade. "Tank is a big boy," he said. "It might even out the odds."

I waved the crowbar several times to feel its weight and slipped it inside my belt. Just short of our boxcar, I stopped and turned to the four of them.

"Why'd you do it?" I asked.

Wade turned to Swartz, who turned to Tanner and Mickleson. Wade scuffed his boot, and the others looked away. The dock was quiet except for a forklift moving up the wharf. A train whistle blew off in the distance, and everyone looked up the tracks. Wade laughed.

"Tonnage, Carr. We've got tonnage to move."

31

I gave no thought to the work I was doing at Bangor until the night the *Caspan Trader* arrived. The *Trader* was a rusty scow in need of paint, and she was just returning from Southeast Asia where—we heard—she and her crew ran into some shooting. The stories of guerrilla attacks, rockets, guys dead, and mutiny spread all over the docks before she even tied up. I couldn't believe she was going right back, but her new manifest called for small arms ammunition and artillery shells. For four nights, all operations focused on getting the *Trader* loaded, and by early the fourth night the holds were being secured and hatched.

On the *Trader's* last night, I was assigned to load stores and the personal items of the crew. It was then that I learned the rumors about the *Trader's* three dead crewmen were more than idle talk. We loaded cases of liquor, frozen meat, canned goods, cigarettes and several crates of movies. I had never seen so much food, liquor and tobacco for so few people in my whole life, and when I smelled the food cooking in her galley, going to sea seemed very exciting.

The crew arrived just before ten as we were loading the last of the stores. None of us wanted to go back to the boxcars for the rest of the shift, so we agreed to get lost on board. Three guys slipped into the galley and drank coffee, and I wandered back to the fantail. I was standing at the railing, trying to find something to do when a taxi pulled up on the dock, and a man in blue dungarees got out. He unloaded several bags and two suitcases from the cab. I ran back forward, down the gangway and offered to help get his things aboard ship. His plastic tag read, "Kemp."

"You the captain?" I asked.

"Oiler," he said.

I grabbed his suitcases and followed him aboard ship. We went down the main passageway and up a narrow ladder into a cabin. I set his bags near a gray, metal desk. The cabin was smaller than Gimp's room at the hotel.

"The *Trader* looks like she's been around."

"She gets the job done."

"Anything else I can help you with?" I asked.

"That's everything." He handed me five dollars.

"Thanks. You sure there's nothing else? If I stand around out there, they'll just send me back to the boxcars."

He laughed and said a quick tour of the wheelhouse was the best he could offer. We went to the galley for two cups of coffee and then up forward. The bridge was huge compared to the cabins and dimly lit. I turned the large wheel and examined the gauges.

"Heard you guys saw some action," I said.

"You did?"

"Was it really a mutiny?"

"Where'd you hear that?"

"On the dock."

Kemp laughed again. This time he wasn't smiling. He told me they were off-loading in Saigon at night when the guerillas attacked.

"They came over the side," he said. "Six or seven of them. Next thing we knew there was gunfire and explosions. And our holds were still half full."

"What did you do?"

"We shot back."

"Did you get any?"

"I saw at least two from up here," he said.

"Right here?" I said.

He pointed to the corner of the wheelhouse. "That's where I was."

I walked up to the plate glass window and looked down on the bow deck. "Right out there?"

"I'm glad they build this gal thick." He pointed at the sill. Four round bulges protruded inward as though the metal had been sculpted. The gray paint was cracked, and a sharp sliver pricked my finger.

"That must've been something," I said.

"Yeah something. We lost three good men."

Kemp escorted me out of the wheelhouse to the gangway. He thanked me for carrying his things aboard, and I thanked him for the tour.

"How old are you?" he asked.

"Nineteen."

"My boy would've been twenty next month. Lost him six months ago at Da Nang. It's not how it sounds over there."

"I don't know anything about it. I just have a friend over there."

"Believe me, it's bigger than one friend. Everyone's friend is going to hell."

The *Trader* sailed shortly after seven that morning, and with it went our work load. All shifts were given Saturday off—our first in thirty-one days.

᪣

When I got home that morning I found a note from Sara saying she wasn't feeling well and was going to the doctor. I left her a note saying I had the night off, and then headed down to the cabin. The tide was up, and the sound was smooth as glass.

Jack had heard that big steelhead were being caught near the mouth of Chico Creek, and he was feeling very lucky. After he left, I lay on the couch and listened to the waves lap beneath the cabin. I couldn't have been asleep long when my father, knocking at the door, woke me. He said he had things to do in town and gave me a stack of mail. "Your mother wants to know about Thanksgiving," he said.

"I don't know," I said. "When is it?"

"Next Thursday. She'd like you and your girlfriend out for dinner."

"I couldn't be there before three," I said.

"You'll bring what's-her-name?"

"If Sara wants to come."

My father looked very tired. He stuck his hands deep into his pockets and walked away. I felt bad that we weren't happier with each other.

I sorted the mail. There was a letter from Scooter Hayes, the return address was an army hospital in Hawaii. I started to open it when I saw two letters from the U.S. Government. I tore open the first letter from the Selective Service. They had changed my status from 4-F to 1-A. The second letter, postmarked a week later, was my draft notice. My reporting date to the Army Transfer Station in Seattle was December 17th. I looked at the envelope again. The name was mine all right. I reread the letter, and the words did not change. I couldn't believe it. I was stunned. I wanted it to be yesterday. But the letter was real. The government was real. The words on the paper were real. And none of it would go away, no matter how hard I wished it.

I got dressed and went up to Sara's. She had just gotten home and still didn't feel well. My news about the draft made her sick to her stomach. When I saw Danny, he suggested I send the letter back with the word "Deceased" written on the front. Mooch's idea of changing my identity wasn't much better, and neither was Jack's about getting married. Jack also mentioned Canada.

"If things get bad enough," Jack said, "they might come after all of us. Flat feet and all."

"I don't know," Danny said. "Canada's kind of serious."

"So is getting killed," I said.

"But moving to Canada?"

"What are you going to do, Danny, when the army wants you?" I said.

"I haven't thought about it," he said.

"You better. You want to kill people or get shot?"

Danny shrugged his shoulders. "Maybe it's all going to blow over."

"How long's Scooter been gone?" Jack said.

"Five months," I said. "So it's not getting better."

"I say we go to Canada," Jack said.

"I'm game," Mooch said.

"Danny?" I said. "How about you?"

"Okay," he said. "Unless we come up with something better."

"Better?" I said. "What the hell could be better?"

32

In all the years I had lived on Olive Street, the only type of sickness I had paid any attention to was the cold, the flu, the mumps or measles we caught as kids and got over. I had never thought about the sickness that was around us and never passed. But driving up the street with Sara on Thanksgiving Day, I realized it was rampant in the neighborhood. Many of the people had always had sickness.

"That's a pretty house," Sara said. "The little well is cute."

The Turner house, I told her. Two of my best friends had lived there. Their mother was a deaf mute. Everyone on the street knew when Mr. Turner was drunk because you heard screams inside the house and later saw bruises on my friends.

The pink and white house two doors up was where Ted had lived. He had had polio, and we were good friends in grade school, but his parents never seemed happy. Then one day his parents went grocery shopping and never came back. Ted stayed with us for a week until an aunt came and took him to Oregon. A "For Sale" sign was in the front yard a couple months later, but the house stayed vacant for almost two years. I never saw Ted again or ever heard what became of him.

Karla, who lived a few houses down from us, had also had polio, but none of us ever thought anything of it. She wore metal braces on her legs and walked with metal canes. Every summer for five years she had operations on her knees, and at the beginning of every school year, she had new scars. Karla was a strong girl, and she made jokes about her legs, and none of us ever felt bad around her. Her mother, though, never accepted Karla's disease and always reminded us what her daughter couldn't do. I remember thinking Karla's mother should have had the polio. She was already beaten by it.

I parked the "Beast" in my father's driveway and pointed out the rest of the neighborhood to Sara. The brown house at the head of the street was where the Johanson's lived. I told Sara about the three brothers I had seen beaten by their stepfather. He was a big man, an ex-marine, and a county sheriff. The youngest of the brothers had been disrespectful to their mother in the presence of the other two brothers. So their stepfather beat them, one by one, in the front yard for everyone in the neighborhood to see.

"Those are awful things to remember," Sara said.

"They're true."

"I don't want to hear anymore."

"You're not going to be sick again?"

"I'm fine. Do I look okay?" Sara said.

"You look fine."

"Is there something else?" she said.

"No."

"Shouldn't we go in, then? Everybody knows we're here."

"I don't feel like I belong here, anymore."

"Of course you belong here," Sara said.

We sat quietly in the car for a moment.

"Are you going to tell them?" Sara said.

"Maybe it won't even come up today."

"You'll have to tell them sometime."

The kitchen smelled of hot turkey.

"Oh Eddie," my grandmother said. "That hair!"

"This is Sara, Nana."

"Hello, dear. Nice to meet you. Couldn't you get him to cut his hair?"

"I trimmed it myself," Sara said, politely. "Just for the holiday."

My brother Cliff came into the kitchen. "Hi Eddie," he said. "Guess what? I'm learning drums in band at school."

"Great," I said, and patted a drum roll on his head. I introduced Cliff to Sara.

"Heard a lot about you," she said. "You're even cuter than your brother."

Cliff got embarrassed and blushed.

"I got some new records, Eddie. You wanna come in and hear 'em?"

"Maybe later," I said. "So what else is new?"

Cliff shrugged his shoulders and stepped aside when my father came up behind him.

"Well, you finally made it," my father said.

"Dad, this is Sara."

"Couldn't you talk this guy into getting a haircut?"

"I like it that way," she said.

"Where's Mom?" I asked.

"She'll be right out." He walked Sara to the living room. "Here, sit down Sara. You want a drink?" I pulled two beers from the refrigerator. My grandfather stood in front of his chair. He didn't look as tall as he once did.

"How are you, Papa?"

"Fine, Eddie. Just fine. Heard you got a big money job."

"Pretty big," I said.

"You saving any of it?" my father said.

"Been catching up mostly. Own my drums now."

"You and them drums."

My mother wheeled into the living room. She wore a pink sweater and a string of pearls. Immediately she started to cry. I hugged her. Sara gave my mother a hug too. That made her cry more. We all laughed. Mom always cried when she was happy.

My grandmother asked, "What is it that your father does, Sara?"

"He's a doctor," Sara said.

"Oh, that's wonderful."

"Say, kiddo," my mother said, "tell me, what kind of doctor is he?"

"Now Margaret," Nana said.

"That's okay. He's a pediatrician."

"A baby doctor," I said.

"Yes, Eddie," Nana said, "we know what a pediatrician is. That's a good specialty. Can't have a baby without a doctor these days. I bet your father does very well."

"He's happy."

"I'm sure he makes good money," Nana said, "and buys the best of everything."

"He collects books," Sara said. "Some are quite rare."

"Yes and I'm sure your mother dresses very well, too."

"She always looks nice. Like you and Mrs. Carr."

"These old things!" Nana laughed. "I haven't bought a new dress in—how long's it been, Papa?"

Papa straightened up. "Hell, I don't keep track of new dresses," he said.

"And everybody notices, too," Nana said.

Water boiled over on the stove and hissed on the hot burner.

"I'm sure your mother doesn't have to run after boiling water, though."

Sara said, "Mother does all the cooking."

"But it has to be nice," Nana said, running back to the kitchen, "knowing she doesn't have to."

My father sat forward in his big chair. "Any of those people arrested friends of yours?"

"What people?"

"Those communists or whatever they were at the college."

"Don't know anything about it," I said.

"We got a few of them in Seattle," Papa said. He scooted his chair closer. "Troublemakers. Kids with nothing better to do than protest and cause trouble."

"If you're smart," my father said, "you'll stay away from that crowd. They're in for trouble."

Papa lit a Chesterfield and offered me one. I declined and lit one of my own.

"I wish you would talk about something pleasant," my mother said. "That's all you talk about. Depressing things." My mother turned to Sara. "Say, kiddo, what do you do for Dr. Brinker?"

My father turned to me. "Sounds like they got some real trouble over in that Vietnam."

I glanced over at Sara. "A friend of mine, Scooter Hayes, is over there."

"From the TV, it looks like things are heating up."

Nana said, "You won't be going, will you, Eddie?"

"Not if I can help it," I said.

"They're calling up a lot of boys," Papa said. "Heard something last night where they're talking about calling up the Reserves and the National Guard."

My mother broke off from Sara. "You're not in any of that, are you, Eddie?"

"No, Mom."

"I don't understand why we have to send our boys over there," Nana said.

"They shot at one of our ships," my father said.

"It's the communists," Papa said. "They're after everything. We can't just let them take what they want. Somebody's got to stop them."

"That turkey sure is smelling good," Sara said. "Can I help with anything?"

"No," Nana said. "We're just waiting on the gravy."

"Everything's done?" my father said. He took his cue, and went out to the kitchen and started the gravy.

"So you don't think you'll be going?" Papa said.

"I don't think so," I said. "What was war like for you?"

"For me?" Papa looked embarrassed.

"Weren't you in World War I?"

"It was during my time."

"You must've done some fighting."

"When there's a war," he said, calmly, "you do what you can."

"Tell him the truth, Papa," Nana said.

"I am."

"Eddie, your grandfather missed them all. He never even saw a rifle, thank God."

"How'd you do that?" I said.

"I was too young for the first war," he said, "and exempt from the second."

"Exempt?" I said.

He extended the stump of his right index finger. "Lost this in the meatpacking plant."

"And that kept you out?" I said.

"Can't fire a rifle without one," he said.

"Uncle Sam felt he was needed more making sausage," Nana said.

"I bet you were glad." Papa smiled and cocked his head. "So you never had to worry about any of this?" I said.

"I wanted to go, but they wouldn't take me."

"But he knows all about the fighting though," Nana said. "The only books he buys are war books. Big picture books with maps and the most awful photographs."

"Reading's good for you," Papa said.

"Dinner's ready," my father yelled.

Sara and I went into the dining room, where Papa cut the turkey in the center of the table. My brother Cliff sat next to me.

"There's no room over there," my father said to him.

"Sure there is," Cliff said.

"Move your chair around," my father said.

"He's fine," I said. I pulled Cliff's chair closer.

The turkey steamed on the table. Papa carved with all the expertise that comes with thirty years working for a meatpacking company. The slices of white meat fell off the carcass in perfectly whole planks, and the house smelled spicy from the hot gravy and the browned turkey skin. The subject of Christmas came up. It would be the first Christmas I would miss at home. The longer the talk of Christmas continued, the less I felt like eating.

"Something wrong with the turkey?" my father asked.

"Everything's fine," I said.

"You sure?" Nana said. "You're not eating very much."

"Just taking my time," I said.

"He's been learning to eat slower," Sara said.

"Sure it's not love?" my father said. Sara got embarrassed. "I thought it might be something like that."

"Dad."

"I can spot love on a girl's face."

Cliff was staring up at me. "You're really not in love, are you, Eddie?"

"Don't talk with your mouth full," I said.

Cliff swallowed what was in his mouth with a loud "glump".

"You aren't, are you Eddie?" he asked again.

"Now see what you started, Dad?"

"I only asked a question." He laughed. "And you answered."

"You're embarrassing me, Mr. Carr," Sara finally said.

"Maybe you can straighten him out," my father said. "I certainly haven't had any luck."

"None of us have," I said.

"The way I see it," my father said, "everybody gets what they deserve."

"Does that include Mom?" I said.

"Eddie!" Nana said.

"Well?"

"What happened to Margaret was an accident," Nana said. "Nobody deserves to be paralyzed—ever. Now, Frank, I want you to never say she deserved that ever again."

"I didn't mean her," he said.

"You said everybody," I said.

Sara stopped eating. "Eddie's been working very hard, Mr. Carr."

"Must we argue?" my mother said. "This is Thanksgiving, you know."

"Who's arguing?" my father said. "We're discussing."

"This is not a discussion, Frank. It's an argument," Nana said. "What's Sara going to think about us?"

"This is such a beautiful dinner," Sara said, thumping my leg under the table. "We should be enjoying each other's company."

"I thought we were," my father said.

"Well, we're not," my mother said. "So stop it."

I excused myself from the table and went to the back bedroom. I closed the door, but I could still hear their voices. The room was a tiny box that had been mine up until that spring. I sat down on the bed that also had been mine and looked at the pictures of the Beatles that Cliff had put on the wall. Cliff had my old snare drum set up in the corner of the room, and I ran the back of my hand over the new clean white head. The bedroom door cracked open, and Sara looked in.

"What are you doing back here?" she said.

"Getting away."

"It's Thanksgiving, Eddie."

"Nothing's changed. It's the same old crap. I knew it would be like this."

Sara closed the door and sat down on the bed next to me.
"Eddie I think there's something—"

"I'm going to show him," I said. "I'm going to make it, and
nothing is going to get in my way."

"I know you'll do well."

"You're still with me, aren't you?"

"If you mean Canada, I'll do what's best for us."

"I couldn't do it without you," I said. "Not now I couldn't."
Sara looked at me, started to say something, and then smiled.
"What?" I said.

"It's nothing."

"You were going to say something."

"It wasn't important. Come on. Let's get back to dinner." I went into
the bathroom, flushed the toilet, and went back to the dinner table.

"You've hardly eaten your dinner," Nana said. "Is something
wrong with my cooking?"

"Everything's fine," I said. "I've been drafted."

"Oh no, Eddie," my mother said, and she started to cry. My
father and Papa remained silent.

"You going to the war?" Cliff said.

"You don't think you'll have to go?" my mother said. "Do you,
Eddie?"

"Course not," Nana said. "Now all of you stop scaring her with
all this talk of killing and dying. My god, this is Thanksgiving."

Cliff pulled on my shirt sleeve. "Huh, Eddie? You going to
fight in a war?"

"Eat your pie," I said.

"Will you bring me a helmet, Eddie, and a Japanese sword?"

"Did you hear your brother," my mother said. "Eat your damn
pie and be quiet."

"When did you find out?" my father said.

"It was in that mail you brought by. I'm suppose to show up
the seventeenth of December."

"The seventeenth!" Nana said. "What about Christmas?"

My mother wiped her eyes. "Oh, they wouldn't make you go before Christmas, would they?" I looked over at my father. "They wouldn't, would they Frank?" she said.

"If they said the seventeenth," my father said, "that's what they mean."

"Can I have your drums?" Cliff said.

"Cliff, eat your pie!" my father said.

"I'm not going, though," I said.

"You're not going?"

"We're going to Canada."

"Canada!" my mother said. "My God, first the war, now Canada."

"Who's *we*?" my father said.

"I'm going with Eddie," Sara said.

"And some friends," I said.

"You think that's going to help?" my father said.

"I'll be alive."

"But Canada," my mother said. "That's another country. How will we ever see you?"

"You won't solve anything," Papa said, "by running away."

"Papa you hush up now," Nana said. "This doesn't concern us."

"Your grandfather is right," my father said. "Running away never solved anything."

"I'll have bigger problems if I stay."

My father turned to Sara. "Talk some sense into him."

"We have talked about it," Sara said.

"Tell him to think this over. You just don't run away from your country. It's something he'll have to live with forever."

"At least I'll be alive."

"They won't let you back."

"I'm not going off to kill people."

"Nobody wants you to kill anyone."

"That's what they're doing over there."

"We do what we have to do. It's our duty."

"Not my duty," I said. "We're not at war with anybody. Hell, nobody even knows where this damn place is."

"It's on the TV every night," Papa said.

"Hush, Papa."

"Well, it is," he said. "They show what's going on."

"Did the TV show the 412 Americans killed last week?"

My father stood up, angry. "If they catch you Eddie, they'll put you in jail. That's what they do if you don't show up. They put you in jail."

"Jail is better than dead."

My father threw his napkin on the table. "You're stupid, Eddie. Throwing away your life because you think you're going to be killed. Chances are you'll never see any trouble. But if you don't go, you're life is ruined. You'll be running or in jail. Call that a normal life?"

"I didn't ask for any of this. It's all crazy."

"You're stupid, Eddie. Stupid. I went along with the hair and the music and you moving into that shack, but this is the stupidest thing you've ever pulled."

I looked at Sara. "Are you ready to go?"

She set her napkin on the table. "Where are you going?" my father said.

"I'm very sorry about this," Sara said.

My father walked into the kitchen, and I went and got our coats.

"Don't go, Eddie," my mother said.

"Sorry to ruin your dinner," I said, and kissed her on the cheek.

"Thanks for dinner," Sara said. "Sorry there wasn't more to be thankful for."

"You're a smart girl," my father said to Sara. "Talk some sense into him. Don't let him do this. Believe me, they'll get him, and you'll both be sorry."

"Come on," I said to Sara.

"When all the shooting is over," my father said, "you'll still be wanted."

"I'll see ya, Pop." I closed the back door behind us. I started the car and sat silently.

"Your father may be right, Eddie."

"Don't you start on me."

"I'm not starting on you. What he said about not coming back and you being arrested is something to think about. Is that what we really want?"

"I want us to be happy—and alive. That's all I want."

"Can we go now," she said, softly. "I'm not feeling very well."

33

After Thanksgiving the work load at Bangor got heavier. Instead of just two ships at dock and one at anchor, we had two at dock, three in the bay, and each ship was "on push". Everyone was exhausted, and tempers started to unravel. Twice the M.P.s were called down to break up fights.

I was working the dock for the *Elsinore* as a "hooker". It was my job to connect the rigging hooks to pallet loads. You worked one on one with your rigger, and mine was Tank Jacobson.

Late in the shift, Mickleson dropped two seventy-five pound boxes of 105-mm shells on his foot. The steel-toed boots saved his toes, but it took us half an hour to catch up. In no time at all there were six pallets backed up on the dock, and I had Tank breathing down my neck.

"Move it, lady," he'd yell. "We haven't got all night. Come on hooker, hook! Or get a man down there." Tank didn't let up. "You're making me look bad, lady. Hey Wade, I want a man down there hooking."

Suddenly it seemed like everyone on the dock was staring at me, and I felt about two inches tall.

"Get me a real man down there, Wade. I can't rig with a goddamn woman."

"You got that right," I finally said. "Just ask your old lady."

Pockets of laugher echoed along the dock. I kicked the hooks under a pallet and waved off the load.

"You got a big mouth, lady," Tank said. I felt cocky and waved him off. The rigging snapped taut, but instead of easing the load straight up, Tank jerked the pallet abruptly, snapping two pallet boards. I jumped back when one end of the pallet dropped to the dock.

"Do your fuckin' job, lady."

I reattached the hooks, stepped back, and waved the load away. This time Tank eased the load straight up. Once I saw the pallet clear the hold hatch, I walked over to the next load and leaned against it, watching Tanner and Swartz tear shoring out of the boxcar. Swartz was banging away at two-by-fours with a sledge hammer, and Tanner was prying boards with his crowbar.

"You guys should've stayed with medical school," I said. "There's a shortage of good surgeons in the world."

Tanner stopped prying and tapped Swartz on the shoulder. "How cold would you say that canal water is about now?" Tanner asked.

"I don't know," Swartz said. "About fifty degrees. Maybe thirty with the wind chill."

"Sounds like Carr needs a cooling down."

"I think you're right," Swartz said.

Tanner and Swartz stepped out of the boxcar.

"Come on, you guys," I said, backing away from the pallet. "I was just messing around."

Tanner took another step, but Swartz stopped and pointed above me. "Eddie!" Tanner yelled.

"Look out!" Swartz said.

I turned, and just as I looked up, I caught a blurred stringy mass moving straight at me. I no sooner saw it than I felt the powerful *thunk* against my hard hat, and I hit the ground. My hard hat flew off, and the impact left me momentarily dazed. My body felt loose and tingly. Swartz and Tanner ran over and helped me up.

"Jesus Christ, Eddie, you all right?"

I nodded and rubbed the top of my head. "What the hell was that?" I asked.

"Rigging," Swartz said.

"You're lucky," Tanner said, rubbing his fingers over the scraped crown of my hard hat. I saw Swartz look up to the ship, and I followed his eyes to Tank looking down at me from his roost.

"Watch what the hell you're doing up there," Tanner yelled.

"Tell your lady friend to stay awake," Tank replied. "This ain't no ladies' social."

I stared up at Tank and the men looking down at me and the smirk on Tank's face. That was all I needed to see. I grabbed my crowbar and started for the *Elsinore.*

"Eddie!" Tanner yelled.

I ran up the gangway, my eyes fixed on Tank. "Come on, you sonofabitch," I yelled. Tank wasn't grinning anymore. He started to come down from his roost, but I was coming up on him fast. He stopped halfway down the ladder. "Come on you fat bastard."

I swung the crowbar at Tank and caught him on the thigh. Somebody tried grabbing me from behind. I swung the crowbar at him, and he jumped away. Tank was on the deck, and a guy handed him a piece of shoring. Tank lunged at me, swinging the board like it was a bat, and he just caught my arm, tearing my shirt. He swung again and caught me on the shoulder, and I went down. I got up, swung low, and felt the bar hit his arm solidly. Tank cried out, clutching his elbow. I started at him again, but Tanner grabbed the crowbar and pulled me back while Swartz wrapped his arms around me.

"That's it, Eddie. That's it."

"I'll kill 'im! I'll kill the bastard!"

Something hit my face, and everything went black. When I came to, I was in the First Aid shed with two medics and two M.P.s. Wade and Bledsoe were standing over me. Bledsoe stood with his hands cocked on his hips, and he got right to the point. "We're sending you home, Carr." he said. I looked at Wade, and his face didn't change. "The M.P.s will see that you get home." He turned to Wade. "Let's get back to work. We've got a schedule to keep."

Bledsoe left the shed, and Wade looked down at me, shaking his head. "That was a stupid thing to do, Carr."

"I couldn't take it anymore."

"Bledsoe had to do it."

"I couldn't take him anymore."

"If he hadn't, we'd have a circus out there."

"So I was wrong?" I said.

"I don't know about wrong," Wade said. "But I'll tell you this. You're still welcome on any crew of mine."

I smiled, and Wade winked. "Take care, Eddie."

34

The party for Flex came at a time when changes were wholesale. Flex was leaving, I had been fired at Bangor, and my concerns about being drafted had dissolved with our plans of going to Canada.

The day of Flex's going away party was like any other late fall day. A low mantle of slate gray clouds stretched across the sky, softening the color of the trees, the water, and the houses to the flat hue of paste. The tide was high in the morning, but by mid-afternoon it had dropped, and sea gulls picked at beach debris, leaving little more than their foot imprints in the mud.

The letter I had received from Scooter held good news. He was due home soon from Hawaii. But the news from Sara—that she couldn't make Flex's send-off party—wasn't good.

"You sick or something?" I said.

"Just not up to a party tonight," Sara said.

"Must be a reason."

"I have to see my folks."

"What for?"

"Some personal things."

"Are you changing your mind about us?" I said. I pulled Sara close to me to kiss her.

"Don't Eddie."

"What did I do?"

"Just don't be so rough. Maybe later if I'm feeling better. But you have a good time."

Mooch came out of the cabin with Jack and Danny, who had both called in sick for work. Mooch was carrying two pints of wine. Jack and Danny each had one.

"Dis stuff is good," Mooch said. He wore a big heavy coat—about three sizes too big—and grinned like a fool.

I took one of the bottles and inspected the label. "What the hell is Whistle Bark?"

"The only thing me and Amy drink around the truck," Mooch said.

The tide was still out, and Mooch stood at the railing surveying the barge resting on the beach below us. He took a long swig of wine and set his bottle down on the railing. Then after telling us to keep our eyes on the beach, he ran back inside the cabin.

"Danny's going to San Francisco," Jack said.

"Why?" I said.

"Legwork, he says."

The toilet flushed inside the cabin, and Mooch came hobbling out to the porch holding up his pants. "Stand by," he said. "This should be like a V-2 rocket."

"When's Danny going?" I asked.

"I don't know," Jack said. "Soon, maybe."

"For how long? I mean, we're still going to Canada, aren't we?"

"That's all I know," Jack said, and then he turned to Mooch. "Sure is taking it's time. You been in training?"

"This is going to set a new record," Mooch said.

"Well if there was a change in plans," I said, "Danny would have said something, wouldn't he?"

"Sure," Jack said. "You know Danny."

"Whole anchovies," Mooch said. "Three cans. Fins and all."

The sewer pipe gurgled and groaned below us. "Sure they weren't tunas?" I said.

We could hear water running in the pipe, but all the noise was back up under the cabin. Then, the water stopped. There was a deep, guttural growl inside the pipe followed by the tiniest dab of water trickling out the end of the pipe.

"What the hell happened?" Mooch said.

"They *were* tunas!" Jack said.

I turned to Mooch. "What did you do in there?"

"Nothing," he said. "I didn't do nothing."

"You did do something, you creep. What was it?"

"It wasn't nothing. Just some paper."

"How much paper, Mooch?"

"Some."

"How much, you cretin?"

"What was on the roll. I was going for distance."

"Distance!"

"Pull up your pants, Mooch."

The three of us watched over the railing, waiting for something to move. "You, my friend, have only one task left in life," I said. "Clear that pipe."

ᕲ

Mooch was still mopping up the bathroom floor when Flex and Lolly arrived for the big send-off. Tony and Lana came in with the Carver brothers and their girlfriends, followed shortly by Whitey Johanson who showed up with Amy Swertz. She immediately wanted to know where Mooch was. She followed Jack's outstretched arm and disappeared into the bathroom.

There was such a constant stream of people knocking at the door that we finally just left it open. Joe the Squid surprised us with a bottle of Jack Daniels, and Margy brought in a large sheet cake she had baked. Margy was friendly and gave no indication that anything had ever happened between us. The cabin quickly filled up with people bringing beer, records and plates of food. By nine every room in the place was full, including the bathroom. People spilled out onto the porch, small groups stood on the grass and others took up seating along the bulkhead.

The size of the crowd did our hearts good. People Flex didn't know were shaking his hand and clapping him on the back, wishing him luck. I had the feeling everyone thought he and Lolly were getting married.

"This is strange," Lolly said to Jack. "Are you sure this is for Maxwell?"

"Everything," Jack said.

"But we don't know any of these people. There's even a cake here somewhere."

"I like it," Flex said.

"This feels very strange," Lolly said. "Where's the bathroom?"

Jack gave directions to Joe's, and Lolly begrudgingly excused herself. Jack drew up close to Flex and slipped him a rubber-corked vial. "The bedroom's all yours tonight," Jack said. "You just give me the word, and I'll clear everybody out of there."

Flex held the vial up to the light. "What the hell is this?"

"Tea," Jack whispered. "Results guaranteed."

"Well," Flex said, "I don't know."

"What's to know," I said. "This is the big send-off."

Flex discreetly slipped the vial into his shirt pocket. By eleven, there was guitar music and singing coming from the living room, and in the back bedroom a Beach Boys record was booming at full volume. The smoke and body heat turned the inside of the cabin into a steam cooker, and a thin layer of beer and food covered the kitchen floor. Somebody had taken a half-eaten wiener and stuck it on a wall nail, and there were several hand-gouges missing from Margy's cake. Even Lolly seemed to be having a good time. Mooch got pantsed right in front of her, and she didn't even flinch. Nobody appeared to have a care in the world except having a good time. For me, the only thing missing was Sara.

Motherbright and Danny arrived close to midnight. Motherbright wore tinted glasses and a long, brilliantly flowered cape. Her fine hair hung long and straight to the base of her back, and it danced like corn silk as she moved. But it was the large peacock feather curving up from the side of her hair that caught everyone's attention. She walked across the kitchen and handed Flex a small box, nicely wrapped in gold foil. She told him not to open it.

"It may keep you alive," Motherbright said. Then, right in front of Lolly, she embraced Flex. "I hope your travels are safe."

"Well, yeah," Flex said, looking at Lolly. "Thanks." Jack cleared his throat. "This is Motherbright. She lives in the blue place."

"Yes, of course," Lolly said. "Motherbright. That's a cheery name." The tea had clearly taken hold. Lolly turned to Flex. "Do we know a Motherbright?"

Flex smiled. "The blue place."

"Yes, of course," Lolly said. "How nice. Little blue places wherever you go." Then abruptly to Motherbright, "I love your feather."

"The Hindus believed that one of their gods changed into a peacock to hide from a demon," Danny said.

"Is that right?" Lolly said.

Motherbright smiled. "Some say their feathers prevent decay."

"Now that's a cheery thought," Lolly said. "Do you always give gifts to men you don't know?"

"We all know him," Motherbright said.

"But we don't know you," Lolly said.

"The gift is all we have to give, wouldn't you agree?"

Lolly turned to Flex. "Are you sure we know this woman?"

❧

The rumor was innocently passed in the kitchen, and Bill Carver's girlfriend said she was just saying what she had heard. "No big thing," she said. "It'll be great knowing somebody in California." I found Danny on the front porch, and he tried laughing off my question.

"Why so damn serious?" he said.

"What about Canada?" I repeated.

"It's like I said. A change in plans."

"We have to go," I said. "We planned it all out. Everybody agreed."

"I agreed—if nothing better came along. And something better has come along."

"So what about me?" I said. "What about the goddamn army? The bastards are going to draft me."

Danny shrugged his shoulders.

"Is that all you've got to say?"

"What else is there to say? I'm into legwork."

"We made plans," I said. "I thought we were in this together. What the hell am I suppose to do?"

Danny chuckled. "Whatever you feel like." I hit Danny without even thinking. Jack jumped between us and pinned me up against the cabin. "That cuts it," Danny yelled.

"And you cut it," I said.

Jack held me until Danny was pulled off the porch. Jack told everyone to go back inside, and then he dragged me to the front of the porch.

"I've got nothing holding me down here now," I said. "Sara and I'll go."

"You shouldn't have hit him," Jack said. "We could've worked something out. You know Danny."

I pulled my arm free and started off the porch.

"Where you going?"

"I've got things to do."

❧

There were four cats on Sara's porch, and the plates were all picked clean. I opened the door. A lone light was on next to the sofa and the apartment was quiet and empty. The bed was made, and the room was in perfect order. From Sara's bedroom window, I could see her car was not in the parking lot. I found an open letter on the kitchen counter from her friend Tal. The return address was Pleiku, Vietnam. I unfolded the pages and read them.

". . . My real fear is not really knowing from day to day if I will see you again. There is no yesterday and no tomorrow here. Just living through today. The future is a luxury. I miss the world, especially you."

I returned the letter to the envelope, took two beers from the refrigerator and walked down to the First Avenue dock. I sat there on the ferry slip, drank my beers, and thought about Sara and Canada. I thought how bad everything would be without her. I finished my beer and dozed against a piling. About one-thirty the last ferry arrived and woke me, and I slowly walked back to the beach.

35

On the stairs I heard screams and music. Mooch raced by me naked chasing Amy Swertz. I heard glass break on the beach and people splashing in the water. Our cabin was dark, and I approached the open door cautiously, listening to the oriental music inside. A porch board squeaked at the far end of the cabin. I peered into the darkness; Motherbright turned and the moonlight caught the side of her face.

"We've been waiting for you," she said.

I looked around. "Where is everybody?"

She gave me a glass. "Some couldn't wait."

The drink smelled like Kool-Aid. Motherbright touched my arm and went inside the cabin. The kitchen floor felt cushioned. The bedroom door opened, and Jack stepped out. He was stark naked, rubbing his eyes.

"Seen Sara?" I said.

"Nope," Jack said. "What's with your clothes on?"

"Where are yours?"

"You changed the color of your hair," he said. "That's beautiful." He went back into the bedroom.

Out in the living room, the needle on the record player was scratching around the center hole, and I gingerly made my way toward it in the dark. Then something moved on the couch. In the faint light, I saw two bodies. Without looking further, I went out into the kitchen and drank the Kool-Aid.

"Eddie, is that you?" Margy was in my face, naked, her arms around my neck. She kissed me, and her body felt slippery.

"What is this stuff?" I said.

"I'm glad you're back." She pressed her body against me.

"You're a mess," I said. "What is it?"

Suddenly the inside of my head exploded, and I dropped the glass. Margy led me into the bedroom where the music was strange and wonderful. I could feel the sound in my head as though my skull was a speaker. Someone silhouetted against the bedroom window moved to the music in the gauzy blue light. The figure writhed and swayed and made the entire room seem as though it too was moving. The smell of perfume and sweat made me dizzy.

Margy straddled my legs and chest. She pulled my shirt off, undid the buttons of my pants. Margy lowered herself to the floor and led me down with her by the hand. The plastic on the floor and the mattresses was wet and slippery. Soft, friendly voices filled the room. I heard Flex and Jack and Danny. Motherbright whispered, and Mooch giggled in response to one of Amy's cackles. "Come closer," I heard Motherbright say. I tried to move but nothing worked. I could see only her outline, and after a moment I felt myself slowly being drawn toward her. I heard a lid pop and felt a cold liquid drop onto my shoulder. A warm hand rubbed the liquid across my chest, my arms, my legs. When I felt Motherbright's skin, I knew I had stepped into something very different from anything I had ever known.

Margy's hand slid up the inside of my leg, as Motherbright guided mine over her own hips. There was someone lying on the other side of Motherbright, and when I touched the patch of hair, I pulled my hand away abruptly. Flex cleared his throat. Motherbright placed my hand on her breast. It was soft, full and slippery. Margy kissed my thigh, lightly biting the skin, while holding me. Hands and bodies moved everywhere in a strange unison over the oily plastic. I slid down between Motherbright's legs, into the softness of the music. Everywhere hands moved over me.

36

The splitting wood slowly cracked and then snapped much like a gunshot. At first I thought it was in my head. I closed my eyes and lay my head on the body beneath me. Then the screams woke everyone. They were harsh, hysterical screams that were quickly echoed by the screams of someone else. I followed Jack and Danny into the living room where Tony and Lana stood at the front windows, draped in a blanket.

"What the hell is it?" Jack said.

"The porch," Lana said. "Look what it's doing!"

A four-by-four was sticking up through the porch boards, rising and falling with the waves and tearing up more of the porch with each swell.

"Jesus," I said. "What the hell is it?"

"Help! Somebody!" a girl's voice cried out. "We're down here."

Danny opened the window, and we all looked out. The tide was at the cabin floor, and the water rolled in full swells. With each swell the chunk of wood rose up through the hole in the porch. Part of the corner railing was broken off, and it dangled out over the water.

"Who's down there?" I yelled out.

"Me! Mooch and Amy!"

"We can't get out," Amy cried. "Please!"

Jack stepped through the window out onto the porch. He crawled through the railing, dropped into the water, and disappeared under the cabin. Danny and I crawled out behind him.

"I need some help!" Jack yelled.

I lowered myself into the water and held onto the lip of the porch, pulling myself along to the nose of the barge. Huge swells broke over me as the barge banged against the cabin piles. Jack was at the side of the barge, trying to slide Amy into the water. Jack told me to stay where I was, so I waited. With Mooch's help, Jack finally slid Amy off the barge, and she cried even louder when she touched the water.

Jack had his arm around Amy, and while holding onto the barge, he slowly inched her closer to me. I kept hold of the porch and reached out to hold Amy's arm. She leaped toward me, hooking her arms around my neck, and almost pulled me under. I inched my way to the front of the porch until outstretched hands slowly lifted her out of the water.

I looked back under the cabin to see how Mooch was doing, and Jack already had him in the water. Suddenly there was a loud crash back under the cabin. Chunks of wood dropped into the water, and water poured down in a steady stream.

"Jesus," Jack said. "Now what?"

We got Mooch out from under the cabin and topside by the stove under a blanket with Amy. Jack and I ran to the bathroom, and when we turned on the light, Bill Carver and two girls were crawling out of the bathtub that had half fallen through the floor. Water from the faucet ran straight down through the hole in the floor. The girls were screaming and crying.

"I can't deal with this," Jack said.

"How we going to fix that?" I said.

"Fix it! The whole damn floor's gone."

Jack sat down on the toilet seat and shook his head. I crawled over and looked down at where the floor under the tub had once been.

"This is too depressing," I said, and went back into the bedroom. I turned off the light and collapsed on the plastic covered bed with Flex, Lolly, Motherbright, and Margy. For what seemed like the next half hour, Mooch ran in and out of the bedroom, and I was getting sick of seeing him.

"You come in here one more time," I yelled, "and I'll rip your heart out!"

The bedroom door slowly opened. "Is that you Eddie?" I bolted straight up at the sound of Sara's voice. Then the light switched on. Sara's face stiffened with shock. Her eyes scanned the room, and I looked around me. Lolly covered her eyes and Margy rolled over, her pantied bottom and bare back exposed. I stood up immediately.

"It's not how it looks," I said, covering myself.

Sara turned and walked out.

I started out of the cabin after her, until I saw some people coming down the hill. "Sara, damn it! Come back here. Do you hear me? Come back."

Sara kept running. Then a moment later I recognized Frog and saw two uniforms.

❧

Amy dashed for the bedroom with the blanket, and left Mooch naked on the floor. The two policemen looked down at him and shook their heads. Frog ran around the cabin and came back into the kitchen screaming.

"Just look at this place," he said.

Mooch stood up, grabbed a shirt off the floor, and tied it around his waist, but all he covered was his butt. Frog pointed to Mooch. "You there!" Frog yelled. "My God, cover yourself. See! It's just like I said. Degenerates, all of them degenerates."

"Is this it?" Mooch said to Frog.

Frog backed up. "It sure as hell is not," Frog said.

"Where is it then?"

"Get away from me you—you—" Frog drew close to the policemen. "What are you looking for?" the taller policeman said to Mooch.

"You know," Mooch said.

"No, I don't know."

The second cop stepped forward. "How about getting dressed partner?"

"That's not the answer," Mooch said.

"Get dressed," the cop repeated. "The party's over."

"It can't be over," Mooch said.

"Oh Lordy," Frog yelled from the bathroom. "Look what they've done. They've sunk the bathtub."

One of the cops inspected the other rooms. They looked amused at people being naked. They told everyone who didn't live there to leave. Frog was in tears, and Mooch kept walking through the kitchen, zombie-eyed, carrying the record player. He was still only wearing the shirt tied around his waist but now with his little butt sticking out.

"Holy Christopher," Frog yelled, running in from outside. "They've destroyed the front porch."

"Music," Mooch said, walking back through the kitchen. "More music."

Frog grabbed the record player. "You! Get dressed!" He turned to Jack and me. "That's it! You're out! All of you! Out!"

37

For the next three days I called Sara, but there was never an answer. I phoned Dr. Brinker's four times, and each time I was told she hadn't been to work. Her apartment was dark day and night, with the cats waiting on the porch.

Jack came and went for two days, and with each trip more of his things disappeared from the cabin. He never said where he was moving, and I took that to mean I wasn't invited. Anyway, my first choice was to move in with Sara. The day before Jack and I were to be out of the cabin, I went to her apartment and this time the lights were on. Sara was standing at the kitchen sink. When she opened the door, her eyes were swollen, and she looked tired.

"Where have you been?" I said. "I've looked everywhere."

"I'd rather not talk right now, Eddie."

"Please—talk to me."

"I have nothing to say."

"I want to know what's happened."

"I'm just not in the mood to talk, Eddie."

"I'm not leaving until we straighten this out."

She turned away and continued washing the dishes. The apartment was cluttered with boxes. Several paper sacks were stacked behind the door, full of shirts I recognized. Two fishing poles stood in the far corner next to the couch.

"What are Jack's things doing here?"

"He needs a place to stay," Sara said.

"Well, so do I."

"Not here, Eddie."

"What the hell is going on?" I walked over and faced Sara around. "Remember me? I'm the guy you said you loved."

"Things change, Eddie."

"Not that fast."

"Then I made a mistake."

Sara looked pale.

"What's wrong?" I said.

"Just leave, Eddie. Right now!" She ran from the kitchen, and I heard the bathroom door shut. I waited and then went to the bathroom door and knocked. Water was running in the sink.

"Sara, what's wrong?"

I heard her cough. I tried the door, but she had it locked.

"Just go away, Eddie. Please, just go away."

I stood outside the bathroom, listening. I lit a cigarette. Finally the toilet flushed, and the water went off. A moment later Sara opened the bathroom door. She looked at me, and for a moment I saw something of the way she had once looked at me when I knew she loved me. I stepped toward her, but the look passed, and she walked by me. I followed her back into the kitchen where she opened the back door.

"Good-bye, Eddie." Her forehead was dotted with tiny beads of sweat, and she brushed her hair back. "Please just leave."

"Look Sara, I don't know how to explain the other night. You're the only person I've ever wanted. That's the truth."

"The truth is, Eddie, we just won't work." She lowered her eyes. "Please go."

"There is someone else, isn't there?"

When Sara finally looked up at me, she rubbed her forehead like she was confused. "Yes, Eddie."

"Why?"

"Because—because I don't love him," she said.

"I don't understand this. There's somebody else—that you don't like? All I want is us to be together."

"I wish you'd just go, Eddie."

"Not until you tell me you don't love me."

"The truth is—the way things are—we would never be happy." I stepped toward her, and she shook her head. "Goodbye, Eddie Carr."

I stood in the doorway, and we just stared at each other. I couldn't take my eyes off her. She started to close the door, but I stopped the door with my foot. We looked at each other through the narrow crack in the door, and then she closed it.

38

I had been at my parent's house on Olive Street less than a week when Scooter Hayes called. Except for the slight stutter, he sounded great. He said he was temporarily assigned to the Naval Hospital in the shipyard, and I could hardly wait to see him. We agreed to meet at Olberg's at the end of the week.

I was in town, waiting for a bus home the following day, when I saw the front page story in the *Sun*. A building had burned down on Washington Beach. I walked to the foot of Sixth Street, just above the beach, and I saw where the grass and the shrubs were matted down. There was a yellow ribbon wrapped around the bushes off the stairs. As I approached the barrier, the air was heavy with the smell of damp, burned wood. Then I saw what used to be the Blue House. It was a flat pile of charred rubble. The only thing that still remained was one of the round doorways. The once blue spot beside the walkway was now nothing more than a burned hole on the hillside.

I went back to Pacific Avenue and waited for the bus. I half listened to the sound of a radio nearby—still at a loss about the Blue House. The music was just loud enough for me to pick out

the words to "The Orange Blossom Special". I looked around
and noticed the birch trees next to the post office. The way the
sun caught their white bark and the way the bark was split and
outlined black, for some reason reminded me of home and all
the things that had sent me back there.

Witts Sporting Goods was directly across the street from me.
There was a camper truck parked outside with the passenger door
open. The short leg of a boy stuck out the door, his small foot
tapping along with Johnny Cash.

An older man came out of Witts wearing a cowboy hat and
boots, carrying two new sleeping bags. Another man, in an apron,
followed him with a fishing pole. The boy stopped tapping his
foot when the music stopped and the news came on.

*President Johnson made a surprise visit to Vietnam today,
visiting selected troops at Cam Ranh Bay. Johnson is the first
U.S. President to visit Vietnam, and he reaffirmed our
government's support for democracy in Southeast Asia.*

The man in the cowboy hat opened the rear of the camper and
put the bags and the pole inside. Watching him made me think
of Jack and going fishing myself. The faint clink of the truck's
blinker ticked off time with the rhythm of the news. The boy kept
another time with his foot.

*U.S. sources in Saigon reported today that Viet Cong
guerrillas attacked an American position north of Pleiku
killing 17 Americans and wounding 39 others.*

The man in the cowboy hat closed the rear door of the camper.

*It was the worst attack on American forces to date, but
intelligence sources report the toll of Viet Cong dead and
wounded far exceeds those . . .*

The boy leaned out as my bus pulled up and grabbed his door.
A moment later the doors closed, and the boy was gone.

39

The burning of the fish was an old Skomish ritual begun, according to Dravis, after Modac was taken by the Keeper. The Skomish lived off the waters and the changes in the weather, and they believed only the Gods controlled these things. On the first day of the harvest moon, Lootol, chief of the Skomish, ordered a sacrifice of the water's harvest to the Keeper to insure prosperity for the coming year. Great numbers of salmon were caught and cleaned and the meat smoked over large hickory fires. The Skomish believed that the fish smoke would refill the rivers, and the fish bones—once returned to the Keeper—would replenish the waters for the coming year. The bones were saved in a ceremonial basket made of young willow twigs. Chief Lootol desired knowledge of the winter rains that swelled the rivers and the routes of the salmon. To insure good fortune he believed he must know the Gods to satisfy them. Thus Lootol sought a guide to the gods.

The crow was a common sight in the village of Tlintot. It was the color of storm clouds with a voice as melodious as Modac was beautiful. Because it walked with the Skomish and flew with the clouds, the crow was believed to be a prophet of weather. For

Lootol and the Skomish, the black bird was to be their messenger of the gods.

Lootol sent two tribesmen out with a net and balls of deer fat to capture a large crow. The tribesmen eventually returned with a bird of extreme beauty, marked with a spot of red on its chest. Lootol held the crow skyward, spoke of bounty and richness, and then released the bird into the heavens to divine the wishes of the Gods.

The bird did not return, and Lootol, having held the ceremony and the villagers in wait all through the night, suffered a loss of esteem. The following day he sent many men of the tribe to find the black bird. When the bird with its red mark was found and returned to the village, it was different. The black bird was fatted— too heavy to fly and too full to sing. The tribesmen said they found the bird beneath a berry tree waiting for more fruit to ripen.

Lootol was a wise man and said to hold many powers of the higher Gods. He took the black bird in his hands and condemned it to suffer from thirst in summer. Alone, Lootol sang out to the Gods, and without knowing for certain the wishes of the Gods, he proceeded with the burning of the fish.

"The long fertility of the waters," Lootol spoke, "rests on these spirits remaining beyond us," and he cast the fish bones into the sound.

The black bird lost its songful voice and ever after lived in scorn over its harsh croak, but for the Skomish, the following winters and springs were plentiful.

ই

That night, after seeing the charred remains of the Blue House, I borrowed my father's car and told him the truth: I had a date.

I drove to the college, parked behind the science building, went to the lab, and jimmied the door open. Within twenty minutes, I had the hinges of the storage cabinet doors removed and replaced, and I was out of the lab. I drove across town and spent the early morning hours on the hillside—on the west side of the narrows.

40

I signed the first sheet of my enlistment papers and slid it across the desk to Sergeant Omeris. While he checked my signature and social security number, I again looked up at the row of photographs on the wall above his bookcase. There was a thin, square outline of dirt framing the glossy paint where a picture had once hung. There were eight pictures to the right of the space and four to the left. Sergeant Omeris signed his name below mine on the first sheet and then stamped it.

"You're making the right decision, Eddie," Omeris said. "Believe me. The smarter man always plans ahead."

"I hope so."

"You're safe, if that's what you mean."

"Three years is a long time."

"Let me be quite candid, Eddie." His voice was soft and calm. "This thing in Vietnam isn't going to last forever. Nothing lasts forever. By the time your hitch is up, you'll have a skill, something negotiable. I pointed that out to these men." Omeris waved his thumb over his shoulder at the photographs on the wall. "Just like I'm telling you. You're planning your future."

"I just don't want to die," I said.

"No one wants to die, but you can't stop living." Omeris shook his finger at me like it was a pointer. "To survive anywhere takes thinking for yourself."

"I just never saw myself as a mechanic."

"Flexibility, Eddie. That's the future. Think of plans as friends. They're cushions. Things that make life more comfortable."

I looked down at my papers, skimmed the bold print, and touched the official seal at the top of the page. I signed my name to the last document.

"That's it, Eddie."

"Do I get anything?" I asked.

"What did you have in mind?"

"A certificate. A card. Isn't there some ceremony?"

"You'll be sworn in at the induction center. Until then, it's life as usual." Omeris stuck out his hand, and I shook it while looking up at the row of photographs behind his desk. The silver frames shone brightly under the overhead lights like a string of polished trophies. Omeris packaged my papers into a long folder and stepped from behind his desk. There was a green metal bookcase behind his chair, and when Omeris stepped out I saw another silver-framed picture on the middle shelf. It was cocked against the wall at such an angle that, between the dusty glass and the shadows, the faces were hard to see. I glanced back up at the photos on the wall.

"The Buddy Plan," Omeris said. "One of the best ideas the army ever had."

"Can I look closer?"

"Help yourself."

I walked behind the desk and looked at each of the pictures.

"You probably know a lot of those boys." I nodded my head. "Friends can make this kind of experience easier," Omeris said.

I looked down at the picture on the shelf. "In this picture down here," I said. "Is that—"

"Two fine boys from Silverdale," Omeris said. "Couldn't be prouder of them both."

I reached down and grabbed the picture. Scooter and Henderson still had their hair, and they were smiling. The photograph was out of the frame; I wiped the dust off their faces. "I know these guys. I'm seeing Scooter tomorrow."

Omeris reached over and took the picture from me. "Our biggest group isn't up there yet." He set the picture on top of the shelf. "We had ten guys from Mason County walk in and sign up last week. Damn near the whole football team."

"I'll tell Scooter you were putting him in a new frame. I think he'll like that."

"No need for that," Omeris said. He turned the photo face down on the shelf.

"Scooter was always big on having his picture around."

Omeris went to the photos on the wall and moved the picture on the far left into the blank space, so the row was continuous, neat.

I glanced back up at the wall of photographs. "It's funny," I said. "I used to wonder what happened to those guys. And there they are."

"That's right, Eddie. Welcome aboard."

41

At Olberg's I made my way to the cafeteria in the rear of the store. There were only two people at the counter, and neither looked like Scooter. The waitress aimlessly stirred her cup of coffee. The guy a few stools down from her looked like he had been in a car wreck.

I checked the back booths, saw no one, and then took a seat at the counter. Small overhead lights made little yellow circles the length of the counter, and one light caught the head bandage of the guy hunched over his coffee. He had his head propped up with one hand pressed against the side of his face.

I looked at my watch. Scooter was ten minutes late. The waitress came around, and I asked for a cup of coffee. On the way back she asked the other guy about a refill. When he dropped his hand from his head, I recognized his face. I stared at Scooter's head. There was no hair below the wide bandage, and his scalp was flaky and red where the bandage had rubbed. The way Scooter hung over the counter made him look as though something was missing from the center of his body. But it was Scooter. I would know Scooter anywhere. I walked around to him and put my hand on his shoulder.

"Scooter?" I said, and he slowly raised his head. "Good to see you."

Scooter's face spread out in a broad smile. "Eddie," he stuttered. "Thought—thought you weren't coming."

"Been a long time," I said. "Didn't recognize you at first."

"A few—few changes," he said.

"How long you been back?"

He couldn't catch his words at first. Then he wiped his mouth and stuttered that he had been back a week. The waitress brought my coffee and refilled Scooter's cup. When she went back into the kitchen, Scooter reached into his coat pocket, pulled out a small sack, and poured a shot into his coffee. He offered it to me, and I accepted. Scooter's stammering took me by surprise because I hadn't heard it on the phone. The whiskey in his coffee was a surprise too. Nobody had ever brought liquor into Olberg's. Scooter's hand shook as he grabbed his cup.

"Not so used to the cold anymore?" I said.

Scooter gave me a half grin and shrugged his shoulders.

"It's time you get back to the real world," I said.

"I'm tryin'. But the army hasn't decided what to do with me yet."

"Do with you?" I followed his eyes up to the bandages. "What is all that?"

"All the rage," he stammered and laughed.

"You look—great. Kind of a swami look."

Scooter pressed the palms of his hands together in front of his face, bowed his head, and I chuckled. He held his hands there long after I had stopped laughing and kept bowing and looking at me, but it wasn't funny anymore. I finally laughed again, and he stopped.

"It's really good to see you, Scooter. Hell, I've lost track of everybody else."

Scooter laughed. "Hell, I've lost track of everything."

"So how's the other guy look?" I said, jokingly.

"The other guy?"

"The other guy that looks worse than you."

"Oh, yeah, the other guy." Scooter cocked his head like he heard something. "I don't know."

"Over a girl, I bet?"

He turned toward me slowly, and the blank look on his face left me cold.

"I never saw 'em, man! You never see 'em." He looked away and then slowly turned back to me. "Just a flash."

The waitress refilled our cups, and I lit Scooter's smoke.

"I'm a little fuzzy," Scooter said. "The coffee alone don't clear nothing. Know what I mean?"

I just nodded. He reached back into his coat pocket and pulled out the bottle. He looked for the waitress before pouring another heavy shot into his cup. He offered it to me, but I passed.

"Does that help?" I said.

"Never give booze to a head wound," he said. "Medic's code." He slapped the counter hard. "Fuck it! That's Scooter's code."

"Sure, Scooter."

He took a drink of coffee. "Know where I was six weeks ago?"

I shook my head.

"In the belly." Scooter looked at me intensely. "Know what I was?"

"No."

He shaped two fingers into circle. We stared at each other, and then Scooter broke out laughing. It was a strange, silly, almost hurtful laugh that I had never heard from Scooter. I wasn't sure if I should laugh or say anything at all.

"You look good though, Scooter. Real good."

"Army surgeons are good, but the nurses are prettier."

We both smiled.

"I was just lucky," he said. "I must've got laid."

"Oh yeah?"

"Least everybody looked at me like I got laid."

"Where's this?" I said.

"In hell man. They got a head shop in hell, Eddie. Everybody gets laid there."

"Like a whorehouse?"

"Yeah. It's just like a whorehouse."

Scooter winced and rubbed the bandages around his temples. "Is it still twenty-one to drink around here?"

"You haven't been away *that* long."

"Hell!" he said, laughing. "I've died, Eddie, and come back. That's a long time. Where the hell is everybody. You used to say this was the place. Hell, this place is dead, man."

"Changes. Everything's gotten worse."

"But where is everybody? There's got to be somebody else, besides you."

"Some of the old crowd is still around," I said, "and others, who knows? You remember Jess Waldrun and Barry Tibbits? They're in Canada now. Some others are working at Bangor."

We drank our coffee, and we both lit up another smoke. The waitress returned with more coffee.

"So—" Scooter said, abruptly, "what's all this—this important business you said—said over the phone?"

"I'm finally going to California."

Scooter's eyes narrowed. "With a band?"

"I've enlisted." A half smile, that could have been a smirk twisted Scooter's mouth. "They drafted me," I said, "but I didn't want to kill, so I enlisted. Going to Fort Ord, California."

Scooter looked into the mirrors behind the shelves of soda glasses. I waited for him to ask me something more— anything—but he was fixed on the mirrors with such intensity that I looked to see what he saw. It was just our faces. When Scooter caught my eyes in the mirror, he whirled around.

"What outfit?" he snapped.

"Maintenance. Same as you. They say helicopters are the coming thing. The safest thing this side of four years."

Scooter nodded and smiled, like he was pleased. Then he started laughing. He laughed harder and harder until I thought he was going to cry.

"What's so funny?" I said.

"The joke."

"What joke?"

"We thought we were safe, too." He started laughing again. Then he looked down at his watch. He brought it closer, moved it away and tilted it slightly from side to side. "Tell me what time this says."

"Two thirty-five."

"Tests, man. That's all those people do is test this and test that. I been tested for everything but—but—" he stuttered. "What the hell was that one big test?" He snapped his head around at me. "That ain't the way it was. It was like I said."

"Sure, Scooter."

"You gotta know, Eddie. Don't ya see? You gotta know how it is now."

"Sure."

"They all wanna know. Every white jacket with a smile wants to know. The shrinks, man. Can you believe it! The goddamn shrinks don't even believe me."

"What shrinks?"

"The Big Shrink. That's what this is, you know. The Big Shrink! There ain't nobody coming out right. They wanna know you civilians will be safe, if they let me out now. They're votin'. They vote all the time. One ballot FOR. Three ballots AGAINST. Two ballots FOR. Two ballots AGAINST. Maybe today it'll be three ballots FOR and only one AGAINST. Or maybe—all four AGAINST."

"Hell," I lied, "you look fine to me."

"I've got to go, Eddie. The verdict's due."

"Right now? I just got here."

"I got lots of time—except today."

"So is Henderson home?"

Another smirk crept over Scooter's face. It was like he was thinking over another joke to himself, working it over in his head, savoring it quietly before passing it on, and I smiled along with him.

"What's so funny?" I said.

Scooter just laughed, and I laughed with him. He slid a quarter under his saucer and pulled a wood cane out from between his legs.

"Hendy bought this off a gook in Saigon."

"Nice." I grabbed the cane below the knobbed handle and ran my hand over the smooth, red wood.

"Rosewood," Scooter said. "Strong as hell. Said he was getting it for when he got old." Scooter looked away. "It wasn't like Hendy. He never made plans."

I slid off my stool and put a quarter next to my saucer. "So, Hendy's still over there."

Scooter stared back up at himself in the mirror. "He's a hero," Scooter said. He looked serious, but the longer I stared at him, the bigger the grin got on his face.

"Where'd you get so funny?" I asked.

Scooter tried clearing his throat, but he couldn't remove what was stuck. Then, just as quickly as his expression had become intense, his face went flat, his eyes vacant. It was hard for me to read all the changes I saw in his face. Finally, Scooter held his watch toward me. "Is it three yet?"

"About a quarter till."

"I got a shuttle bus to catch," he said.

I apologized again for being late, and Scooter waved it off.

"We'll do it again," he said.

"Maybe some pool at the Y." He slapped his coat pocket. "And some juju water."

Scooter slipped a green baseball cap on his head and nodded toward the front door of the store. I stepped aside for him to pass. His cap sat funny on his head, with much of the bandage showing beneath the brim. It wasn't until he walked ahead of me that I saw he wasn't wearing shoes.

People at the front of the store stared at Scooter. He didn't have much of a limp, but it was clear that his right leg was bad. He scratched at his bandage and dragged his bare foot over the floor. Heads turned toward us with each step, and each face had the same freakish look I had seen too many times when I was out with my mother after her accident. I always started talking to her whenever I saw people staring, so they would know that it was only her legs that were bad.

I put my hand on Scooter's shoulder. "So you and Henderson are heroes," I said, loud enough for everyone around the check stand to hear.

Suddenly Scooter was all over me, swinging and yelling and screaming about Henderson. His arms were like steel rods, and his hands gripped my neck as tight as a vice, but finally someone pulled him away.

"It's okay," I said. "It's okay."

"Don't say that!" Scooter bellowed. "Don't ever say that, you hear?"

I told the guy holding me to let go. Scooter continued fighting the grip of the guy holding him. "It's okay," I said. "Really — we're friends. Let him go."

The manager wanted to call the police, but I convinced him it was just a misunderstanding. "It was just a mix-up," I said, "Don't call the police." I picked up Scooter's cane and guided him through the door.

Outside, Scooter calmed down, and I was no longer afraid of him. I apologized for saying anything about Henderson, and I told him that I didn't mean anything by it. Scooter didn't say anything.

We walked down to one of the public moorings on the First Avenue dock and sat on a makeshift bench. We didn't say anything for some time; we just stared out at the water. Finally, Scooter pulled the bottle out of his pocket, took a drink and passed it to me. I had said enough and had no idea what was safe with Scooter anymore, so I didn't say anything. We sat quietly for a long time, staring across the narrows, passing the whiskey back and forth. Then Scooter cleared his throat, and when I looked at him, his eyes were swollen and wet.

"The gooks got Henderson, Eddie." Scooter turned away and closed his eyes. "Caught two rounds in the face," he said, "and I saw it happen, Eddie, I saw it explode, and it won't go away."

"Jesus, Scooter."

"It happened so fast, Eddie. One minute we were talking and joking, the next I heard it and saw his face go like a fuckin' melon."

Scooter's lips quivered, but he caught himself. He took a deep breath and another drink.

"I didn't know," I said. "If I'd a known—"

"I can't shake it, Eddie. All I see is Hendy's—I see it go, man, and feel him. Know what it's like to feel chunks of your buddy hit you in the face?"

I couldn't say anything.

It had been a routine flight, Scooter said, but neither he nor Henderson liked working the door gun. Too exposed, he said. "We were only mechanics," he kept repeating, and I felt sick inside.

Scooter wasn't even looking at me anymore, his eyes just fixed straight ahead, the words tumbling out. He told me about Henderson's camera and all the pictures he had taken over there.

"I didn't want the door," Scooter said. "It had been a great flight over beautiful countryside. Then we hit a stretch where the B-52's had been. It looked like the moon. Snap. Snap. Click. Click. It was amazing. I got Henderson to work the door."

Scooter stopped.

"What?"

He stared away for the longest time, finally coming back. "If I had been on the door, I wouldn't be here. And that's the truth. They would've hosed me off the bulkheads instead."

Scooter rubbed his temples and took another drink before handing me the bottle. I wiped my mouth. "You all right?" I said.

"Just the chill," he said. "The headaches get tough. This stateside doctor told me a warm climate might help. Steel and the cold don't mix."

"I mean about Henderson."

"If it wasn't for Hendy, I wouldn't be here. He was a good buddy. I'm glad we were together. But, you see, Eddie—I'm alive."

"I'm glad, Scooter."

He tapped his forehead. "They decorated me. Got the Purple Heart and this." He tapped his head again. "That's funny, ain't it? I mean real fuckin' funny. Hendy shags all the rounds, and I get the metal. I call it, 'Hendy's Medal'. Pretty good, huh?"

"He'd like that."

"He saved my ass. But they still got me pretty good. Won't ever see the real moon, Eddie."

Scooter's face went flat, like all his muscles gave out. His eyes flicked, and his lip tightened and quivered. I didn't want him to do it, not in front of me, but he did.

"I threw my boots away," he said, through the tears. "Threw them right out the chopper."

I reached out and touched Scooter's shoulder. He looked at my hand, covered his face, and bawled. When he wasn't looking, I wiped my face.

"He was all over my boots, Eddie." Scooter wiped his face and looked up at me. "How could you wear boots like that? Tell me, Eddie. How could I wear 'em with Henderson's—" I rubbed his shoulder, and he straightened up. "They say I'm crazy, but I've never cried over anybody. I just can't wear them anymore."

"It's okay."

"I wish I had a picture of him, now. I can't remember how he looked before."

We sat on the bench until Scooter was together enough to go back to the hospital. At the intersection across from the anchor memorial, the shipyard bus sat idling. Two women in front us turned around, and when they saw Scooter's bandaged head, his cane, and bare feet, they smiled and stepped aside.

"We'll do it again," Scooter said. "A booth next time, though. Something back in the corner."

"Sure, Scooter. Before I leave." I decided not to cross over to the bus with him but just say goodbye. "Take care, Scooter."

He smiled. "You too."

The light changed, and Scooter limped across the street. He waved his free hand at the bus when the driver revved the engine. For a moment Scooter's jerky movements reminded me of a pheasant I had once seen thrashing in tall grass in the blueberry fields near home. It had been neck shot, and it tried hopelessly to fly away. It only took the pheasant about a half hour to bleed to death, but that was because it lay still and didn't flutter very much.

I had wanted to say something to Scooter. I wanted to tell him about his picture on the recruiter's bookcase. I wanted to tell him he could have that picture of Henderson, but how do you tell a friend, crippled, with steel in his head, he's been disowned? The longer I watched Scooter, the more I knew it would be better if he didn't know. There was only so much you could know before nothing seemed right.

42

My first leave from the army came four months after I had left Bremerton. I was nervous about being back. I wanted to see Jack and familiar faces, eat a burger in Olberg's, and listen to old friends play music upstairs at Sherman Clay. I wanted to ride the ferries again and know how Scooter was doing.

I had received two letters from Sara while I was away, yet nothing she said in them implied that things had changed between us. She was sorry, she said, for the way things turned out and that it would be good to see me. She had also enclosed a clipping from the *Sun* about the disappearance of the Indian bones. I saved that letter and thought of nothing in Bremerton the way I thought of Sara. I spent almost a week just trying to locate her. I traced her through three moves before I ran out of leads.

I went down to the beach hoping to find a familiar face, but the beach had changed. Toshi's name was still on his mailbox, but there was no one home when I stopped by. A group of sailors was now living in Joe the Squid's old place. One of them said Joe was a civilian now, back in Chicago. He had gotten married before he left, the sailor said, rolling his eyes when he mentioned Margy's name.

Our old cabin was boarded up with a CONDEMNED sign posted across the porch. The grass was uncut, slats were nailed across the windows, and weeds were growing up between the porch boards. The barge was no longer tied up under the pilings.

❧

I ran into Mooch one afternoon in Olberg's, sitting at the counter like old times, pouring the remnants of leftover coffee into his cup. He had a stack of yellow fliers, and he was handing them out to people walking by the counter. He recognized me immediately and didn't even seem to realize that I had been gone four months. I offered him a cigarette, and in return he handed me a flier.

PEOPLE'S DEMONSTRATION
Saturday April 29th, Evergreen Park
1:00 P.M.
Get the U.S. out of Vietnam and end the war.
Stop capitalist imperialism that enslaves the world.
Show your support for peace.
Bring Americans home. Get America out of Vietnam.

"We're going to stop the war," Mooch said. He tore open another packet of sugar and emptied it into his coffee. "You gotta be there, Eddie. We need a big crowd."

"Where is everybody?"

"Everybody?"

"Everybody from the beach. Jack, Danny—"

"I did see Danny once on the ferry a few months back. Jack? Let's see. Think he went fishing."

"Fishing?"

"Can you beat that?" Mooch said. "Haven't seen him since."

"Have you seen Sara anywhere?"

"Nope! We weren't very close."

I lit a cigarette, and without thinking, offered Mooch another. He took three and then relit a butt he had behind his ear.

"So where you been?" Mooch said.

"In the army."

"So what's it like?"

"Like the army. So how's Amy?"

"Fine, I guess. We broke up."

"What the hell happened?"

"Her face cleared up, and she got popular. But I'm real busy these days with the war. Bet you never thought you'd see the day, huh, Eddie?"

"How about Scooter. You seen him around?"

"Scooter? Let's see—yeah—seems to me I saw him. Where was it now? Hell I can't remember all this shit. I saw him, no—I didn't see him. I heard about him. That's it! Somebody—let's see, from somewhere—now where in the hell was I?"

"How was he, Mooch?"

"Shots, man. He shot himself—yeah that's it—right in the head. Figure that!"

Mooch tried telling me about when it happened and about the funeral that nobody he knew attended. It was clear that Mooch didn't have it all together. That part of Mooch had not changed.

"Somebody has to know what happened."

"Don't look at me, man. I don't know anything. I hardly even knew the guy. Here," Mooch said, handing me a stack of fliers. "Pass these around. I gotta go. I'm in charge of downtown. Be there Saturday. Lots of people. We're gonna stop the war!"

I looked at one of the fliers again and left them on the counter.

₰

My brother Cliff had turned twelve a few weeks after I had left for basic training, and since I had missed his birthday, I took him to Seattle to pick out his own gift. We spent most of the morning walking around First Avenue, stopping in all the pawnshops and music stores. Cliff finally chose a guitar we saw in a store window for his present, and I bought it for him. We ate lunch in the Public Market and then walked uptown looking at clothes and records.

The Seattle Cafe, across from the record store, advertised the "Largest Banana Split West of the Mississippi." The cafe was warm and filled with people like us coming in to get out of the cold. We sat at the counter, and I ordered Cliff his banana split and a coffee for myself. A large picture window ran the length of the cafe along Fourth Avenue. There were lots of people out on the street. While Cliff worked on his huge banana split, I stared out the window at all the strange faces. Everyone was bundled up and hurrying against the wind and the cold.

I watched a guy with a long ponytail hawking an arm load of newspapers on the corner, and I couldn't take my eyes off him. From the back he looked very familiar even though I was sure I didn't know anyone in Seattle. But the longer I watched him approach people on the street, the way he moved from person to person, the broad hand gestures, the more sure I felt I knew him. I watched him for some time, but I never got a clear look at his face. Finally I left Cliff at the counter and went outside. I studied him for a moment and finally walked up and tapped him on the shoulder. He spun around. Even with the heavy beard and dirt-smudged face, I knew it was Danny.

"Newspaper?" he said.

I just smiled at him.

"The Seattle Flag?" he said.

"It's me, Danny—Eddie Carr."

Danny got a long, faraway look in his eyes like disbelief or shock or both. He stared at me for a moment, broke off abruptly to pitch a passerby, and then came back to me, rubbing his beard. He looked pale, sickly, and much thinner than when I had last seen him.

"Eddie?" he said. "Eddie from the beach?"

"It's good to see a familiar face from the beach, Danny."

I had a lot of things to ask him about the last four months, but it was too cold to talk outside. I suggested the cafe, but he said they wouldn't serve him. He had an appointment in a short while, but he had to go to his place first. We were welcome there, he said, and we could talk. I got Cliff, and we walked with Danny. "Of all people and in all places!" I said. "I've been thinking about you ever since your place burned down. It's really great to see you Danny."

Cliff looked at Danny cautiously, like he wasn't quite sure what to say or whether he should stare. I knew I couldn't explain anything of what I was feeling to Cliff.

It was a ten minute walk to Pioneer Square, but Danny was not very talkative or especially friendly. He seemed removed from who we had been and the times we had shared together. He was just there, walking next to me, rambling on about the "cause", stopping the war, and hating "pigs". He said he didn't know anything about Jack, and when I asked about the fire at the Blue House, he replied, "She's gone."

"Motherbright?" I said.

"Motherbright who?"

"Motherbright in the Blue House."

"There was no Motherbright," Danny said.

Danny's place turned out to be a storefront clothing and art shop not far from the Union Mission on First Avenue. It was an old building with huge double doors. The "Closed" sign was still in the door. Between the wood paneled walls and draped windows, there was hardly enough light to make out the loft room above the main floor. Danny went straight upstairs, and I heard a woman whispering loudly. Cliff and I looked at the sunburst paintings and glass display cases filled with clips, wood pipes, and bright colored T-shirts. Incense was burning in a brass holder on the counter. I was intrigued by some photographs hanging on the walls that were printed directly onto wood. Cliff liked the top hat and tuxedo coat emblazoned with an American flag.

The loud whispering continued up in the loft, accented twice by loud screams, and I had an uneasy feeling about being there. I sensed we were intruding on something, and what had begun as a reunion was making me feel uncomfortable. Finally, Danny emerged. "I gotta see a man," he said.

I looked over at Cliff, playfully amused with a rack of beads and colorful patches. "Can't we just talk for a minute?"

"I'd take you along," Danny said, "but it gets a little touchy."

"How's Jack? Have you seen him?"

"Jack? He sailed away."

"What the hell's that mean?"

The woman upstairs called Danny's name, and he looked nervously up toward the loft.

"Gotta go," he said.

"Well, have you seen Sara?"

"A few months back," Danny said. "Try her folks. Look, I've got to split."

"Sure." I stuck my hand out, and Danny stared at it for a moment before he half-heartedly put his hand to mine.

"Good seeing you, Danny."

He tried to smile, but it wouldn't come. Cliff and I went outside, and I closed the front door behind me. We walked a few steps. Then I stopped. I started back for the door, and saw the curtain part just enough for me to see Danny's eyes and part of his mouth through the glass. His eyes were like those of a frightened child. Everything I felt inside, I saw in Danny's eyes.

Cliff and I stared at one another. "He's a hippie, isn't he?" Cliff said.

I glanced back at Danny still peering out at us, turned to Cliff, and shook my head.

"No," I said, "that's Danny Peezor. Somebody I once knew."

When I heard Sara's voice on the phone, it took me a moment to speak. She was very cordial, like we were old friends, and she asked a lot of questions about my life. I asked to see her, and she said it would be best if we just met somewhere. I had missed her, and her letters made me hopeful we still might fix things. Over the months I had thought of marriage, and that night I worked the lines over in my head in the hope that things might still be good between us.

I reached the foot-ferry dock to Port Orchard twenty minutes before time, just in case Sara arrived early. When the foot-ferry pulled up and the young deck hand helped her off, I was not prepared to see what I saw. Her hair was longer, and she was prettier than when I had last seen her. She was also quite pregnant.

"Aren't you going to even say hello?" she said.

"You're having a baby," I said.

"Pretty soon."

I forgot everything I had wanted to say to her. "Should we go somewhere?" I finally said.

Sara looked back at the ferry idling behind her. "I don't have very long," she said. "I'm going back on the next ferry."

"Is this all the time we have?"

"It's all there is, Eddie."

The ferry had a ten minute layover before its next run across the bay, so I led Sara up the gangway to the covered bench at the top of the dock, and we sat down. She looked older but just as pretty as when we had loved each other. She talked about Tal and told me they had been married the month before. He had gotten an emergency leave from Vietnam to come home and marry her, and he was back finishing his last six months of duty there. She spoke about the whole thing so clinically that it took me a minute to sort out my confusion with time and events.

"You never wrote about a baby," I said, "or about being married."

"They weren't the things I could say in a letter. I wanted to see you and tell you personally."

"I've sure made a fool of myself in my letters."

"I don't think so, Eddie."

A young couple passed in front of us and walked down the ramp to the float.

"I don't know what to say now."

"You look good, Eddie. Are you happy?"

"I don't know. The army isn't a happy place."

"It won't be forever," she said.

I looked straight into Sara's eyes and saw there was no going back and no catching up. I didn't want us to be through, to just walk away. Then I realized just how little time we had, and I wanted an answer, a way out of what was feeling so damn inevitable. "Did you get the clipping I sent you?" she asked. I couldn't look at her. I just nodded. "Some people in town said you took the bones from the college."

"People say a lot of things."

"Do you know where they are?"

"Where they belong—I hope."

"You never talked to me about the work you did on them."

"Maybe we could get together again, and I could tell you."

She smiled. "I'm going to miss you, Eddie."

"I never thought things would turn out this way."

"None of us did."

The ferry engines revved, followed by a whistle. Sara stood. I followed her down the gangway, and we walked to the edge of the float together. I looked out across the water and remembered the night we had stood in the same place, talking until things were better.

"Remember the last time we were here?" I said.

"We almost made it."

"But we didn't, did we?"

Sara stood apart from me, her hands clasped in front of her.

"I'd like to think we did," she said.

"I wish to hell things were different."

"If they had been different," she said, "none of it would've happened. I have no regrets, Eddie."

"Why did you have to get married?"

The whistle blew again, and several more people ran to the float and stepped aboard the ferry. In a moment Sara would get aboard, and it would be over, and the thought of her leaving, knowing she would be gone forever, was more pain than I had ever thought possible. I could already feel the hole growing in my chest.

"There was a baby to think about," she finally said.

"Then I wish it had been mine."

Sara looked into my eyes and smiled. "You didn't, Eddie."

"But I—"

"Don't say it, Eddie."

She turned her back to me, and I could see her hand wiping at her face. I touched her arm.

"Last call for Port Orchard," the mate yelled.

Sara turned and kissed me. "Good-bye, Eddie Carr. I wish you all the happiness in the world. I really do."

I just looked at her. "Is anyone ever really happy?"

Sara smiled. "We have to believe so, Eddie."

The whistle blew for the last time. Sara stepped aboard. The door slid closed, and Sara was gone.

ﻉﻻ

Two months later, while in Massachusetts, I heard that Sara's husband Tal had been killed in Vietnam. I wrote Sara several letters, but I didn't receive a reply for almost six months. In the letter, she sent a picture of her and her daughter taken on a beach. My bunkmate said my wife was pretty and my daughter looked just like me. I was about to tell him, but I caught myself, and the possibility I was wrong kept me from saying anything. The good memories of Sara came back to me, and remembering how truly we had loved each other made it hard for me not to believe something good still might happen for us. I stared down at their smiling faces, and for just a moment my heart raced, and I felt the same flush of excitement I had known when stepping off those big yellow buses at a fresh, unpicked field, in a place I had never been before.